Welcome to the su...

After a summer in t................................
Dream is geared up ... a winter of fun and sun
sailing the warm waters of the Caribbean.

On our **Creatures of the Caribbean** cruise, we
invite passengers to get up close and personal
with our sea-dwelling friends. Cruise director
Patti Anderson and water-sports instructor
Dylan Langstaff have planned excursions that are
geared to all ages.

Meet the stingrays and find out how gentle and
graceful these creatures can be. And who can
resist the playful nature of our dolphin friends?
The sociable sea mammals are fun to watch, and
those who swim with the friendly creatures are in
for a once-in-a-lifetime experience.

Don't forget our special treasure hunt for the
teardrop pendant. Pick up a brochure in the
ship's lobby and read the romantic legend of the
moon goddess and her shepherd lover. The lucky
passenger who finds the necklace will discover an
array of shipboard perks – and, according to the
legend, a little romance as well.

But even if you don't find the pendant, a cruise
aboard *Alexandra's Dream* is guaranteed to be a
first-class experience for all passengers.

MARY LEO

yearned to live somewhere warm from the time she felt her first winter freeze. She's now a California girl and loves it. The first story she ever wrote took place in Huntington Beach with a surfer chick as the heroine. It was a horribly written story, but it gave her two things: a love of California and a passion for writing.

Mary lives with her husband, author Terry Watkins, in San Diego, where she is surrounded by artists. Her daughter is an actor, and her son is a music producer.

Mary enjoys hearing from readers. You can reach her at www.maryleo.net.

Mediterranean NIGHTS™

Mary Leo
CABIN FEVER

⊛™ MILLS & BOON®
Pure reading pleasure

*First published in Great Britain 2008
by Harlequin Mills & Boon Limited,
Eton House, 18-24 Paradise Road, Richmond, Surrey TW9 1SR*

© Harlequin Books S.A. 2007

Mary Leo is acknowledged as the author of this work.

ISBN: 978 0 263 86700 8

61-0608

*Harlequin Mills & Boon policy is to use papers that are
natural, renewable and recyclable products and made from
wood grown in sustainable forests. The logging and
manufacturing processes conform to the legal environmental
regulations of the country of origin.*

*Printed and bound in Spain
by Litografia Rosés S.A., Barcelona*

Dear Reader,

I grew up in Chicago, which can get cold enough to take your breath away. When I was in my early twenties I had a job that required a twenty-minute walk from the train station up Michigan Avenue and down Congress. I remember being so cold that my toes would go numb before I arrived at my destination. I used to dream of warm sandy beaches and crystal-blue water and so much sunshine I could live in a bikini. It's no wonder that when I was asked to write the first book of the Caribbean portion of this series, I knew exactly what I wanted to convey…BODY HEAT!

So how about this: crystal-blue water, sunshine enough for that bikini – or not – and our transportation to those warm sandy beaches is a luxury cruise ship with a ridiculously hot watersports instructor named Dylan Langstaff, who knows exactly how to warm those popsicle toes! Oh yeah, I'm feeling all toasty just thinking about Dylan.

And did I happen to mention there's the legend of the moon goddess, her lucky pendant, the bad people who are after it, and three charming kids who believe the pendant has magical love powers, especially when it's dangling around Becky Montgomery's neck? Why else would Dylan be so attracted to her? Because he…oops!

Wishing you warm toes and sunny beaches,

Mary

ACKNOWLEDGEMENTS

I want to thank Kathryn Lye and Marsha Zinberg for offering me this great series, Janet Wellington for always being there when I need her most, my niece, Dionna Phillips, for being the beautiful visual inspiration for Tracy Irvine, my husband for coming up with the core conflict for my hero/heroine, the other eleven authors of this series who shared their ideas, thoughts and concerns on our loop, with a special shout-out to Ingrid Weaver for writing a fabulous opening book, Diana Duncan for starting the loop and keeping us informed throughout the process, and Marcia King-Gamble for generously sharing her intimate knowledge of cruise ships.

DON'T MISS THE STORIES OF

NIGHTS™

FROM RUSSIA, WITH LOVE
Ingrid Weaver

SCENT OF A WOMAN
Joanne Rock

THE TYCOON'S SON
Cindy Kirk

BREAKING ALL THE RULES
Marisa Carroll

AN AFFAIR TO REMEMBER
Karen Kendall

BELOW DECK
Dorien Kelly

A PERFECT MARRIAGE?
Cindi Myers

FULL EXPOSURE
Diana Duncan

CABIN FEVER
Mary Leo

ISLAND HEAT
Sarah Mayberry

STARSTRUCK
Michelle Celmer

THE WAY HE MOVES
Marcia King-Gamble

For my daughter, Jocelyn, and my son, Rich…
all my love

PROLOGUE

THE QUARTER MOON sat high in the sky as *Alexandra's dream* slipped peacefully through the dark waters toward her next destination. She was an elegant vessel with sleek lines, a graceful chipper bow and a somewhat squared stern. This was her long, lazy repositioning voyage from Piraeus on the Greek coast to Miami Beach, Florida, where she would spend the winter months in the Caribbean.

Patti Kennedy sat alone in the crowded back office of the ship's library, looking through a cardboard box filled with the remaining reproductions of antiques that the police and the FBI had left behind. Ariana Bennett, the ship's librarian, had decided to send the larger pieces, a bust of one of the Caesars, a Greek vase and an Etruscan plate to a friend of hers who was interested in antiquities. She had asked Patti to go through the box one last time to see if there was anything she might want to keep.

Patti couldn't sleep and decided at one in the morning that now was the time to go through the box. Her mind still raced with recent events aboard the ship that had brought her to this moment and she needed to find closure. She also needed to assuage the feeling of guilt she shared with other senior cruise staff. As cruise director, Patti felt she should have had some awareness that a smuggling operation had been taking place on board the ship during their entire Mediterranean segment.

The incidence had also eroded trust among staff members. Patti didn't know who to believe anymore. First Officer

Giorgio Tzekas had been arrested for his participation in the smuggling—an involvement partly motivated by gambling debts. Then there was Mike O'Connor a.k.a. Father Pat Connelly, who had smuggled aboard black market antiquities and displayed them with the reproductions he used for his library lectures. Both men worked for Anastasia Catomeris, who had set up the scheme to frame Elias Stamos, the ship's owner and her former lover.

According to Ariana, Anastasia, or Tasia, had given birth to Elias's child, Theo, forty years ago. Even though Elias had generously paid support for his illegitimate son, that wasn't enough for Tasia. She wanted Elias to acknowledge Theo publicly as his son. Elias eventually did, and now father and son were busy building a relationship, despite Tasia and her devious ways.

But it was Mike O'Connor who had fooled everyone, even Gideon Dayan, the head of security. He'd had his suspicions but could find no evidence the guy was a fraud. Thanasi Kaldis, the hotel manager had actually defended the man at one point.

Patti sat back in her chair when she thought of Thanasi, and played with the silver necklace she'd found in the box. The man owned her heart, but there was no way she could even tell him, at least not in the foreseeable future. For now, it was enough they worked together and besides, as cruise director she didn't have time for a love affair. But she could dream, couldn't she?

The necklace slipped out of her hands to the floor, and when she bent over to retrieve it, a clear blue light flashed from the teardrop pendant.

"That's odd," she said out loud.

There was only a small window in the office, but as she glanced through it, she caught the sliver of moon winking in the dark sky.

As she sat upright again holding on to the silver pendant a shiver swept through her and she rubbed her arms to get rid of the tingling sensation.

When she carefully placed the pendant down on the desk in

front of her, she remembered the Greek legend Mike O'Connor had said was attached to the pendant. It was something about the moon goddess and her love for the sheppard, Lexus, and how the sun god, jealous of their love, had the shepherd killed. The silver pendant was supposed to hold the diamond that had been in the clasp of a magic cloak the goddess had made to conceal her lover. After Lexus's death, a teardrop from the moon goddess hardened over the diamond and covered it. The moon goddess told one of her attendants to hide it where she and Lexus had spent their days together and whoever found the pendant would have good luck, especially in love.

"That's it!" Patti said, grabbing the pendant.

The rest of the stuff could be sent off to Ariana's friend but the pendant, even though it required a little polishing and a few repairs would serve as a fun way for the crew to get past the scandal.

She'd hide it in a randomly selected stateroom and make a game out of it for the passengers. "Find the pendant and find your true love" or "Whoever finds the pendant will be lucky in love," or something like that.

She'd have to get the details worked out, but she was hoping Ariana could help her with that. Now that Ariana had found her own true love, a former Italian undercover police officer, perhaps she would know what slogan to use.

She wanted to go to Ariana's cabin and talk about it right now but she knew she needed to wait until morning.

Patti grabbed the necklace closed the box of reproductions, turned out the light and headed for her own cabin, tired but feeling content.

As she walked by a bank of windows and gazed up at the crescent moon, she had to smile at the romance of it all. It was childish to think a piece of inexpensive jewelry could change a person's life, but with all her heart she wished and hoped it was true, not only for the passenger who would find the pendant, but for her, as well.

CHAPTER ONE

THE ONLY REASON Becky Montgomery had agreed to this Caribbean Christmas cruise aboard *Alexandra's Dream*, with her late husband's family was because of Laura, her fifteen-year-old niece. The girl knew her way around Becky like no one else, especially when it came to dealing with Becky's mother-in-law, Estelle, the matriarch of the family.

"You don't even have to see her," Laura had said with that assuring voice of hers. "You know how much she hates the sun. She'll probably stay in her cabin all day sleeping, or annoying the staff telling them how to run things. Besides, I need you and the kids to keep me sane. Between my mom nagging me all day and Grandma reciting the proper rules of etiquette over and over again I might end up hurling myself overboard. You wouldn't want that on your conscience, would you?"

"If I go, I may have to hurl myself with you," Becky had told her. There was no doubt in her mind that she would be going on any cruise with Estelle Montgomery. The mere thought of being trapped on a ship with the woman had given her instant heartburn.

"Then we can save each other once we hit the water. Please, Aunt Becky. You have to come. I'm your favorite niece and I'm begging you."

"You're my *only* niece."

"That may all end soon if you don't come on this cruise."

"Are you threatening me?"

"I'm desperate."

"You're fifteen. All fifteen-year-olds are desperate."

"Yes, but I've got Estelle and Kim for my role models. My desperation is on another level."

That was the precise moment when Becky's resistance had tumbled and she had agreed. She always was a sucker for an underdog and she really felt for Laura.

However, now that the departure date had actually arrived, Becky was having second thoughts. The suitcases were packed, the shore excursions were purchased, and Becky had secured a neighbor to come in and water the plants, feed Brad and Angelina, Sarah's lovebirds, play with Lance Armstrong, Connor's tabby cat, and walk John Wayne, the family bulldog. Now Becky wasn't so sure this whole thing was such a smart idea. She was so nervous about the adventure that the Mickey Mouse pancakes she'd made for her kids for breakfast had given her the dry heaves, and the headache she'd been trying to ignore since waking was now about to blow her eyes out of their sockets.

Still, the fact remained, she had made an agreement with Laura and it was too late to back out...or was it?

Wouldn't a simple phone call to Estelle solve all her problems? She could merely say she was really sorry, but she and the kids couldn't make it this year...or next year, or ever.

Becky sat down at the table with her favorite mug filled to the brim with hot tea and a bowl of dry Cocoa Puffs cereal, her favorite breakfast treat, and seriously pondered the idea as she watched her seven-year-old daughter Sarah gently eat around Mickey's ears. She liked to save them for last.

"I think this whole thing is dumb," Becky's ten-year-old son, Connor, announced. He hadn't touched his food.

"You think everything is dumb," Sarah countered.

"Yeah, including you," he shot back.

"Please, kids. Let's try to be nice to each other while Mickey's at the table." Becky liked to discipline with whatever aid she had at hand. Usually she used the various pets as negotiating tools, but for some reason they weren't in the room.

"Mom," Connor reasoned, rolling his eyes. "These are pancakes."

"It doesn't matter. They represent Mickey, and while he's a guest at our table, there's no arguing."

"Whatever," Connor said, stabbing the pancake with his fork.

Becky stared at her young son. Laura had convinced her to agree to the cruise, but there was another reason that it might not be a good idea in the end: Connor. She hoped the trip would bring him out of his shell. Ever since his dad had died almost two years ago, Connor had slipped further and further into his own world, and now he hardly spoke or ate. And when he did converse, he was usually sarcastic or contrary. She'd tried everything she could think of to get him to come around, but nothing seemed to work for long. He seemed more distant with each passing day.

Becky watched as Connor made little circles with his fork in the syrup, not really eating, his mind obviously somewhere other than the present.

"Connor, two more bites, and finish your milk, then you can leave the table," Becky said, knowing he just wanted to get back to his room.

Without saying a word, he did as he was told, then picked up his dish, placed it in the sink and left the room.

"Don't worry, Mom." Sarah patted Becky on the back. "Mickey understands why Connor's so sad and he's not mad at him for not liking the pancakes."

Becky's eyes watered as she hugged her sweet little girl.

"THE PURPOSE OF A CRUISE is to relax, especially a Caribbean cruise," Lacey Garnett told Becky. "Take in the sights. Float on a breeze. Enjoy yourself."

"Easy for you to say. You don't have a mother-in-law like Estelle Montgomery," Becky snapped.

The two women were standing in front of their shop,

Frock U, a trendy boutique in Hillcrest, the uptown district of San Diego. Lacey turned the lock in the door and they stepped inside.

"She's technically not your mother-in-law anymore. She's simply your kids' grandmother."

"I know, you're right, and I *do* want to keep that relationship strong."

"Good. Then sit back and enjoy the perks."

Becky flipped on the lights and the little shop came to life with color and bling. The women knew all about fashion trends and were constantly on the lookout for the next big craze.

"But I've hardly spoken to Estelle in two years, other than those phone calls every other week so my kids can keep in touch with their grandmother," Becky said, putting her purse down behind the counter. She started to fold some T-shirts. "It's just that she's so controlling. Last week I received a detailed outline on the appropriate attire for each formal dinner and event on the ship. Not for my kids, but for me!"

"She's just being helpful."

Becky stopped folding and glued her fist to her hip. "No, she's not. Helpful is what baggers do at grocery stores. Helpful is when you open a map in the middle of New York City and someone steps up to point out the way. Telling me what to wear on a cruise ship suggests that I don't have a clue even though she knows I co-own a fashion boutique!" Becky's arms were flailing now.

"I think you're reading too much into this. Maybe she's changed, but because you never really talk to her, you can't see it. I still think she was simply trying to be helpful." Lacey joined in the folding.

"Impossible. Her spots go all the way down to the bone."

Lacey walked closer to Becky. "Hey, shouldn't you be home right now, packing all those outfits for all those dinners and events or something? Doesn't your plane leave in, like, three hours?"

"I'm not going." Becky walked over and picked up the retro rotary phone behind the desk and started dialing.

Lacey stopped her mid-dial. "You need this vacation. Your kids need this vacation."

"I know what I'm doing. I'll take the kids to Disneyland for a long weekend. I don't need a family cruise. *We* don't need a family cruise." Becky put the phone down, grabbed her purse and pulled out her cell phone. Lacey snatched it from her hand. Becky was getting really angry now.

"You can't meet a guy in Disneyland," Lacey said.

Becky stopped struggling. "What?"

"A guy. A man. Someone with a penis…who's available. Guys at Disneyland are most likely going to be there with their families or girlfriends."

"I don't need to meet a man, Lacey, I'm perfectly happy with my life the way it is." Becky stared at her best friend and business partner incredulously. She couldn't possibly be serious. Could she?

"No, you're not perfectly happy. I can tell. You need a guy. If only for a couple of nights. Just some meaningless sex under the stars to relieve some of that tension." Lacey took a couple steps back, giving them both some breathing room. Becky did the same.

"I am not tense!" Becky snapped. "All right, maybe I'm a little tense, but meaningless sex certainly won't fix it. Besides, I'm a mother. I have responsibilities. I'm fine."

"I know you when you're fine, remember? We've been friends since we could walk, and you are far from fine. I love you to death but you're an overworked, single psycho-mom who can't even take the morning off on the day she's supposed to be flying to Florida. You're wound up so tight, if someone gives you a nudge you'll spin for the rest of time."

Becky's eyes watered. There was truth in Lacey's words, but she didn't want to admit it, and she definitely didn't want to think about "sex under the stars," even though—if she was being absolutely honest—she *did* long to be held again in a man's arms, and kissed and…

Lacey walked forward and hugged her tight. "It's okay, honey. I know you're hurting, and you don't want to see Estelle, and you miss Ryder. But Becky, he would want you to move on. It's been almost two years since he passed away. You know he would want you to be happy."

Becky pulled away. She couldn't even think about having a relationship with a man…not yet. It was too soon, wasn't it? "I can't. It's not time yet."

"Okay. I understand. I do. But at least get on that plane and go on the cruise. Relax a little. Hey, maybe you can find some new merchandise for our shop while you're on Saint Thomas Island, some exotic dresses and jewelry. I hear it's a fab place to shop. Go discover some struggling designer and bring his or her designs to the States. Look at this as a working vacation. Would that make you feel better about it?"

Becky thought about it for a moment, and the idea actually sounded good. "You know, we could use a little more color in this place to go with all our plans for next year." A smile spread across her face.

Lacey grabbed Becky's purse, slipped her cell phone back inside and handed it to her. "You better get going if you want to make that plane. That designer is out there on some island waiting for you to discover him…if you know what I mean."

Becky smiled and took her purse. "I get it, but I'm really not ready for romance. Honest. Besides, I'll have my kids with me."

"They can't be with you every minute."

Becky gave her a look. "I'm a dedicated mom."

Lacey walked her to the front door, turned and hugged Becky. "And I'm a dedicated friend. Remember, sex doesn't equal romance. You can keep your heart perfectly safe and *still* relieve some of that tension all bottled up inside. Having sex is healthy."

They separated. "Okay. I'll consider the sex, but only on one condition."

"What's that?"

"Can I have the meaningless but healthy sex in a cabin? I'm not one for public displays."

"Honey, you can have sex in a vault for all I care, just make sure you don't come home without it."

"I'll do my best," Becky said, going along with the idea to placate Lacey. Secretly she had no intention of having sex with anyone.

"You're lying. I can tell when you're lying, but it doesn't matter because I've thrown the idea out into the universe, and once it's out there, only the moon, sun and stars know what will really happen. It's out of your control."

Becky never believed her somewhat mystical friend, but this time a slight shiver washed over her as she walked out of the store. For some reason she felt as though Lacey's wish had truly been ordered and she couldn't help wondering if the universe was listening.

ALL THE NUDGING in the world couldn't keep Connor from being anxious for most of the flight from San Diego to Miami Beach, Florida where they would board *Alexandra's Dream* for their cruise. While Sarah, the girly-girl who already knew how to work Becky's new digital camera better than Becky did, had busied herself on the flight with the continuing adventures of Ken and Barbie on holiday—her dolls and outfits had been carefully packed in her backpack. Connor had sat with his nose in a *Lemony Snicket* novel, speaking to no one.

Sarah was such a clever and easy child that sometimes Becky would forget that she was only seven years old. Nothing seemed to faze her, and her laugh was infectious. She had an imagination that knew no bounds, and a curiosity that kept Becky busy trying to figure out answers. She could read by the time she was four, and wrote her first story when she was barely six. Her teachers couldn't keep up with her, and most of her classes were at advanced levels.

Connor, however, had changed dramatically since his father's death two years ago. Gone was that happy, carefree little boy who loved to swim and play baseball and ride his bike for countless hours. Connor's approach to life was more somber, but then, so was Becky's.

"The ship is going to sink just like the *Titanic* and we're all going to freeze to death in the water." Connor looked up from his book as the plane made its final descent. "I think we should turn right around and go back home."

Sarah rolled her eyes. "There aren't any icebergs in the Caribbean, silly. They would melt. And I looked up *Alexandra's Dream* on the Web—we each get our own lifeboat."

Connor shook his head and made a face. "Yeah, well, maybe we'll get locked in the bottom of the ship and won't be able to get out to find a lifeboat, and we'll all drown."

"Then I'll get an ax and break the lock," Sarah declared while making hand gestures as if she were breaking the lock at that very moment. Sarah liked to give a demonstration for clarity whenever possible. "Then you and Mom can take my hand and I'll lead you to the lifeboats."

"Like you would know where to go."

"Of course I would. I'm Wonder Girl and I can do anything!"

"Oh, yeah." Connor turned in his middle seat to face her. Sarah sat next to the window, while Becky was on the aisle. Connor had insisted on the arrangement because he didn't want to see what was going on either down below or on the plane. "If you're Wonder Girl then why didn't you fly here on your own?"

Without missing a beat Sarah said, "I thought about it, but it would mess up my hair." She primped her naturally curly blond hair. Usually it fell into her eyes, but today she had worn a lavender-and-pink sparkly barrette that matched her outfit to hold it in place. She also wore lavender sandals, and Becky had polished her nails a bright pink to match her backpack. Sarah was a fashion diva.

Connor burst out laughing, and Becky was finally able to relax a little. It had been a long flight, but the journey was just beginning. If this little incident was any indication of things to come, she was hoping that Sarah would continue to use her magic on Connor to get him to lighten up. Of course, the way Becky was feeling, she could use a sprinkling of Sarah's magic herself. Her stomach was still in a knot and her nerves were wound tight. She had wanted to buy a drink during the flight, but she just couldn't justify it with her kids sitting next to her, so instead she tried to simply ignore her own apprehensions… not the best solution.

The plane landed and Becky escorted her children to baggage claim, then they caught a cab to the cruise ship without crisis. Connor, although somewhat distracted, was at least cooperative, while Sarah skipped her way through the entire journey.

It would be the first time Becky and her kids had ever been on a ship. They'd seen them before, docked in San Diego, but knowing they were going to be living on one for a week was exciting. They stood in line on Pier Five at the Port of Miami, filling out forms, then gave their luggage to a stevedore and handed an agent their passports to check. Connor kept lagging behind, studying the exterior of the ship, while Sarah bounced around in happy anticipation. The heads of Ken and Barbie popped out of her backpack, as if they were doing their own happy dance.

BECKY KEPT BOTH Sarah and Connor close as they went through the embarkation process, which was held in a comfortable covered area on the pier. There was even a band playing island music in the far corner, and a private seating area for the VIP group, which Estelle had seen fit to bestow on Becky and the kids. However, Becky was sure all this executive treatment came with a high "you owe me" price tag. She could only speculate what that might be.

Becky kept the kids close by her side, not wanting them wandering off before they even found their cabins. Her ticket stated that she and her kids had a penthouse with a veranda.

Sarah had looked it up on the Web, and when she discovered the cabin had a DVD player, she insisted on bringing along *Alice in Wonderland, The Little Mermaid, Pirates of the Caribbean, Cars* and various other movies to torment Becky and Connor with during the cruise. Becky brought along *The Princess Bride*, the one movie the entire family could agree on, even Connor. They'd all seen it countless times, and could quote from it, but there was something almost magical about the movie that usually put them in a good mood.

Sarah had this belief that anyone they met who loved the movie as much as they did would eventually become part of their family, and so far, Sarah had been right.

Becky, of course, was hoping to distract her from watching so many movies with all the water activities this cruise had to offer. After all, it was billed as A Creatures of the Caribbean encounter, a chance to get up close and personal, and Becky intended to take full advantage of every encounter offered... well, at least within reason. She had already signed up for a dolphin encounter—too good to pass up—and snorkeling around a coral reef sounded like fun. But she'd been forced to leave herself and the kids open because Estelle had her own plans, and Becky knew better than to try to disrupt those. The ship was scheduled to drop anchor at Grand Turk Island, the Cays, Tortola Island, St. Maarten and, of course, Saint Thomas in the U.S. Virgin Islands. She was sure Estelle had plans for each stop, only she hadn't yet bothered to tell Becky.

Once they stepped on board and into a huge lobby with glass elevators, large baskets of fresh flowers everywhere and enough room to accommodate half the people on the ship, Becky let out a sigh of relief. They had actually made it. Maybe she could, in fact, relax.

A charming woman with dark hair and a warm smile handed Becky a brightly colored brochure announcing an onboard treasure hunt. "Be sure to join in the fun, looking for the treasure," the woman encouraged. "It's all explained in this brochure." Becky noticed her name tag: Patti Kennedy, Cruise Director.

"What's that about?" Connor asked Becky, obviously curious.

Becky handed the brochure to Connor instead. "Here. You read it and tell us what it says."

"Is it a real treasure?" Sarah asked. "Like in *Pirates of the Caribbean?* Will we be rich if we find it? I'd like that. Then Mommy could stay home more and only go to work when we're at school."

A pang of guilt ripped through Becky. She really had been working too many hours since Ryder had died. It wasn't about the money; Ryder had left them more than enough to be comfortable. Plus each child had a college trust fund. The Montgomerys had set that up as soon as the kids were born. But work was the only thing that seemed to keep Becky from thinking about Ryder. It hadn't been very fair to her kids. She could see that now, especially with Connor.

She made a promise to herself to spend every moment of this adventure with her kids. Perhaps, in some small way, that would make up for all those long hours they had spent with their babysitters.

She let out a heavy sigh, suddenly seeing the cruise in a whole new light. She watched as Sarah took Connor's hand and pulled him in closer so she could see the pictures on the brochure. Connor didn't put up any resistance. He merely opened the brochure, lowered to her level and began reading.

"May I see your boarding papers?"

Startled by the deep voice, Becky looked up and into the impossibly green eyes of the handsome man standing in front of her.

"What?"

"I'm here to escort you to your cabin."

She handed him the papers.

"Oh, I see you're in a penthouse, Ms. Montgomery."

"Becky." She felt her cheeks heat up. Now why had she wanted to tell him her first name?

"Welcome aboard. Follow me."

Becky tapped the kids' shoulders to get their attention and they all fell in line behind the man. She caught bits and pieces about the treasure hunt as Connor kept reading while they walked. It looked as if they were being given the VIP treatment with a special escort, something Estelle had likely set up.

As they walked, Becky sneaked a glance at their escort. He was very good-looking, dressed in white shorts and a white polo shirt, with the ship's insignia discreetly stitched over his heart, along with a small name tag: Dylan Langstaff—Newfoundland. He wasn't dressed in a steward's uniform, and there was no indication of his title, so Becky could only guess this wasn't part of his regular duties. He looked more like the fit outdoorsy type to her.

"'…and the sun god was intensely jealous of the beautiful moon goddess and wanted her all to himself.'" Connor continued reading the legend in the brochure. "'He didn't like it when she was on the far side of the earth and he couldn't see what she was doing. In one of these periods, the moon goddess fell in love with a beautiful shepherd from Arcadia named Lexus…'"

Becky could only imagine this cute guy's backlist of women, probably the proverbial "girl in every port" routine. He didn't seem the type who would choose to spend weeks on a ship, working far from home while he had a wife or steady girlfriend waiting his return. No, he definitely looked more like the dyed-in-the-wool bachelor type.

"'…they had to keep their love a secret from the sun god and could only be together at night. The moon goddess went to the celestial seamstress Athena and begged her to weave a beautiful cloak of shimmering moonbeams that would shield the goddess and her lover from the eyes of the sun. The cloak worked beautifully until one day when the sun was searching for them, the cloak slipped and nearly revealed them…'"

But Dylan *was* the perfect specimen of the type of guy she had expected might work on a cruise ship: handsome and tall—she guessed just over six feet—wavy brown hair with those natural blond highlights from being out in the sun, thin and tan with muscular arms and straight shoulders. She thought he probably handled the athletic activities the ship offered, maybe helping passengers climb up those rock-climbing walls that were so popular. Connor had been to a birthday party at a rock climbing gym in San Diego a few years ago, and all the men there looked like Dylan—powerfully built, fit, ready for adventure.

"'The moon goddess arranged for a blacksmith to make a clasp to secure the cloak and couldn't resist having a large diamond inserted in the clasp. The sun was becoming increasingly jealous because he knew the moon goddess was in love with a human and he was determined to put an end to their relationship…'"

Becky kept sneaking peeks at Dylan as he led them into one of the glass elevators, then down a corridor with plush carpeting under their feet, where creamy white doors lined both sides of the hallway. She noticed his hands, the long fingers, his neatly trimmed nails and the silver and onyx ring on his right pinky. Perhaps the ring was a gift from a pining girlfriend patiently waiting for him in some exotic port of call?

"'…and once again, the sun god carefully scanned the area with his beam, and this time he noticed a flash of light. When he moved his beam over the same spot, he realized it was the facets of a diamond flashing in the light. He grabbed the diamond clasp and tore the moonbeam cloak from the lovers. Then he struck Lexus, and sent the moon goddess back to the sky. In his anger, the sun god had melted the bronze clasp, freeing the diamond, which the moon goddess snatched up to remember her lover…'"

"Here we are," Dylan said.

"That mean old sun god—I want to know what happened to the poor moon goddess," Sarah whined. "Did she ever see Lexus again?"

Dylan turned, knelt on one knee to get down to Sarah's level and shook his head. "No. Poor Lexus died, and the moon goddess cried for so long that the earth was about to be flooded with her tears."

"Like my mommy did when my daddy left to go to—" Sarah began, but Becky reached out and pulled her back to make her stop talking. Sarah liked to tell everyone that her daddy had left to go to heaven, but he was watching them every minute from his cloud. He didn't want to leave, but God needed him to be an angel, just like in *It's a Wonderful Life*. Becky was never really comfortable talking about Ryder with anyone, especially not a stranger.

But it was too late. Sarah had already said too much.

Dylan looked up at Becky and his face seemed so full of concern that it took Becky's breath away. It was neither sympathy nor pity. It was something she couldn't put her finger on.

Here was this charmer, this obvious babe magnet, yet he seemed to have a soft underside, and for a split second Becky thought she could see into his soul.

Something shifted inside her, something she couldn't explain.

He looked back at Sarah, and the compassion was replaced by the friendly smile of a man telling a child a story.

He stood and opened their cabin door. "The goddess Artemis came to visit the moon goddess and convinced her to stop crying before she destroyed everything on earth, and she agreed, but not before she shed one final silver teardrop that hardened around the diamond. Then she sent the jewel off to be hidden, but she said she would always cry one day a year for Lexus." His voice turned into a whisper. "And she still does, but on the very next night—" he waved an arm over his head and grinned "—the moon goddess sends a cascade of moonbeams and shooting stars across the sky to remind everyone of Lexus."

"So when we see a shooting star, that's the moon goddess reminding us of Lexus?" Sarah asked him, wide-eyed.

"You bet it is," Dylan answered, still smiling that dazzling smile.

"Right," Connor mumbled, slumping down on the sofa.

"Don't pay any attention to my brother. He's no fun anymore." She motioned for Dylan to bend down so she could tell him something, then she blurted, "He doesn't even want to read about Harry Potter. He doesn't like movies, not really, and he won't play Wonder Girl with me."

Connor pulled a pillow up over his head.

"I knew there was something different about you." Dylan winked at Sarah.

As Sarah did her cute Wonder Girl pose, Becky could tell Dylan had won her heart. And could win Becky's if she wasn't careful. It was his eyes. He had those sensitive, innocent eyes, but Becky knew it had to be something he could turn on and off at will. He worked on a cruise ship. He was trained in the art of making people, especially women, feel special. Wasn't he?

Becky put her arms around her daughter's shoulders, and pulled her in tight from behind. She suddenly felt as if this man had learned enough about her family. "Thanks for escorting us to our room, and finishing the story. I think I can figure everything out from here."

"Okay. But don't hesitate to contact someone if you need assistance, Ms. Montgomery." He turned to leave, but then stopped and slowly turned back around. "Oh, there's one more thing about that diamond the moon goddess hid." He directed his charm at Sarah. She stared up at him as if he were telling her a special secret.

"What is it?" she asked, never blinking. He had her full attention. Even Connor slipped the pillow off his head.

"It's hidden somewhere on this very ship. In one of the cabins, to be exact, and whoever finds it will have good luck." Dylan looked directly at Becky. "Especially in love."

A slight shiver danced up her spine as she stared into those magical jade-colored eyes of his, and for a moment she actually considered Lacey's advice. But before she could genuinely second-guess herself, the oh-so-charming Dylan Langstaff was gone.

CHAPTER TWO

"I CAN'T BELIEVE you pulled this off, Patti, that this treasure hunt idea is actually happening." Thanasi Kaldis walked up behind Dylan, who was handing out brochures in the lobby with Patti Kennedy, the cruise director.

"Look at them," the ship's hotel manager continued, "half the people aren't even glancing at their brochures. I still say that no one will bother looking for that silly pendant. I thought the whole idea was rejected, Patti."

Thanasi was in his late forties, wore his navy-blue blazer over meticulously pressed whites; he had a crop of black wavy hair and a charismatic smile…most of the time. However, at that precise moment he directed a teasing scowl at Patti.

"It was never rejected," she told him in a confident voice. "You must have dreamed that, so stop your stressing. Just go with it. Besides, it's going to be fun."

Patti, also dressed in a navy blazer and whites, was a brown-haired dynamo who had celebrated her thirty-ninth birthday in Venice on a gondola, alone. If Dylan had known about it beforehand, he would have surprised her with a party or dinner. They'd become friends, and he hated to hear that his friend had been so alone on her birthday, especially when she loved people so much and wanted nothing more than to see everyone around her happy.

Her title usually went to a man, but Patti was possibly the best cruise director Dylan had ever worked with. She anticipated the needs of the passengers and was always looking to enhance their cruise experience. Plus she was just fun to be around.

She turned back to a young couple approaching her. "Find the hidden pendant and receive extra perks the entire cruise!"

Dylan watched as the woman took the brochure, glanced at it then stuffed it into her large straw handbag. Perhaps Thanasi was right. The pendant hunt could be a complete bust. He hoped not, though. He'd liked the idea, and he would be taking part in a few fun excursions set up for the passenger who found it.

Patti turned to Thanasi. "Somebody will find the pendant and the entire ship will be buzzing about it. It's romantic. And you might want to lighten up—our passengers don't need to see an officer frowning." The smile she offered would have melted anybody's heart.

People filed by happily, but Thanasi was still scowling Patti's way. She was right, Dylan thought. Not a good image. He could tell that all the hotel manager could think of was possible damage to the cabins as the passengers searched for the pendant.

When the idea had been discussed at an activities planning meeting, Thanasi had voiced his concerns. But even then Dylan thought it was simply his way of teasing Patti. As if they were school kids on the playground and he was vying for her for attention by being uncooperative.

One thing Dylan simply didn't understand was why Thanasi didn't just tell Patti he was attracted to her. The entire crew could see it, and it was obvious Patti felt the same for him. Dylan decided what the man needed was a dose of good sex to help him lighten up, but Thanasi went by the book, and apparently that book didn't include onboard romances.

"Find the pendant and find your true love," Patti said to a group of twenty-something women. They each took a brochure. One of them mumbled something and they burst out laughing as they walked away.

"See, look, they think it's a joke," Thanasi announced.

"Hey," Patti said softly, so only Thanasi could hear, "I'm work-ing here. If you can't help, then maybe you should just leave."

Thanasi stared back at her for a moment as though trying to think of something clever to say, but before he could respond, a petite lady with white curly hair and a bright pink visor walked up to him and tapped him on the shoulder. "Could you please tell me where my room is located? It's my first cruise and I'm not very good at this sort of thing. I've been waiting for a steward, but they all seem to be busy with other people."

Thanasi smiled at the woman, then turned on his charm as he bowed, his entire demeanor transforming. "I'd be delighted." He extended his elbow, she slid her arm through the crook, and off they went. "Let me tell you about *Alexandra's Dream*," he said, but Dylan could tell by his tone that he was still a little ir-ritated about the pendant search.

Patti had told Dylan about the necklace she and librarian Ariana Bennett had found among the personal things of Mike O'Connor, the guy who'd been posing as a priest and smug-gling stolen artifacts aboard. Apparently the pendant was left behind with a few other reproductions after the police investi-gation. The whole scandal had required a deft PR campaign to keep the cabins on *Alexandra's Dream* at capacity although Dylan had a feeling the press coverage had also gained the cruise ship a few new bookings.

He loved his job and really didn't want to lose it. Being in charge of the ship's dive staff paid well, and in the world of cruise ships, it was a tough job to come by. It was his first real managerial position and allowed him to teach water sports and diving, and run a few of the water-themed activities off the ship.

Dylan was happy the ship wasn't docked somewhere and he was out looking for another job. If that had happened, it would have given his brother the perfect excuse to press him even more to return home.

His absence was a sore subject between them, even though Dylan tried his best to make up for it by sending half his pay

home to Newfoundland every month, something he'd been doing for the past eight years, never missing a month. And besides,
jobs were still scarce in his hometown, further confirming he
was doing the right thing. It gave him great comfort to know
that at least his mom didn't have to worry about money.

But, he admitted, a job shortage wasn't the only reason
he was reluctant to go back. The place had too many sad
memories, and Dylan was doing his best to avoid them.

He loved the routine of welcoming passengers and a week
or so later bidding them farewell and getting ready for a new
group. But today's boarding had been different. Today he'd felt
a totally unexpected personal interest in one of the passengers—the woman he'd just escorted to a penthouse suite.

Becky Montgomery.

He remembered what the adorable, little blond-haired angel
had told him about her mommy crying when her daddy left, just
like the moon goddess who'd flooded the earth with her sad
tears. How could any guy leave that perfect little family, let
alone such a fine-looking woman as Becky? And from what her
little girl implied, Dylan assumed it must have been one nasty
divorce, and her mom hadn't taken it well. The hurt was still
there in her pretty eyes.

Plain as day.

The son seemed distant, maybe still harboring feelings he
didn't quite know what to do with. A boy needed a father,
though Dylan would bet a year's salary his mother bent over
backward to keep those kids safe and happy.

Strange, how he'd picked up on all of that in just those few
moments.

Then he stopped himself. Stopped the feelings that had
rushed through him as he'd been thinking about the beautiful
woman, the charming little girl and the obviously troubled boy.

He admitted to himself this could be trouble. Big trouble.
He couldn't deny he felt a strong attraction to her, but there were
strict rules about passenger/staff onboard relationships.

He'd never broken that rule before, but Becky Montgomery might just cause him to bend it a little if he wasn't careful.

He could only hope she and her kids hated water sports.

"BUT WHY DO WE HAVE TO wait until after dinner to go to the pool?" Connor asked, giving his suitcase a little kick while he stood in front of the twin beds.

"Can we at least unpack first?" Becky liked settling in when she was in a strange place.

"Don't you want to look for the pendant first?" Sarah asked, still hopeful.

"No, I don't want to look for that dumb old pendant," her brother grumbled.

"Well, I do," Sarah said, and flung herself across her bed.

A knock at the door stopped further arguments as the kids ran to answer it, nearly tripping over themselves trying to get to it first.

When they opened the door, both Sarah and Connor squealed with laughter and excitement. Their cousin Laura slowly entered the room, both kids hanging on her.

"Mom wanted me to wait until dinner to see you guys, but I couldn't wait. I am *so* happy you're here." The kids tumbled Laura to the floor in a heap of tickles and laughter.

Becky couldn't believe her eyes. All Laura had to do was walk into the room and Connor's whole disposition changed. Whatever magic Laura was dispelling, Becky wanted the potion.

"I'm so glad you're here," Becky echoed.

"Save me, Aunt Becky," Laura spluttered as she tickled Connor's belly. Sarah lay on Laura's stomach, one hand tickling Laura under the arm. Laura fought to get her off, but Sarah was persistent. Finally, after a few minutes, both Connor and Sarah rolled away, scrambled to their feet, grinning from ear to ear. Laura stood, then walked over and gave Becky a warm hug.

"Let me look at you," Becky said as they pulled apart.

Laura backed away and Becky was pleasantly surprised by

how much this fifteen-year-old had grown. She had almost reached Becky's height of five-seven and her hair was a rich golden-brown cut short and shaggy around her face. She definitely looked like a Montgomery with those thick eyebrows and that chiseled nose. Her skin had cleared up and was now glowing, and although she was several pounds heavier than Becky had remembered, it seemed to suit her well. However, her makeup was rather thick and her clothes were simply too tight, but Becky didn't care if she wore vampire makeup and arrived in a toga. She was thrilled to see her, and instantly realized just how much she'd missed her.

"You're beautiful," Becky told her.

"I'm fat," Laura countered.

"Aren't we all?"

"Not my mom. She's perfect."

"Impossible. Nobody's perfect."

"Tell that to my grandmother."

"I'll do that."

"Can I watch?"

"Only if you hide any and all sharp objects first."

"It's a deal."

They hugged again, laughing, then parted. Sarah joined them and tugged on Laura's hand. "I want to find the magic pendant."

"How could *you* ever find it on this big ship?" Connor said with more than a little sarcasm as he stepped closer. Apparently it didn't take long for his mood to change.

"Yeah, but somebody has to find it," Laura suggested, ignoring his crankiness and supporting Sarah's excitement.

"And it won't be us," Connor scorned. "Nothing good ever happens in this family."

Laura tousled his hair, and Connor let her, but Becky could tell his attitude was deteriorating quickly. "Oh, I don't know. We're all on this cruise together. That's something good."

"You know what I mean." He moved away from her hand. "I mean to my family, like me and my sister and my mom."

"Well, maybe if we find the pendant, your luck will start to change," Laura said.

"I seriously doubt it." He walked away and plopped himself down on the sofa.

"If we all think positive thoughts, maybe we'll have a better chance of finding it," Laura decreed, sitting next to him.

Connor shrugged. "Whatever."

Sarah looked pensive for a moment. Becky could tell she was trying to figure something out. Suddenly her face brightened. "Thoughts like raindrops on roses, and whiskers on kittens, bright copper kettles and warm woolen mittens?"

"Don't get her started," Connor whispered.

Ignoring him, Laura added, "Sure, whatever makes you the most happy."

Suddenly, Sarah started singing "My Favorite Things." Connor slid down on the sofa. Laura joined in the tune, then got up and grabbed Sarah, spinning her around, laughing. Becky joined in, as well.

When they'd finished dancing around the room, and bugging Connor whenever they got the chance, his attitude picked up slightly.

Becky relished the fact that Laura had such a positive effect on her kids. She knew Connor was just as thrilled as Sarah to see his cousin, but he purposely didn't want to show too much enthusiasm. However, it was almost impossible when Laura was in the room. It was as if he was fighting against his true self and couldn't trust his own emotions. As if he was afraid to be happy.

It tore Becky apart.

At least so far it didn't seem to be affecting his schoolwork, and he still participated in some school activities, so she didn't think he needed a therapist yet. However, if this family cruise didn't change his somber disposition, she had already decided to make an appointment with a good family therapist when they returned home.

"I think I'm going to find the pendant and we're going to be the luckiest family in the whole world," Sarah announced.

The chances of them finding the pendant were next to zero, Becky figured, but Laura's enthusiasm was infectious. Becky wished, for Connor's sake, that by some miracle the kids would find the pendant.

"This is bogus," Connor mumbled. "We can think positive thoughts for the next million years and we still won't be able to find it."

"No deadbeats allowed," Laura insisted, grabbing hold of Connor again and tickling his belly. He smiled briefly, but then turned away. Becky knew Laura was working her happy magic on him, and the ice was at least melting around the edges. "Come on, Connor, have a little faith, at least for a few hours. You don't want to break our positive vibes, do you?"

Connor shrugged.

"I sometimes believe six impossible things before breakfast," Sarah said.

Connor stared at his sister then rolled his eyes. Becky knew how much he hated it when she quoted from *Alice In Wonderland*. It was one of those movies Sarah had watched over and over until Becky couldn't take it anymore and had actually pretended to lose the darn thing for two whole weeks. When she found it again, Sarah was into *The Little Mermaid*, thank you very much.

"Tell you what," Laura said to Sarah. "What would make you the happiest right now?"

Sarah thought for a moment. "Swimming!"

"I don't think we can do that right now, so what else?"

She thought again. "A really big chocolate ice cream cone with sprinkles."

"That's something we can do," Laura confirmed. She turned toward Connor. "And what would make you happy?"

"Nothing," Connor grumbled.

"Come on, Connor. There must be something."

"No. I don't want to."

"You don't want to be happy?" Laura argued.

"No. I don't want to play your stupid game," he announced, and stomped into the bathroom and shut the door.

"Connor," Becky called after him, but the only thing she heard was the lock turning in the door. Laura gave Becky a quizzical glance, but Becky didn't respond.

"Pickles. Those great big sour ones," Sarah said, her eyes dancing.

"Pickles?" Laura asked.

"Connor loves pickles," Becky told her.

"Then let's get you a double-scoop ice cream cone and Connor the biggest pickle on the entire ship." Laura grabbed Sarah's hand and headed for the door then stopped. "If that's okay with your mom." She looked at Becky.

"It's perfect," Becky said, "In the meantime I'll stay here with Connor and we'll unpack."

Sarah looked up at her mother. "Tell him he can have the bed next to the wall if he wants. I don't care." And with that, she and Laura went skipping out of the cabin, leaving Becky alone with Connor.

Suddenly, Becky realized the ship was moving. It was almost surreal. She glanced out the sliding-glass doors that opened onto the huge, private patio. Not only were they moving, they were well away from port and headed out into open water.

She had wanted to be on deck with the kids when they sailed away, a glass of champagne in her hand, toasting this cruise meant to appease her mother-in-law and somehow bring her son out of his shell. But instead she was in her cabin, alone, with no champagne in sight, and a somber Connor locked in the cabin's bathroom. She sighed, knowing it would be a few minutes before he'd emerge. Becky had learned to let him have his quiet time. Time to think. But she was worried her ten-year-old spent way too much time thinking.

She gazed out the sliders. At least the view was spectacular.

Dusk had descended and the sky was ablaze with color, the lights from Miami fading in the distance, but Becky didn't seem to really care. The person who now held the power to make this trip work or turn it into a complete nightmare wasn't Estelle, it was Connor. Becky was terrified that she'd lost her sweet son, and she had no idea how to find him again.

Connor walked out of the bathroom, staring down at the floor. His smile was gone, replaced with his usual scowl.

"Your sister said you could have the bed next to the wall," Becky told him.

"Whatever," Connor mumbled. But Becky could see that he was happy about the turn of events. She watched as he pulled his suitcase closer to the bed, unzipped it and began sorting out his clothes.

While Connor figured out just what drawers he wanted, Becky continued to unpack her own bag. Connor was a neat freak, as his dad had been, and it would take him the next couple of hours just to make sure all his clothes were lined up properly in the drawers and in the small closet.

He liked to keep his clothes color-coordinated, and his shoes lined up according to usage, with his flip-flops closest to the door. Clothes were never something he took for granted, but a statement of his mood, and lately Connor favored camouflage military attire. However, when he'd packed he'd taken along one orange tee, which Becky saw him hang in the back of his closet. She couldn't figure out why he'd brought it along. She knew he would never wear something so bright.

The suite had ample closet space, but Becky had packed light. When she carefully hung up her turquoise cocktail dress, a memory flashed of the day she'd bought it for the company Christmas party. She hadn't wanted to go, but Ryder had insisted saying it was good for them to get to know some of his employees at Wireless Technologies. They had actually shopped for the dress together, and when she'd tried it on, his eyes had lit up and she'd known she'd found the right dress.

Afterward, they had hurried home before Connor had to be picked up from preschool. They had made love on the stairs leading up to their bedroom. The buttons on her silk shirt had popped off, and Ryder hadn't even bothered to remove his pants.

When they were both spent, they lay sprawled across the steps, Ryder's knees and shins sporting rug burns and her own elbows a little raw. Memories of the waves of pleasure that had surged through her still brought a flush to her cheeks. She was convinced that had been the precise moment she'd conceived Sarah.

The turquoise dress never did get worn for the company Christmas party. Estelle and Mark, who owned and ran the company, had sent Ryder to New Jersey on urgent business, so Becky had made her excuses to Estelle. But Estelle had insisted she make an appearance for Ryder's sake, and even sent over a car on the night of the party.

But Becky was stronger than both Ryder and his sister Kim. She knew how to say no to Estelle and mean it.

As her fingers touched the dress, a classic style, it slipped off the polished wooden hanger and onto the floor. Becky picked it up and reached for a satin padded hanger from the other end of the closet. It would prevent the gown from sliding off and ending up in a heap on the closet floor.

As she pulled the hanger toward her, something glittered in the center of the pink satin. At first she thought she was seeing a reflection from the hook, but as she slid the hanger closer, she saw that something was wrapped around the center. On further inspection, she realized she was staring at what had to be the moon goddess's pendant.

As she reached for it, Connor's voice startled her. "I've looked everywhere in this darn room and it's not here." His voice was heavy with despair. "We're just unlucky, that's all. We're one unlucky family."

Becky had become so lost in her memories that for a brief moment she didn't know what he was talking about. Then reality came rushing back.

She pulled the pendant off the hanger, walked into the next room and leaned against the doorjamb. Spinning the necklace around her hand, she said, "Now, just what were you saying about us being unlucky?"

CHAPTER THREE

"I DON'T CARE what you have to do, but if you ever want to see your son again, you'll find my diamond." Sal Morena's voice was harsh and menacing and it made Tracy Irvine shake right down to her very core.

"How do I know he's all right?" She pleaded into her cell phone, tears streaking her face. "I need to talk to my son."

"He's fine," he said lightly. "Never been better. A boy needs his father. I don't know why I stayed away so long."

"A court ordered you to," Tracy reminded him.

"That was your fault," he yelled. "If you weren't cheating on me, none of that would have happened."

She wiped the tears away with shaking fingers as she remembered the beatings she'd suffered. Being involved with Sal and his scheme scared her more than she could imagine, but she knew she had to be strong for her son.

"I never cheated on you, Sal."

He laughed and her knees went weak. "Don't lie. It won't help the situation. You're a whore. Everybody in Vegas knew it, but I was just too blind to see it. Hell, if it wasn't for that blood test I got on this kid, I wouldn't even know he was mine."

"He looks just like you."

"Yeah, lucky kid."

"I want to talk to my son," she repeated, forcing herself to sound calm as she sat on the floor of her tiny cabin and nervously picked at the tan carpet. The floor was strewn with brochures announcing the silly, gimmicky pendant hunt. Brochures that she hadn't even finished passing out because Sal had tried to call her several times on her cell phone. It was only now, after the ship had left the pier, that she had time to finally take the call.

"I want my diamond," he insisted. "That bastard Giorgio Tzekas owes me. He's in prison, but my payment is still on that ship and I want it."

Sal had loaned Giorgio Tzekas, who had been the first officer of the ship, a lot of money. Tzekas had been going to pay him off with the diamond, but had been arrested before it ever happened.

"It's a big ship, Sal. It's going to take time."

"Honey, the longer it takes, the more the kid and I are bonding. How old is he now? Five? Six? He's a pretty smart kid."

Her mouth felt dry and her throat tight. "He's five, Sal. He just turned five."

"Yeah? I bet he knows what a whore is."

Tracy squeezed the phone tighter, praying she could keep her voice calm, not let him hear her fear. "Sal, put Franco on the phone."

"Let me see if I can say this in words you might understand. Find my damn diamond!" He swore, and then her cell phone gave her those sweet tones to indicate that the caller had hung up. Tracy called him back several times, but Sal never answered.

She slowly pulled herself up from the floor and began picking up the brochures, when suddenly it was as if a light had gone off somewhere inside her head. Why hadn't she made the connection before? She quickly skimmed the brochure again, excited about the possibility.

Could this be the necklace she'd been looking for? The necklace that was hiding Sal Morena's diamond? She'd heard that water sports instructor—Dylan somebody or other—mention how Patti and Ariana had found the pendant among Mike O'Connor's things. He was that fake priest who'd smuggled real antiquities among the reproductions he lectured about when *Alexandra's Dream* was cruising the Mediterranean. She'd simply assumed it was a piece of costume jewelry. However, now that she saw how big the silver teardrop was in the brochure, her heart skipped a beat. She knew with every fiber of her being that she was actually looking at Sal's hidden diamond. The coincidence was too strong.

Could she really get her hands on the pendant? One of the passengers would need to find it first, of course. There were almost a thousand passengers on board and all she had to do was find the one wearing that pendant. God help her, she would do whatever it took to steal it away so she could get her son back.

There was a knock at her door. Two of the other dancers were calling her for the bingo game they were working together. The other dancers seemed to love the extra duties they had to perform, but she'd been secretly dreading them, especially bingo. But now she was thinking of ways she could take on more duties.

That way she'd have greater exposure to passengers.

"Coming," she yelled through the door as she touched up her makeup in the mirror above the small dresser. When she looked human again, long chestnut hair combed behind her ears, golden eye shadow caressing her brown eyes, red-apple on her lips, she opened the door, smiling. "Can I take the floor first? I really can't wait to meet our passengers."

"Sure," one of the dancers said. "But I thought—"

"Never mind what I said before. I'm loving all this extra duty. It's exactly what I need to, um, get over a really bad relationship."

The other girls started comparing bad breakup stories as the three of them made their way to the Bacchus deck and Caesar's Forum casino. With each step, Tracy could feel hope blossom as she formulated a plan to find the passenger with the pendant.

BECAUSE THE KIDS WERE SO excited about Becky finding the pendant they wanted to eat dinner early and at the Garden Terrace buffet instead of the formal dinner in the dining room. Of course Estelle wanted nothing to do with casual dining, but relented when the kids were so persistent.

Laura, Connor and Sarah had all insisted that Becky wear the pendant to get her luck started right away. She had contacted Patti Kennedy to report that she'd found it, and within thirty minutes a steward had brought her another large basket of goodies—there had already been one in the room—and a list of the perks she and her family were entitled to. Becky hadn't had time to go over everything, but was definitely considering the free massage in the spa.

Of course, the leaflet also made it quite clear that the pendant had to be returned at the end of the cruise for even more surprises. Sarah couldn't wait to see what those were.

Reluctant to attract attention as they made their way to the Garden Terrace, Becky compromised and told the kids she would wear the pendant once she had a chance to tell the rest of the family.

Laura had helped her convince the kids of the plan. The reality was, both Becky and Laura knew that if Becky took all the attention away from Laura's mother, Kim, and her grandmother, Estelle, on the very first night of the cruise, the rest of the trip would probably turn ugly.

The dining room was surrounded by large picture windows and the tables were positioned in tiered seatings. There was a relaxed attitude about the place that Becky liked. She didn't have to worry about what she wore, or if her kids were using the proper fork. It was the first night of the cruise, and now that she had found the missing treasure, she was feeling rather comfortable about the entire adventure.

That was until the rest of the Montgomery clan walked up to the table and everyone began a marathon of hugs. Estelle was wearing some sort of purple cowboy hat, matching purple jacket and leather pants, her blond hair perfectly styled. Then there was her ex-husband Mark. According to Laura, he'd only agreed to come on the cruise because of his grandkids. He and Estelle had recently divorced after being married for nearly forty years, and Estelle was probably going to use this cruise to try to win him back. She hated losing a fight, and theirs had been a whopper.

Mark looked his usual handsome self, dressed in a white polo shirt and khaki shorts, brown deck shoes and no socks. His face had aged since Becky had seen him last, but in a good way. The lines around his steel-blue eyes only added to his charm. For what it was worth, Becky had always liked Mark, even though he would sometimes push Ryder too hard. It amazed her how much Ryder had resembled his father, and for a brief instant a wave of sadness washed over her until Kim, Laura's mother, emerged from behind Mark, hanging on to what had to be her latest boyfriend.

He was briefly introduced as Bob Ducain. He was an average-looking guy, with thinning gray hair and enough of a stomach that even his loose-fitting island shirt couldn't disguise it. He had a ruddy complexion, pale blue eyes, and a smile that seemed to lack sincerity. There were gold chains around his neck and gold diamond rings on each pinky. No doubt Estelle had handpicked this guy for Kim. He must have been from one of her social clubs, or the son of a wealthy friend. At any rate, in Estelle's eyes, he was probably Kim's perfect match.

"I hate buffets," Kim announced before she even sat at the table. Her hair was its usual shade of blond, hanging straight down her back. She wore a Chanel black-and-white sleeveless sweater, a black short skirt and sandals. Kim was somewhere around Becky's age, thirty-six, but Botox had removed any hint of aging, so she still looked as if she was in her twenties. She had the same blue eyes as her dad, and a perky paid-for nose that she'd changed at least two times.

Kim bent over and briefly hugged Sarah and Connor, then continued to whine about the buffet. "The food is never good, and I have to serve myself. I hate it."

"You sit and I'll fix you a plate," Bob offered, pulling out a chair for her to sit on. Then he took off toward the rows of steaming food.

Kim made herself comfortable and glanced over at Becky, who was across from her at the large tan-speckled table. Kim sat with her back to the buffet. She obviously didn't even want to look at it. Instead of sitting by her mother and new boyfriend, Laura sat next to Becky, while Sarah and Connor moved down to the end of the table to sit with Estelle and Mark.

"Isn't he great? He does everything for me. I don't know how I ever got along without him," Kim remarked to Becky.

Laura turned sideways in her chair and rolled her eyes at Becky.

Becky nodded as if she was listening, but her attention had fallen on Dylan Langstaff. He had just walked across the room toward an officer dressed in white who was talking to a few passengers standing in the food line. Dylan looked even better than she had remembered from that afternoon. His hair was somehow darker in the dimmer lighting and his demeanor even more friendly and casual. He had the look of a genuinely nice guy. Someone Becky wouldn't mind getting to know, as a friend, of course, but she was sure deep down he must be a flirt.

So why was she so attracted to him? A little voice inside whispered, *Because he makes you feel something.* And it had been a long, long time since she'd felt anything for a man.

Kim droned on. "I know he's not very pretty, but I find that the cuter the guy is, the more he's into his own needs."

Becky heard herself saying, "Uh-huh." But she didn't believe that for a moment. Dylan was over-the-top cute, and from the way he'd treated her kids, she just knew he was a guy who didn't think of himself first.

There was a commotion of some sort right in front of Dylan, who just happened to be standing next to Bob, who was busy piling fried chicken on a plate. Suddenly a rather large woman staggered into Bob. He froze, still clutching his plate of food.

"And I just don't have any time for that kind of guy in my life," Kim said, while a waitress poured her an iced tea.

"Uh-huh," Becky mumbled as she watched Dylan grab hold of the woman from behind. She was so large he could barely get his arms around her. From what Becky could tell, the woman was choking on a piece of food and Dylan was administering the Heimlich maneuver, pushing air up from her diaphragm and into her throat.

"So, naturally, when I met Bob at Mom's charity auction three months ago and he told me how he loved to pamper women, well I just had to have him all to myself."

"Yeah. That's great," Becky agreed. Half of the people in the room were watching Dylan, while Bob just continued to stand there motionless, both hands on his plate as though he was annoyed at the interruption.

Becky stood and was ready to try to help that poor woman and Dylan when something flew out of the woman's mouth and landed on the floor in front of her.

"We've been dating ever since, and let me tell you, he really knows how to care for a woman, if you know what I mean." She sighed as if to make her point.

Becky let out the breath she had been holding and smiled. "You don't say." She watched as Dylan and what looked like two women from the ship's medical team, helped the now-panting woman into a chair.

Bob turned back to the buffet and continued moving down the line, filling his place.

"But I know you're still mourning my dear brother, so you couldn't possibly be interested in anyone, could you?" Kim asked with a flourish.

Becky stared at Kim for a moment in complete silence and disbelief. It was as if someone had rung a bell and everyone had turned their attention to Becky, waiting for her reply. Even Laura stopped what she was doing to listen.

"I, uh, no, definitely not. I'm not interested in anyone,"

Becky spluttered. But Laura, who had also been watching the whole incident between the choking woman and Dylan, threw Becky that kind of look as if she knew better.

Becky was just about to set Laura straight, when Kim reached across the table and grabbed Becky's hand. "You poor thing, but I understand. No one can replace my brother. If you ever need a shoulder to cry on, just call me and I can put you in touch with some of the best shrinks in San Diego. I'm here for you, Becky. You can always count on me."

"Thanks," Becky muttered, slowly pulling her hand away.

"We've got something to tell everybody," Sarah blurted in a loud voice.

"Let's get our meal first," Becky countered, hoping that would be enough to stifle her excited daughter.

"But we want to tell everyone now," Connor chimed in.

Becky was glad Connor seemed kind of excited about the whole thing, but she just wasn't in the mood to show the pendant off at that exact moment. Besides, now that the room had settled down again after that poor woman's near-death experience, Becky didn't want everyone to now turn their focus on her.

"Your mom's right," Laura said, getting up. "Let's have our dinner first."

Estelle, of course, supported Connor and Sarah, not Becky.

"But the kids seem to want to tell us something now. We should see what they have to say."

Becky stood.

Mark stood. "I say we should honor Becky's wishes, Estelle." He walked to the buffet, taking Connor with him.

Laura went over and took Sarah by the hand, then led her to the buffet. They passed Bob, who was returning with a plate of food for Kim.

"Fine," Estelle conceded. "Bob, darling, you did such a good job with Kim's plate, do you think you could do the same for me? It's been such a long day that I think I'll pass out if I have to get up and pick out my own food." She peeked over at Kim's plate. "No chicken, darling. Do they have any baked white fish? I would love a little baked fish. It digests so easily and my poor little tummy has been slightly upset ever since we boarded. Do you think you could find some, dear?"

Bob nodded. "It would be my pleasure, Estelle."

Becky shook her head and walked away from the table, knowing perfectly well that by the time this dinner was over, Estelle would have everyone at the table waiting on her, including Becky.

She headed straight for the nearest buffet, grabbed a white plate and began the process of deciding what she wanted to eat. Her stomach was actually growling for food.

"There's this great broccoli salad you should try," a voice said just behind Becky's right ear.

Becky turned to see Dylan's tanned face smiling at her.

"I saw what you did for that woman," Becky said, ignoring his opening suggestion, "You were incredible. How is she doing?"

"She's fine. Resting in her stateroom."

"You saved her life. That was amazing."

"Thanks, but she was the amazing one. She never put up the least resistance. That's what saved her."

"I'll remember that the next time I'm choking."

His grin widened. "Good idea."

There was a moment of awkward silence while Becky searched for something to say. "Wh-where is that salad?" she stammered at last.

She loved broccoli, but ever since Ryder had died, she found herself eating more and more comfort foods like pasta and homemade breads. She'd put on about ten pounds in the last two years, even though she still worked out with weights. But the strange part was, she didn't seem to care about the added weight. Or maybe she simply didn't have the time to think about it.

"On the other side of this station," he said, eyes shimmering like pools of sea-green water, and a smile that could make a girl swoon. But she wasn't going to be one of them. Nope, not her. She knew better. Besides, she wasn't ready for romance, especially with this type of guy. His interest had to be all PR. It couldn't be real. Or could it?

She didn't want to reflect on that. She had her kids with her, for heaven's sake. What would they think of their mother swooning over some man who would sail off again at the end of their cruise. The whole thing was ridiculous. She needed to stop these crazy thoughts right now, before her fantasies got completely out of control.

And she'd start with the broccoli.

"Never mind. I'm not really that fond of broccoli," she said without flinching at her little white lie, meant to prevent him from accompanying her to another buffet station.

"I would have thought you were."

"Is there a broccoli type?"

She was sure there was a teasing glint in his eyes. "Well, actually, there is."

"And just what would that be?" He had her smiling now. She liked how easy it was to talk to him.

"She usually has an athletic body, strong arms and an equally strong opinion on matters that count. She eats whole grains, avoids most carbs and never eats anything with hydrogenated or trans fats, but she loves gelato, all flavors, and only has it when she's on vacation. By the way...Artemis deck, Just Gelato. Best on the ship."

Becky turned back to the cornucopia of steaming food and added a square of lasagna to her plate. She considered lasagna the perfect food, at least lately. "And you've done research on this broccoli-woman theory, have you?"

"It's just an observation. You can tell a lot about a person from the foods they eat."

He followed her down the line as she added scalloped potatoes to her plate, and then some kind of stuffing with thick, creamy gravy. She figured this would do the trick. He was looking for a broccoli babe, and right now she was the carboholic.

"And what if a person doesn't eat vegetables? What does that say about her?" She stopped and turned to him. He looked down at her plate, which was now a mess of carbs swimming in brown gravy. She felt a little of the gravy drip off her plate and onto her toes.

He gave her a sly smile, reached over, swiped the dripping gravy from the side of her plate, and quickly licked it off of his finger.

"They make the best beef gravy on this ship," he said, wearing a pirate's smile. Then he turned and walked away.

Becky watched him for a moment, angry at his audacity, but also charmed by it at the same time.

She spotted a waiter, apologized and handed him her dripping plate, then, wearing her own pirate's smile, she went in search of the broccoli salad.

DAMN IF HE DIDN'T RUN into Ms. Becky Montgomery. And damn if he didn't have to go right up to her and start a conversation. Dylan couldn't understand why he hadn't left as soon as he'd seen her. No. Not him. He'd had to joke with her, laugh with her, and even flirt a little. All right, a lot.

Dylan walked back to his cabin as if he were late for a meeting. He didn't talk to anyone, nor did he gaze out at the full moon that seemed to hang just out of reach in the black sky. If a staff member had seen him swipe that gravy off her plate and lick his finger, he'd be on the carpet in no time. What was he thinking?

That was the problem. He wasn't thinking. Not rationally, anyway. He was being led by his emotions and he knew his emotions always got him in trouble. He had to be more logical about this. After all, it couldn't lead anywhere. She was a passenger.

It had been a long day and he was eager to get to his cabin. He had to admit that when he couldn't get a good hold on that choking woman at first, dread had crept in and almost made him want to give up entirely. He hadn't felt that way since he was a little boy and his dad used to take him out fishing off the coast of Twillingate, in northern Newfoundland. It was crazy, but at the time he just couldn't bear to watch all those cod suffocating around him. He would try to push as many as he could back into the water, and his dad would scold him for doing it, so he stopped. But he never got used to it. Never got used to the thrashing, their need to breathe, their gasping for breath.

He'd had the same feeling with that woman. He'd had the power of life and death in his hands, and for a moment it had scared him to the point of wanting to run. But he hadn't, and that's what he needed to hold on to. He hadn't run. Not this time. He had stayed the course and gotten her through. And because of him, she would enjoy the rest of the cruise and the rest of her life.

He needed a drink to calm down, to stop the internal shaking, but instead he just walked at a fast clip, ignoring everyone around him. He wasn't rude. He would nod when it was appropriate, or smile when someone looked his way, but for the most part he kept his head down and his feet moving forward.

When he finally reached the crew's quarters, he unlocked the door to his small cabin and shut it behind him. Then a sense of ease took hold and the shaking began to subside. He took a deep breath and let it out again, then searched for his cranberry juice, poured himself a tall one, sat in a comfortable dark blue chair, pushed off his white shoes, opened his shirt and let the day fade away.

Too bad that the minute he closed his eyes Becky Montgomery came into focus.

"Damn her," he said out loud, and slammed his now empty glass down on the small coffee table, got up and went in to take a long, hot shower.

THE PLATES HAD BEEN CLEARED from the table and the kids were pestering Becky to make her announcement about the pendant. She was still reluctant.

"It's time, Mom," Sarah urged "You have to tell everybody now."

Estelle, Kim and Bob were at the other end of the table chatting about something that seemed to occupy all their attention. Mark sat sipping his coffee, staring out at the people passing by, seemingly oblivious to anything but the thoughts whirring around in his head.

"Yeah, Mom, you promised right after dinner," Connor insisted. "Well, it's after dinner now."

He was standing next to her, pulling at the necklace's chain, trying to get it out from under her sweater. Becky kept moving his hands away. The whole thing suddenly seemed ridiculous. She really wanted to just give the thing to one of the kids and let them get all the attention.

She leaned over to Laura. "How about if I slip it to you and you tell everyone you found it?"

Laura turned to her. "It's all yours. You need the good luck more than I do. Besides, I want to see the look on Grandma's face when you tell her you found it. She called the captain this afternoon and asked if he could somehow arrange it so that my mom could find it, as a joke."

"You're kidding. What did he say?"

"I don't know, but he invited her to take a private tour of the ship."

"She's unbelievable."

"She's Estelle. Now, please, show her the pendant."

Reluctantly Becky pulled the necklace out from under her sweater. Holding the teardrop pendant in her hand, she took another good look at it. She had to admit that although the silver teardrop was rather large and heavy, the necklace looked as if someone had worn it every day for their entire life. If she wasn't careful, the chain might fall apart with one good tug.

Sarah and Laura had been so excited when they returned that afternoon with ice cream and pickles that Connor had caught their enthusiasm and it still showed on his face. She simply had to go through with this for his sake. It was almost as if the pendant had its own little magic effect on Connor.

"Everybody, quiet please." Connor held out his hands as if that would make his grandmother and aunt stop their conversation. Instead they simply glanced at him and continued talking.

Laura stood. "Mom. Grandma. Aunt Becky has an announcement."

Suddenly, Bob, Estelle and Kim began laughing, but never turned their attention to Laura.

Then Mark reached over and grabbed Estelle's arm. "Becky has something to say."

Estelle looked up at Mark, pulled her arm from his grasp, mumbled something to Kim, leaned back in her chair, rested her hands on her lap and swung her hair off her shoulders. Apparently comfortable, she looked at Becky and said, "You have my complete and undivided attention, dear. What is it that you want to say?"

Becky felt like a total fool and wanted to simply disappear. She mindlessly slid the pendant back and forth on its chain and thought of a million things she'd like to say to Estelle. Hurtful, mean things. Things that had been on her mind for years. She thought maybe she could do it right now. Clear the air. Get the hostility off her chest.

But instead Sarah came to her rescue, preventing her from putting her foot in her mouth and possibly spoiling the rest of the cruise. "My mom found the moon goddess's pendant in our cabin! Mom found it! Isn't she lucky, Grandma? Isn't my mom the best?"

Sarah beamed as she hugged Becky tight around the neck.

Becky let go of the pendant and it settled heavily on her chest. She put an arm around Sarah to steady her as she knelt on the chair next to Becky's, and put her other arm around Connor, who stood beside her. Both kids wore grins that encompassed their entire face.

"*That's* the missing pendant that everyone's been looking for?" Kim asked with a large dose of sarcasm.

"Yes," Becky said, bringing her kids in even tighter.

Estelle slipped on her glasses to get a better look. "But, darling, it's so tacky. And here I thought it was going to be worth something."

Becky could actually feel Connor's enthusiasm waning as his body slumped against her.

"But it is worth something," Becky protested. "It's meant to bring good luck to the person who found it."

"Yeah, especially in love," Laura added.

"Your aunt already found her one true love with my son, Laura, and no pendant will help her find someone to take Ryder's place," Estelle chided. "Once you've had love like that, you don't ever want to replace it. Not ever. And someday, my dear naive child, you might be lucky enough to have the same thing." She turned and reached for Mark's hand, but he picked up his coffee cup before she could touch him. Estelle instantly withdrew her hand, but Becky noticed.

Laura excused herself from the table. Becky could tell she was upset by Estelle's thoughtless reprimand.

Connor moved away from Becky, his expression sullen, but Becky wouldn't let go of his hand. She reached for Sarah's and helped her slide off the chair. "This is just a game, Estelle, a charming promotion that someone on this ship thought would be fun and romantic. I happen to agree and intend to wear this pendant the entire time I'm on this cruise." With those words she led her children away from the table.

"Of course, dear—" Estelle began, but Becky and the kids were already on their way to find Laura.

Part of her had wanted to tell Estelle that she agreed with her about Ryder. She would never find someone to replace him, and wouldn't want to try. But deep down in her heart, she hoped that someday she would be lucky enough to find love again. She hadn't realized that until she'd heard Estelle's presumption that she'd never be interested in romance again.

However, Becky refused to allow Estelle to get the best of her in front of the kids. She wanted them to have a good relationship with their grandmother, no matter what Becky personally thought of the woman.

And at that precise moment, it wasn't anything good.

CHAPTER FOUR

"LAURA, WAIT UP," Becky called as she made her way through the crowded main lounge, bumping into a woman who didn't even stop to let her apologize. It was hard moving quickly because Sarah had wanted to be carried so she could play with the necklace around Becky's neck. At seven, Sarah was too big to be carried, but Becky knew she was dead tired.

Sarah and Connor chimed in for Laura to stop, and she finally did, but Becky could see the torment in her eyes.

Sliding down from her mom's embrace, Sarah ran to meet Laura.

"She's my grandmother and I love her, but sometimes she just makes me so mad I want to scream," Laura said, with the emphasis on "scream."

"You can scream if you want, Laura," Sarah told her. "This room is so big I don't think anyone would notice."

Becky looked around. Sarah was right. They were standing in the Court of Dreams—a huge space with Doric columns and a sweeping staircase with ornate gold railings and marble steps. A fiber-optic chandelier hung in the center and gave the appearance of suspended stars. Cherubs and clouds were painted on the ceiling and Renaissance-style pink, white and gold upholstered chairs and sofas were arranged in small groupings for passengers to sit and enjoy the opulent space.

What Becky really liked were the huge statues of Artemis, Athena, and Poseidon that flanked a black concert grand piano where a woman, dressed in a flowing pink floral dress, was getting ready to serenade everyone.

The place was fabulous and reminded Becky that Estelle had, in fact, paid for this entire trip. She needed to find a way to get along with the woman for a week.

"Let's sit down and talk," Becky urged.

"Thanks, Aunt Becky, but I want to go back to my room," Laura said.

"Okay, but before you do, can I just say one thing?"

Laura's eyes were beginning to water.

"You're a bright and beautiful young woman, and when the time comes, any guy would be lucky if you even smiled his way."

"Thanks." A tear slid down Laura's cheek. "But I know that Gram and my mom think I'm fat, and dumb, and no one will ever love me like Uncle Ryder loved you."

"He loved you, too, honey. And he wouldn't want you talking like this."

"I love you," Sarah said, looking up all doe-eyed at Laura. "And Connor loves you, and so does Mommy."

Laura wiped her tears away and smiled at Sarah. "I love you guys, too."

"Then don't be sad, Laura. The moon goddess wouldn't want any of us to be sad. She's happy 'cause we found her pendant, and she wants us to be happy with her." Sarah took Laura's hand in hers.

Connor handed Laura a tissue, then slipped away and sat on a chair by himself.

Laura wiped her tears and squatted eye level with Sarah. "Tell you what, hot stuff. You catch me tomorrow morning and I'll be my usual happy self. We'll spend the entire morning in the pool. I hear there are some great activities and super instructors. I'll come and get you guys early."

"Before the sun comes up?" Sarah asked.

"Not quite that early, but somewhere around eight-thirty if that's all right with your mom." Laura looked up at Becky.

"Sounds perfect," Becky said, thinking she could use the time alone to explore the ship so she could learn her way around all the decks.

"It's a date," Sarah agreed.

"You betcha," Laura confirmed, giving Sarah a tight hug. Then she stood and walked toward the glass elevators.

She could tell her niece didn't like having the kids see her so upset. When the little family of three finally walked up to the same bank of glass elevators Laura had taken and Connor pushed the button, Becky thought about her strong urge to lash out at Estelle. She was thankful that she hadn't, especially in front of the kids. After all, even though the woman was crass and unfeeling, she still deserved Becky's respect...didn't she?

TRACY HAD PERSONALLY checked out everyone who had been in that bingo room, then scoped out the casino and the main lounge, but that pendant was nowhere to be found. She reasoned that perhaps no one had actually found it, and considering that half the ship hadn't even gotten their luggage yet, most of the passengers probably hadn't stayed in their cabins long enough to start looking for the necklace.

Still, she had hoped against hope that she would be lucky to spot the damn thing dangling from someone's neck. The brochure had promised so many perks that anyone who found it would be sporting it around like some sort of trophy.

Tracy swiped the card on her cabin door and walked inside. The room was dark. Her roommate was probably still down at the crew's bar and on her forth or fifth martini. Tracy had learned a long time ago that if you wanted to thrive in Vegas you didn't gamble or drink. The same thing went for working a cruise ship. Drinks cost money, not to mention the hangover the next morning when you had to be up to monitor a shuffle-board game or to help somebody climb a rubber mountain. Tracy had danced at the Stardust for five years in Vegas before they closed it down, and she could count on one hand when she'd gone out for drinks or to gamble after a show. Besides, she had a kid to raise.

God, how she missed her little boy. She wanted to hold him, like that woman she had bumped into who was holding onto her kid.

Wait. Tracy flashed on the woman and the little blond-haired girl. That little girl was spinning a silver necklace around her fingers. Could it be the necklace Tracy had been looking for the entire night?

Why hadn't she focused on it before? She'd been so distraught about not spotting the necklace earlier that she'd given up right when it was practically staring her in the face.

She grabbed her purse and ran out of the room, praying they were still in the lounge.

She punched the button for the elevator, but when it didn't come fast enough she ran for the stairs, taking them two at a time. The metal felt slippery under her feet and the tinny sound echoed through the stairwell with each step. When she got to the right deck she was almost out of breath, but she swung open the door and ran out as if someone was chasing her.

The room was an expanse of people, but she was only looking for two, a brown-haired woman and her curly-haired child.

Tracy prowled the room, eyes desperately searching for the right features, the right clothes, anyone that even resembled the woman and her little girl.

She climbed a few stairs to get a better vantage point, and frantically continued her search, but with no luck. Then, just as she was about to walk through the lounge one more time, she spotted the little girl's blond curly hair. The child stood with her mom and a little boy in front of the elevators.

Tracy's heart raced as she walked as quickly as she could across the room.

People got in her way, and one guy bumped into her, but she just kept walking, praying, holding on to her hope of getting to that little girl.

The area in front of the elevators was crowded, especially since the glass elevators were such an attraction. By the time she reached them, the woman and her children were nowhere in sight. Tracy stood in front of the elevators for a moment and thought about her next move. She would have to be smarter if she was going to get that pendant, and she would start by asking Patti Kennedy the name of the passenger who found it. Her only problem now was having to wait until morning.

BECKY HAD SPENT MOST of the morning on her private veranda, watching the water slip by along with her angry disposition. When they eventually set anchor near Grand Turk Island for a port stop, she wouldn't move. She had no intention of leaving the ship with the rest of the passengers. It was a fabulous morning with a bright blue sky and an endless sea that reached up and kissed that sky. The sun had drenched her balcony with its warm rays, and Becky soaked the heat up, feeling it deep inside her body. It was wonderful just to lie there, not doing anything, not really thinking anything, floating on a daydream.

She loved it.

It was her cabin that made her edgy. For some reason she couldn't relax when she was cooped up inside that room. Not that it wasn't spacious and lovely, but there was just something about it that made her anxious, impatient to get outdoors.

As planned, Laura had taken the kids for a poolside adventure that had lasted several hours, but now it was time for Becky to go in search of her family.

She was wearing a modest two-piece suit, but ever since she had put on those ten pounds, she mostly wore a one-piece suit—black, of course—when she went to the beach. However, she was feeling a little bold today. After applying another layer of sunscreen, she pulled on a gauzy white sleeveless top and wrapped a bright red fringed shawl around her hips. And even though her thighs weren't as toned as they once were, she didn't have any cellulite, so why not be comfortable?

She grabbed a bottle of water out of the minibar, pulled her hair up in a ponytail, slipped on her large black shades, clasped the pendant around her neck and set off in search of her family.

The swimming pool, or Coral Cove, was on Artemis deck, the same deck as the gelato shop that Dylan had told her about. She had to try it.

She glanced at a small sign that requested guests order only one scoop, and ordered cherry gelato from a friendly girl in her early twenties wearing a bright yellow shirt.

"You found the pendant! Wow! You can have three scoops if you want them."

Becky hesitated for a moment, thinking of the calories, but then remembered she hadn't eaten much for dinner the previous night, just some great broccoli salad, and only had coffee for breakfast. "Sure," she said, smiling back at the girl behind the counter. "Bring 'em on."

When she had her mound of gelato, she sat on a nearby white deck chair to enjoy the sounds and feel of the ship before she looked for the kids. She could hear the water rushing by, people laughing and chatting about silly things as they passed, the occasional announcements about onboard events or port excursions, and the gentle sway of the ship itself when it was under way. The combination seemed to be soothing her restless thoughts. She only hoped it was doing the same for Connor.

Before she could take her first bite of gelato, her bliss was threatened by the Kim and Bob show. The two of them appeared out of nowhere and were headed right for Becky's table.

"Look who's here, Bob, my ill-tempered sister-in-law," Kim teased as she approached Becky. She wore her hair up under a straw hat, large hoop earrings and an outfit that belonged on a runway. The woman really needed to learn what casual attire actually meant.

"Hello, Kim…Bob." Becky nodded and shifted uncomfortably in her chair. "I was a little rough last night, and I'm sorry for that."

"It's part of your character. We expect it." Kim leaned in and pulled her Dior white-rimmed sunglasses down from her eyes. "I see you're still wearing that hideous necklace."

Becky grabbed the pendant and slid it back and forth on the chain. "Yes. I just got three scoops of gelato because of it."

Kim rolled her eyes at Bob. "Well, goody for you." She sighed.

"Would you two like some? It's pretty great."

"Me? I never eat dairy. Besides, that cup must have a thousand calories, or maybe you don't care anymore. I've heard that widows and divorcées usually gain about twenty to thirty pounds within the first two years of living alone." She leaned in closer again and whispered in a loud voice. "Maybe you shouldn't be eating that, what with all the weight you've already gained."

Becky was almost overcome by the desire to smash the little cup of sweet delight right into her sister-in-law's overly made-up face, but instead she said, "You know, you're probably right." She stood, walked over to a trash container and, as painful as it was, dumped the ice cream.

"So, where's Estelle?" Becky asked. "She usually loves to lie out by the pool."

"I think she said she had an appointment at the Jasmine Spa right about now." Bob ran his hand through his thinning hair, trying to straighten it out after the wind had blown what there was of it down on his forehead.

"I was on my way to check on the kids anyway." It cost her to say it, but she added, "Would you two like to join me?"

"Actually, we were just on our way to the demonstration kitchen for a lecture on spa cuisine," Kim said. "Besides, I hate all this sun, and couldn't possibly even think of an outdoor pool. Not with my sensitive skin. I'd burn up in a heartbeat."

Kim actually did have exceptionally fair skin. Of course, part of the reason could have been that she never went out in the sun for more than fifteen minutes at a time. Ever. It was freaky.

"Kimmy is just a sensitive little flower, and I have to look after her." Bob turned to his flower. "We've been out too long, baby. We need to get you under cover."

"Is that a promise, Bobby?" Kim teased, rubbing up against him.

The vision of "Kimmy" and "Bobby" in bed together, naked, was enough to make Becky's skin crawl. She shivered and broke out in goose bumps.

"Are you cold?" Bob asked, all concerned. He touched her arm and Becky instantly moved away as if she was spring-loaded. He gave her a quizzical look, but she kept her distance. No way did she want to be touched by Bobby. There was just something about the guy that she didn't like, and ever since she'd seen his reaction to that choking woman, she didn't trust him.

"No, not at all," She lied. "Warm, actually. I better get going. The kids are expecting me." Thank heavens she didn't have to see the happy couple again until dinner tomorrow night.

When Becky finally arrived poolside at Coral Cove, which wasn't very far from Just Gelato, she was immediately accosted by Sarah and Laura. Both girls were in a tizzy over something and were talking over each other.

"He's just so cute," Laura called from the pool.

"He's the best swimmer," Sarah insisted.

"You have to go out with him," Laura shouted.

"We told him all about you," Sarah yelled.

"He really is the best swimmer, and he's funny, and he doesn't have a girlfriend, and…" Laura swam up to the edge of the pool.

"…and he likes Cocoa Puffs, just like you do," Sarah interjected.

"Well, that alone's enough for me to fall in love with this guy," Becky teased.

"No, seriously," Laura reasoned. "He's perfect for you. I only wish I was a little older." She sighed. "Then I'd take him for myself."

"Does he have any say in this?" Becky asked, trying to spot

Connor. She looked across the expanse of lounge chairs and towels, and scanned the pool, but didn't spot him. Of course, the pool was crowded, and Connor loved the water, so he was probably half submerged somewhere practicing his back stroke. He always had a problem with that one.

"Sure he does, but you have the lucky pendant, so he probably won't be able to think straight when he's around you," Laura said, giggling.

"I didn't know I was that powerful," Becky joked, finding the girls' enthusiasm infectious.

"Only when you wear it," Sarah explained. "If you don't wear it, you're just like any other lady."

"Are those the rules?"

"No. That's the magic part. There are no rules for love."

Becky smiled at her daughter. Sometimes Sarah was simply too smart for her age.

"How do you know such things?"

"I watch a lot of movies. You know that."

Becky and Laura laughed out loud.

"So, where is this Adonis you guys want me to meet?" Becky glanced around the pool area again. The wooden planks under her feet were teak, and the railings were that wonderful, high-polished dark wood. The ship looked elegant and luxurious, and at that moment, she was happy to be able to enjoy it.

"He's right over there," Laura said, pointing. "The guy bobbing up and down in the pool, with the sun-streaked hair and the whistle hanging around his neck."

Becky looked as hard as she could, but all she saw was a tangle of people, young and old, big and small, swimming or wading in the pool.

"You already met him Mom. It's—"

"Dylan Langstaff," Becky said over Sarah.

"Yeah, isn't he a cutie?" Laura swooned.

Becky nodded, smiling. "Yeah, he's a cutie, all right. I kind of guessed he did something outdoorsy."

A bevy of young women and a few kids Connor's age surrounded Dylan in the pool. The girls were probably in their early twenties. She figured Dylan was flirting with each and every one of the women. It was the perfect setup.

Still, she hoped it wasn't true. She had a little crush going for him, and even though she knew nothing could possibly come of it, she was enjoying the momentary fantasy.

"Where's Connor? I think it's time we went back to our stateroom and got cleaned up for lunch. Besides, aren't there some other activities you guys want to do this afternoon besides swimming?"

"Okay, but we told Dylan you would probably come by and he said that sounded great." Laura seemed a little confused. "Don't you want to meet up with him again? He's really nice."

"Not now, thanks. He looks busy."

Becky watched as Dylan entertained the young women and the kids splashing in the water around him. He had such a charismatic smile, and he *was* an absolute cutie. With all that attention around him, Becky was sure he couldn't possibly care if he ran into her or not.

Just then his gaze fell directly on her. He smiled and nodded her way.

Becky smiled right back.

All right, so he looked pleased to see her. But he was probably just being polite. "Maybe I will hang around for a little while. Where's Connor? Did you guys get him to go into the pool?"

"No. He refused, so he's been reading comic books all day," Laura said. "Grandpa bought him some in the gift shop."

"Dylan tried to get him to go into the pool, Mommy, for a water polo game."

Becky sighed. She had hoped that Connor's good mood would continue because he was around Laura.

"Connor started crying—"

"What?" Becky was attempting to remain clam, but she

didn't want anyone trying to force Connor to do anything. He was way too vulnerable.

"Wait," interrupted Laura, "Dylan didn't *make* Connor cry. Connor did that on his own. I think it's Connor's way of forcing—"

Becky turned on Laura and cut her off. "Where's Connor?"

Laura's happy demeanor changed. "He's right over there," she said, pointing to the other side of the pool.

Becky spotted Connor sitting by himself on a deck chair. He had a white towel draped around his shoulders and was hunched over, reading a comic book. Becky was glad to see that at least he was reading something a little more upbeat than his usual fare.

As she approached him, Dylan popped his head up from the pool and must have yelled something to Connor, because Connor shook his head no.

Becky needed to get to the bottom of this situation. She couldn't imagine that Dylan would knowingly make Connor cry. He seemed like such a nice guy and so good with kids, and she knew that Connor cried easily. He'd used this to get out of things before. Dylan was still standing in the water near Connor's chaise when Becky approached her son.

"Hi, honey. How's it going?" She sat on the end of Connor's chair blocking Dylan's view.

"Fine," he said, not looking up.

"Come on in, Connor," Dylan yelled in a friendly voice. "We're ready to start the next game, buddy."

Connor looked up at Becky, tears streaming down his cheeks. "Don't make me, Mom. I don't want to go in the water. I hate the water. It's stupid."

Becky patted her son's legs. "This is your vacation, honey. You don't have to do anything you don't want to do."

"But Dylan needs one more person or they won't be able to play the game," he mumbled, wiping the tears off his face. "Then all the kids will blame me."

"No one's going to blame you for anything. Besides, it's

time for lunch. That's why I came to get you." Becky turned to Dylan. "I'm sorry. My kids need to eat now. You'll have to find someone else to play." But she said it with that mamma bear tone, and Dylan flinched.

He looked up at her, astonishment on his face. "Sure. No problem. I think I can manage that. I just thought he might want to—"

"Mom," Connor whispered, and grabbed his mother's hand.

There were other kids Connor's age in the pool, tossing a ball around.

Becky stood. "He doesn't want to," she snapped, and immediately felt as if she'd been too harsh. "I'm sorry, but maybe some other time."

Connor grabbed his things and slid off the chair, taking Becky's hand. She and Connor headed for Laura and Sarah, who were waiting at the far end of the pool.

As Becky walked, she began second-guessing herself all over again. She felt as though she should never have listened to Lacey or Laura. Her initial instincts had told her not to come on this trip. Connor simply wasn't ready. At least if they had gone to Disneyland the drive home was only a couple hours, but getting home from the middle of the Caribbean—if it came to that—could take a couple of days.

DYLAN COULDN'T LET Becky and Connor walk away in such a stressed state, so he made his apologies to the kids who were waiting for the game to begin, left them in the care of his assistant, grabbed a towel and went after them.

When he finally got close enough, he called out her name. "Ms. Montgomery, please wait."

She turned around and stopped walking. He hadn't noticed it before, but now he saw she was wearing the moon goddess pendant.

"I want to apologize if I offended you in any way. It wasn't my intention, and I'm truly sorry." He looked down at Connor.

"You, too, buddy. I'm sorry if I made you cry. Sometimes I just get caught up in those games and I act like a jerk. Forgive me?" He stuck out his hand. Connor took it and gave him a brief handshake.

"Thanks," Becky said.

"Can I make it up to you? I see you found the pendant, and that entitles you and anyone else you'd like to bring along to a private tour with a power snorkel around the coral reef off of Grand Turk Island this afternoon." He looked at Sarah and her cousin, who had walked over to join them. "It's a great tour. You guys would love it. We only take a few passengers at a time and you get to see the reef up close and personal. If you've never seen a coral reef, and you don't have anything else planned, you really don't want to miss this one. It's beautiful."

Becky hesitated and he could tell she was actually giving it some thought. He really wanted her to say yes. "We've planned the entire adventure, and I'll be bringing two other staff members, so there'd be no shortage of instructors for the kids. We were just waiting to find out who had the pendant."

Connor was tugging on Becky's hand, so Dylan knew the chances of them going were slim.

"That sounds awesome!" Laura said.

"I saw an invitation in the leaflet I received in the goody basket. It does sound like fun, but I'm afraid the kids and I won't be able to make it. But if Laura wants to bring her mom and Bob, they can certainly go in our place."

"Can I?" Laura asked Dylan.

"Sure. I don't think there's any problem with that."

"Wow! Thanks, Aunt Becky."

"You're welcome." Becky turned to Dylan and he caught the sparkle in her eyes. They were warm, beautiful brown eyes. He could get lost in those eyes. "Now, we really need to scope out a lunch. Any suggestions?"

He pulled himself out of his momentary trance and hoped she hadn't noticed him staring.

"I want pizza, Mom," Sarah insisted.

"You always want pizza," Connor protested.

"If you want a little variety," Dylan said, "Sunshine's American Diner is great for pizza, seafood and burgers, and it's right next to the pool."

Becky smiled. "No broccoli?"

He chuckled at the reference, glad that she'd made it. "Nope. Not even on the menu."

The woman was a delight, and he wished he could spend some time with her. He liked the way she made him feel, all warm and a little too eager to fall into temptation...

Connor tugged on Becky's hand. "Let's go, Mom."

"Thanks," she said, still smiling that sweet smile of hers as they walked away.

He couldn't be sure, but if he didn't know better, he'd think she was flirting with him, at least a little, and he liked it.

But Connor was a challenge for Becky, he could see that now. She seemed a little overprotective, just like his own mother had been with him. The difference was his mother *had* smothered him with what she thought was love and understanding, but all it really did was turn him into an introvert. He had become so filled with self-doubt he could hardly even tie his own shoes properly without his mother's help. Or so it had seemed. It wasn't until he headed off to college that he figured out what had happened to him and set out to change himself.

But he didn't see that strong overprotective tendency in Becky's character, and after dealing with so many passengers, he was pretty good at reading people. He couldn't help wondering about the reasons behind her protective attitude when it came to her son.

Dylan's heart went out to Connor, as he thought of his own struggle for independence, and although he had been trying to get Connor to join the other kids in the pool, he knew there wasn't much he could do to change anything on a single cruise.

CHAPTER FIVE

INSTEAD OF BECKY SPENDING the rest of the day with her kids, their grandfather decided to treat Connor and Sarah to a rousing game of miniature golf, then Mark caught a movie with them in the theater, and afterward took them on a private tour he'd arranged of the workings of the ship. Somewhere in there they'd had dinner and attended a dessert extravaganza.

Her first thought had been so much for wanting to spend more time with her kids. But while they were golfing and seeing movies, Becky had shifted gears and made use of her packet of perks, spending most of the day at the Jasmine Spa. She was in a Zen mood when Mark finally appeared at her door. Sarah had fallen asleep on his shoulder and Connor was almost sleepwalking.

"I hope they didn't cause you any problems," Becky told Mark as she tucked Connor into bed.

"Not at all. Matter of fact they saved me from spending the day on some carriage ride tour of Cockburn Town on the island with Estelle. Not that I didn't want to see some of the island, I just wasn't in the mood to see it with Estelle."

"Can I offer you a drink on the veranda? I think that minibar stocks a Scotch."

"No, thanks. I've been trying to stay away from the stuff. My stomach isn't what it used to be."

Becky was still feeling a little guilty for being so curt with Estelle the previous night. "I think I should apologize to Estelle for my behavior last night. I shouldn't have been so aggressive with her. And walking away was rude on my part."

Mark put his hand up. "Please don't. You were fine. I always admired the way you stood up to her. She was totally out of line last night. We both know how much you loved my son, but life goes on and we all have to move on. You're a beautiful young woman, and it's only natural for you to find someone else."

"No one can take Ryder's place. Estelle was right about that much."

Becky looked into his eyes and they reminded her just how much she missed Ryder's love and compassion. She was getting emotional, and tried with all her heart not to let the tears come.

"I think I'll take that Scotch, after all," he said.

Becky poured him a double, then poured herself a glass of Merlot and walked out onto the veranda, where Mark was already seated. It was a balmy night, with a full moon, a sky filled with stars and the whispering sound of the ship gliding across the water on its way to their next port of call.

"You should know that the divorce was final a week before this trip," Mark announced as Becky took a seat next to him.

"I'm sorry," she said mildly, not knowing what to make of his announcement.

"Don't be. It's been a long time coming. If Ryder's death taught me anything, it taught me to grab hold of my life. I sometimes don't always know just what that might be, but I don't think it's living with a woman I don't seem to love anymore."

"It must be difficult for you. You and Estelle have been together for a long time."

"Thirty-nine and a half years, but if I can survive the death of my son, I can survive anything. I used to be full of fire, just like you were, and I want it back. I'd hate to see you give that up, Becky. You always had the ability to know what you wanted and to stand up to anybody who got in your way. Don't give that up. I think it's what my son admired most about you. That, and your pretty smile."

He made her blush, and the sadness seemed to abate for a moment. "I don't know if I have any of that fire left in me anymore, and sometimes when it does come out, I don't think it's for the right reasons. Ever since I lost Ryder I've been afraid to think about what I want for myself, or for my kids. Sarah seems to be all right, but Connor's behavior breaks my heart. I don't know how to reach him."

He took a couple sips of his drink. "Sarah's got a lot of you in her. She's a little spitfire. But Connor takes after his dad. He thinks too much. I wish I could give you some sage advice, but I failed when it came to raising my own son, so how could I possibly tell you how to raise yours?"

Becky couldn't believe she was hearing this. "You didn't fail. Ryder was a loving, kind and generous man. Where do you think he got that from?"

Mark shook his head. "Thanks, but the unfortunate thing was he could never stand up to his mother like you could. He got that from watching his old man while he was growing up, and I can't forgive myself for that. Kids learn from what we do, not what we say."

"Ryder was a grown man and made his own decisions. No one suspected he had a weak heart, not even his doctors. Standing up to Estelle or not standing up to Estelle wouldn't have changed that fact."

"But he could never say no to her, just like I couldn't. He was overworked. I could see that. Everyone could see that, but he pushed on because she demanded it. It's not that I blame her for his death. She didn't realize what was happening. She sat up in our house in San Francisco and gave the orders, but she had no idea what those orders were doing to her son. I know it was simply the luck of the draw. And heaven knows she suffers his loss just like the rest of us, maybe even more. But I can't help thinking—"

"You think too much, Mark. Just like Ryder, and maybe just like Connor. We have to let it go. It's time, don't you think? Maybe that's one thing you and I can accomplish on this family vacation."

Mark nodded, his eyes glistening in the moonlight.

Could she let go? Becky wondered. Could she find a way to let it all go?

Part of her really hoped so, and she hoped Mark could, as well. She took his hand and they sat together, watching the moon dance on the ocean, not talking for a long time.

THE NEXT MORNING, Becky accompanied the kids on an excursion she'd booked from home to a private beach on the uninhabited island of Gibbs Cay. At first she'd felt a little reluctant to go, leaving the comfort of the ship, but then Connor had insisted that he really wanted to see the stingrays. His eager face had made her hesitation vanish.

Becky knew there had been a lot of bad press about stingrays ever since Australian icon Steve Irwin had been killed by one, but she also knew that stingrays were docile creatures, and the babies were interesting to pet and watch.

What she didn't know when she and the kids boarded the tender that would take them to the island was that Dylan would be in charge of the excursion. If she hadn't known better, she would almost believe the pendant really did have some magical powers to bring the two of them together.

She made her way to the front of the boat with Connor in tow, while Sarah and Laura insisted on sitting in the back near Dylan, the man they seemed to love to be around. She had to admit, she liked to be around him, as well.

There were only about fifty or so people, including ten or fifteen kids who were part of the adventure. Becky didn't know if that was because of the fear of stingrays or because the tours were staggered during the day. Whatever the reason, when they arrived on the deserted island, it was almost as if they had been stranded there, and were going to be forced to get to know each other to survive. The dive staff set up a couple tables with food and drinks, and afterward the adventurers listened quietly while Dylan and two female assistants instructed the group on the proper way to approach and pet a stingray.

Becky was positively amazed at the clear aqua-colored water and the lush foliage that bordered the creamy sand on the endless stretch of beach. It was one of the most beautiful and peaceful places she had ever seen.

She pulled out her digital camera case from her bag and snapped a few photos of the island, and one of Dylan as he made his speech. She wanted to remember what he looked like when she returned home. Plus, Lacey would never forgive her if she didn't take his picture. At least she'd have a photo of the best-looking man on the cruise.

The stingrays swam right up to the shoreline, making it easy for everyone to pet them. The larger ones seemed to keep their distance, swimming a little farther out, while the smaller, younger stingrays clustered in the shallow water as if they were waiting for someone to play with them.

"They won't come to me," Connor mumbled after he reached out to pet one and but it slid from under his touch.

"Aw, come on, Connor," Laura urged. "You need to at least try again. Maybe that one was just having a bad day." She reached across and slid her hand right over a tiny stingray that came back for more.

"I don't want to," Connor argued as he made holes in the wet sand with his toes.

Sarah stood next to Laura, staring down at the water. Becky could tell from the way she was clutching her hands in front of her chest that she was scared. Before Becky could rescue her, Dylan walked up next to them and proceeded to make Sarah laugh. Within moments he had her squatting to pet a baby stingray.

The man was remarkable with kids like Sarah. He seemed to bring out their best and knew exactly what to say to get them to overcome their fears. It was the Connors of the world that he couldn't get to respond, and for that matter, neither could she.

"Look, Connor, it's easy," Sarah yelled back at her brother. "They like to be petted." But Connor ignored her and walked up to the beach and sat down hard.

Becky sat next to him. "What's wrong, Connor? I thought you wanted to see the stingrays."

"I changed my mind. They're ugly and dumb."

"Oh, I don't know. I think they're kind of pretty, and they seem rather smart if you ask me."

"Yeah? How?"

"Did you see how they swim? That must take a lot of coordination."

He looked down at the sand and kicked at it as though he was angry at something. "Big deal."

"What's wrong, honey? Talk to me." She stroked his silky hair, but he moved away from her touch.

"Nothing's wrong. I just don't like stingrays. I want to go back and play golf with Grandpa."

"I'm sorry, honey, but we signed up for this, so we're kind of stuck until it's time to leave."

He was silent for a few moments, probably considering the lack of options. "It's okay, Mom. I'm fine here. I just want to watch for now. But you go ahead. Sarah said she wanted to show you how to pet them." He turned away from her, dismissing her and withdrawing into himself.

She didn't know what to say to him, what to do for him to make him laugh again. At that moment she felt useless as a parent. These days, once Connor made up his mind, there was no changing it back. His stubbornness was taking hold in a way that almost frightened her. She was beginning to think her idea of finding him a therapist when they got back home was the right one.

"Mommy, come and pet one. They feel smooth and rubbery. Come on, Mommy, I'll show you." Sarah's excitement raised her voice several octaves.

Becky leaned over and kissed Connor on top of his head. "You sure?"

"I'm okay, Mom. Honest."

At least his voice sounded a bit more cheerful. "I'll just go for a little while and then check back with you," Becky said, then stood to join Laura and Sarah.

As she walked in the warm sand toward her daughter, she noticed that Sarah was busy teaching a little boy how to pet a stingray, her hand stroking the air to demonstrate. It made Becky smile to watch Sarah so filled with enthusiasm over her latest accomplishment.

Dylan walked up alongside of her. "If I'm not careful, Sarah will take over my job," he said. "She's really not afraid of anything, is she?"

Dylan turned, smiling at her. He was truly a beautiful man, and stirred feelings in her she thought had died with Ryder, feelings she'd believed she had learned to live without. But here they were, threatening to make her knees buckle. And when he accidentally brushed her arm with his, it sent a bolt of heat through her. She liked the sensation, and wished she could have more of it.

"She gets it from me," she told him, trying not to give her emotions away.

"I thought so. Look…" He nodded toward Sarah. There she was, instructing a group of kids on the proper way to pet a stingray, encouraging them when they did it right and gently scolding them when they did it wrong.

Becky's mood brightened and she even chuckled when she saw Sara take a little boy's hand in hers and bring him to the water's edge to show him a stingray up close. Becky quickly snapped a couple pictures.

Dylan leaned over to get a better look at Becky's face. "You know you're beautiful when you smile? I noticed that the other night but was afraid to tell you. We have strict rules about such things while we're onboard, but now that we're out here—"

He smiled that smile that made her legs weak and she had a strong, sudden urge to kiss him.

She cleared her throat and pushed the image right out of her head.

"Thanks, but I'd hardly say we were alone," she said, looking around.

He sighed. "Technically we're alone, but—" One of his assistants was motioning for him to come join her. "I have other obligations. Maybe we can continue this conversation later?"

Without thinking Becky said, "Maybe we can."

Dylan took off up the beach to meet his assistant.

It was as if she was bewitched or something. Truth be told, she wanted to have that conversation with Dylan right now. Right here, sitting next to him in the soft, warm sand. She wanted to get to know him, his likes, his dislikes, his dreams and goals. And she wanted to tell him her own.

FOR THE NEXT HALF HOUR, Dylan watched Sarah and Becky play in the water. Oh sure, he helped some of the other kids and passengers when he needed to, but his attention was mainly on Becky and her little girl. They were wonderful together, laughing, dancing, running, and even getting the other kids and adults to enjoy the water and the baby stingrays with them.

Then, just when Dylan was getting up the courage to approach Becky again, Connor started making fun of Sarah. "So who cares if you know how to pet a stingray? They're just dumb old fish, anyway."

Becky tried to get him to back off, appealing to his compassion. "Connor, please don't make fun of the stingrays. You'll hurt their feelings."

"They don't understand me, Mom. You can use that stuff on Sarah, but you can't use it on me. I want to go back to the ship. This is bogus. I hate it!"

Dylan couldn't help himself from stepping forward. Connor's behavior had quickly escalated and was spinning out of control.

He knew the boy was hurting, that his behavior was affected by his emotions, and he certainly empathized with him. "Hey, buddy. We're going to get ready to leave in a few minutes. Until then, maybe you can help me load everything onto the boat."

For a brief second it looked as if Connor was actually going to help, but then Becky walked up. "I can handle this."

Dylan ignored her. "But he obviously wants to help." He turned to Connor.

Connor looked at his mom. "I want to go back to the ship."

With sadness in her voice, Becky said, "Is there any way to get off this island right now?"

Dylan could hardly contain himself. He wanted to urge Becky not to give in to her son so quickly. He knew full well what was going on. He had tormented his own mother with this kind of behavior when he was a kid.

"Are you sure this is what you want to do?" he asked gently.

Becky hesitated for a moment but then she said, "Yes." He could tell she was uncomfortable with the entire situation, as though she was almost second-guessing herself.

"Then I'll see what I can do." Her grateful gaze was all he needed. Her sad eyes melted his heart as he now tried to figure out how to support her decision.

Fortunately for Dylan, he could see another tender was on its way out to the island with the next group of passengers, plus three more staff members from the dive team. As soon as it arrived, he made arrangements for Becky and her kids, along with Laura, to be taken back to the ship. He also invited any other passengers who were ready to leave.

When everyone was onboard, Dylan put one of his more-than-capable assistants in charge of the stingray excursion and escorted Becky and the group back to the ship.

Laura sat next to Dylan, while Connor and Sarah sat on either side of Becky on a long bench in the middle of the tender.

"Connor wasn't always like this" Laura told Dylan once they were on their way. "He used to be a lot of fun."

"According to Sarah, he's no fun anymore," Dylan replied.

Laura smiled back at him. "He used to be able to dive into the deep end of the pool from a diving board. His goal was to be on the Olympic diving team. He and his dad used to practice every chance they got. He even had a professional coach interested in him."

Dylan got angry at a father who would disappear out of his son's life like that. He would have given anything for his dad to have been able to do something like that with him. "Not that it's any of my business, but I'm kind of curious. How long ago did your aunt and uncle get a divorce?"

"Who told you that?"

"Sarah said her dad left and I just assumed…"

"My Aunt Becky and uncle Ryder didn't get a divorce. Uncle Ryder died about two years ago. Sarah thinks he's an angel now, just like the angel in *It's a Wonderful Life*."

Dylan's heart actually hurt as he watched Becky cuddle her two kids. He now understood all the hostility that Connor carried around, and all the sadness he'd seen in Becky's eyes on that very first day of the cruise.

He didn't know if he could help, or how he could help. He only knew he wanted to do something for this family.

And he had a week to figure it out.

CHAPTER SIX

"How DO I LOOK?" Becky asked Sarah as they stood in front of the full-length mirror on the back of the closet door.

"Turn all the way around and let me see," Sarah demanded.

Becky whirled around. She was wearing the turquoise dress, and even though she was a little heavier than the first time she'd put it on, it was the kind of fabric that seemed to adjust to her body, hugging it in all the right places.

She hadn't wanted to wear it, but Sarah had insisted.

"You look beautiful, Mommy, but you should wear my pretty blue butterfly clip in your hair. It matches your dress, and butterflies are beautiful, just like you."

"I'd love to wear your butterfly clip, sweetheart."

"I'll get it." And off Sarah went in search of her clip.

Estelle had planned a private Christmas party in the Polaris Lounge on deck six. It was something she'd set up months before. Estelle always was one for planning ahead. Sarah was excited, but Connor and Becky were both apprehensive about the event. They had made a deal with each other to only stay for a few hours.

Sarah returned with her sparkly butterfly clip. "Here, Mommy. I think you should pull one side of your hair back with it."

Becky followed her daughter's directions and clipped her hair with the butterfly. She really wasn't one for hair adornments, and would have rather not worn it, but she knew how much it meant to Sarah. "How's that?" she asked, turning to her daughter.

"It's perfect. You really look like the moon goddess, especially once you put on your pendant."

"But I thought I'd give the pendant a rest tonight."

Becky wanted to wear her own simple gold chain with one black pearl. Besides, her neck was starting to be irritated by the chain, and she really wasn't enjoying all the attention she was still getting from the other passengers.

"Oh, but you have to wear the pendant. The moon goddess wouldn't like it if you didn't." Sarah looked so innocent and sweet standing there in her black-velvet, white-taffeta party dress. The freckles on her cherub cheeks and nose were more prominent now that she had been in the sun. She was clicking her patent-leather shoes together as if she were going to start dancing at any moment. There was no way on earth Becky could refuse her.

Becky grabbed the pendant off the dresser and fastened it around her neck. Her next thought surprised her. She found herself hoping the pendant would work its magic tonight and that somehow Dylan would be at the party. She wanted to continue the conversation he'd started on the island that afternoon.

"How's that?" Becky asked Sarah.

"Perfect. You look like a fairy princess ready to go to the ball and meet her prince."

"So do you," Becky said, giving Sarah a great big hug.

"Are you two done? Can we go now?" Connor yelled from the other room, dampening Becky's happy disposition just a tiny bit.

"Don't worry, Mommy. You look too pretty to be sad. Connor will cheer up once we get to the party. Grandpa will see to that."

"Do you know what it is?"

"You're so silly, Mommy. It's a surprise!"

TRACY COULDN'T BELIEVE she had been pulled from the main show to dance at a private party. Usually, this would never happen, but whoever was throwing this gala was more than your ordinary VIP. Apparently this evening had been in the works for quite some time and the troupe had been compensated for it months ago, but because Tracy had only recently been hired, she hadn't been aware of the situation until that afternoon when the dancer who should have worked the private party came down with a sprained ankle.

Just her luck.

She had learned Becky Montgomery's name from Patti Kennedy and was hoping to spot her in the audience when the houselights were turned on at the end of the main show, or maybe before the show when everyone came in. Sometimes a few of the dancers would hang out to greet the passengers, and she had eagerly volunteered, but it wouldn't be happening tonight.

As she sat in front of a large mirror applying her stage makeup, tears kept filling her eyes, making it tough to brush on her mascara. Even if by some miracle Becky Montgomery was at the party, there was no way in hell she would wear the pendant to such a formal event.

Just her luck.

THE POLARIS LOUNGE had been transformed into a winter wonderland. Even the windows that looked out onto the ocean had been sprayed with fake snow. Garlands and greenery hung from every ledge and tabletop. A floor-to-ceiling Christmas tree, complete with ornaments, flying angels and wrapped presents stood in one corner. Tables of festive desserts were set up along the back of the large room, and twinkling lights swung like stars from the ceiling. Soft Christmas music filled the air as a quartet serenaded the guests.

Estelle had spared no expense in bringing a traditional Christmas to the Caribbean.

"Mommy," Sarah sighed. "This must be where Santa takes his vacation. Is he here?"

"I don't think so," Becky said, trying to come up with an

answer. "It's his busy time of year. He just let your grandma use the room."

"Wow! Grandma sure knows a lot of important people."

"She sure does."

Becky wondered how Estelle did it. How she managed to get to know so many passengers, officers and crew members in such a short time. The room was crowded with people Becky had seen around the ship, and some she hadn't. How could Estelle, who spent most of her day either in her room or getting a massage, have accumulated so many instant friends?

"My dear, you made it!" Estelle squealed as she approached Becky and the kids, arms outstretched for kiss-kiss, hug-hug. "And don't my sweet little darlings look fabulous? Connor, you look so distinguished in a black suit." She turned to Sarah. "And, Sarah, my precious, that dress is simply the sweetest thing. Your mommy always did have good taste in clothes."

She then focused on Becky. "You look lovely, dear." She moved in closer, whispering in Becky's ear. "But lose that tacky pendant. I have a wonderful sapphire necklace you can borrow. I'll have my butler bring it down for you. And what in God's name is that thing in your hair?"

Becky kissed her on each cheek and told herself to ignore what Estelle had just said. Instead she tried to focus on the good stuff. At least Estelle thought Sarah and Connor looked nice and, even if she hadn't meant it, she'd complimented Becky in front of the kids. No, she needed to be the adult and just let it go. Estelle was...well, Estelle, just as Laura had said.

"Estelle," Becky began, "you look gorgeous as usual."

Estelle was wearing an outfit by her favorite designer, an Armani black silk-and-lace gown with a deep round neckline that showed off her diamond-and-emerald necklace.

"Thank you, my dear."

Mark stood next to Estelle, as handsome as ever in a black

tuxedo, white shirt and a matching bow tie. He leaned over to welcome Becky and the kids. "You look beautiful tonight, Becky," Mark offered. "And I especially like the jewelry."

He winked.

"Thanks. It's just a little something I picked up from a moon goddess," Becky teased.

Sarah giggled, while Connor rolled his eyes.

"By the way," Estelle began, "I have something extra-special planned for my two granddaughters when we get to St. Maarten." She looked at Connor. "And your grandfather has something special planned for you, dear, only he refuses to tell me what that is." She smiled and tapped Connor on the nose. He grinned up at her. "Anyway, please make sure Sarah's ready early in the morning with sunglasses and suntan lotion and all that protective stuff. I'll send Laura around to fetch her."

"Sure," Becky said, but she really wasn't that pleased about giving up Sarah to Estelle. If Laura hadn't been part of the deal, it would never happen. She remembered the stories Ryder would tell her about the times his mom would forget he was with her at the mall and go home without him. He always made sure he had enough money to make a phone call whenever they went out together.

"What are we going to do, Grandma?" Sarah asked.

Estelle bent over. "It's a surprise, kitten, and it's not ladylike to ask me to tell you. Now run along and open your presents under the tree."

Becky would make sure she knew exactly where Estelle was taking the girls before she'd let Sarah out of her sight.

The kids looked at Becky to get her approval before they ran off together. She knew they were anxious to get to the presents, so she nodded and they scurried off.

A woman in her midfifties, dressed in a deep red satin gown, walked up to Estelle. "Oh, Mark, honey, I'd like you to meet Jan Milton. She's the CEO of Ambling Meadow Entertainment, out of L.A. She's responsible for some of those fabulous lounge shows we like so much in Vegas. I just had to get to know her so she can help us with the entertainment at our next company party."

Jan put out her hand for Mark. Mark took it in his, and in that instant Becky caught the sparks radiating from that hand-shake.

Unfortunately so did Estelle, because she instantly dismissed Jan and went on to greet the ship's captain, Nikolas Pappas, who had just walked in behind Becky along with Patti Kennedy, the cruise director. Because he was sharing host-duties with his ex-wife, Mark had no choice but to extend his hand to the new guests and ignore Jan. But Becky knew the special moment had already taken place, and there wasn't anything Estelle could do about it.

"I see you're wearing our pendant," Patti Kennedy remarked to Becky.

"Yes. My daughter insisted."

"Smart girl. Isn't it fun? Oh, let me officially introduce Thanasi Kaldis, our hotel manager. He keeps your home away from home in top form," Patti added, eyes twinkling. "Is the pendant bringing you good luck?"

Obviously the woman was really into the pendant game. Becky decided to play along when she caught Estelle looking their way.

"I love it! Whoever came up with the idea was a genius."

Estelle looked away and Becky felt a little upset at herself for rubbing it in. She had thought again that she might apologize to the woman, yet here she was causing her more grief.

"Do you really think so?" Patti asked.

Estelle interrupted. "A true genius. It's simply a delightful game and I'm so glad my daughter-in-law found it, and wore it tonight. It's really quite charming," she said to Thanasi, but Becky could tell she was reeling on the inside.

"Yes, quite charming," Thanasi agreed, but somehow Becky

got the impression he felt the same way Estelle did about the
pendant search.

He and Estelle both chuckled as if they got each other's joke,
while the cruise director walked off and disappeared in the
crowd.

Becky watched as Mark greeted the remainder of the guests
with distracted enthusiasm. She had the distinct feeling his
mind was preoccupied with a woman named Jan Milton.

Eventually, Becky slipped away from the reception line and
mingled with the crowd. She could see Connor and Sarah sitting
on the floor, comparing gifts, a look of absolute delight on
their faces. Becky could only imagine the expensive electronic
wonders Estelle had gotten them. She'd deal with that later.
Right now, she kind of liked the anonymity of mingling with a
crowd. It was nice to be alone at a party of mostly strangers.
She didn't have to talk to anyone if she didn't want to. She could
simply disappear into the crowd and blissfully enjoy the evening and the entertainment, completely unnoticed.

THE LIGHTS DIMMED, and Tracy and the three other dancers
took their positions on the small dance floor. When the music
started, they went into their routine. It was a shortened version
of their act in the main showroom, except that the women wore
blue chiffon knee-length dresses instead of all the bangles and
sequins they normally wore. Their male partners had black
shirts and long pants rather than the black tights and the tiny
vests they wore for the main show.

As soon as Tracy stepped out onto the small dance floor, she
scanned the room as best she could for that damn pendant, but
in her heart she knew it was hopeless. Still she couldn't help
but steal a quick glance whenever she faced forward. It broke
her concentration a couple of times and she missed two slow
counts, but she had been dancing this kind of swing for so
many years that it was easy for her to make up for it, and even
her partner didn't catch her mistake.

No pendant.

Then somewhere in the middle of a Lindy routine, she spotted a woman at the very back of the room with something silver dangling around her neck. She looked exactly like the woman Tracy had seen the other night. Could it be Becky Montgomery? Tracy couldn't be sure. This time she missed the two quick counts completely, but her partner twirled her around to hide the mistake. "Stay with me here," he ordered.

She merely nodded, but her heart raced, and no matter how hard she tried to relax, she could feel the stiffness building up in her arms and legs.

Tracy glanced out again and this time she couldn't see anything but a blur. Would this dance never end?

Finally, after a few more spins and a wave rhythm break, it was over. The audience applauded their approval, while Tracy looked as hard as she could for the Montgomery woman. She couldn't see her anywhere. The foursome bowed, Tracy's partner gave her one more twirl and they walked off the floor.

"I'M WORRIED ABOUT MY MOM," Laura told Becky once the applause died down.

Becky took a step back to admire Laura's beautiful soft pink dress. "You look fabulous in that dress. It fits you like it was made for you."

"It was. Mom hired a seamstress when I couldn't find anything off the rack. According to my mom, they don't make stylish dresses in my size. Of course I know that's a bunch of crap, but I let her have her way because I love the dress." Laura twirled around in a wash of luminous pink.

"So, why are you worried about your mom?"

"Because Bob's been walking around here like he's anxious about something, and he and Grandma have been whispering to each other all night long. It's giving me the willies." Laura fussed with the matching pink satin bag that hung over her shoulder, sighing and pulling on its fragile-looking strap.

"Well, maybe they're planning another event or excursion or something. It doesn't necessarily have to have anything to do with your mom." Becky was grasping at straws. She just wanted Laura to calm down.

"Come on, Aunt Becky. You know as well as I do that Grandma has been trying to get Mom married off ever since she and my dad got divorced."

"Bob seems like a nice enough guy," Becky said, knowing that was a complete lie.

Laura stared at her for a moment. "You're talking to me now, not my mom."

Becky didn't want to get in the middle of anything, especially when she had no influence with Kim or Estelle, and especially Bob. If she interfered, there would be hell to pay, and besides, her real goal was to keep the peace for the rest of the cruise. "Maybe you should give him the benefit of the doubt. Your mom seems to really like him."

"Yeah, 'like' is fine for a friend, but not for a husband. I'll die if she marries him."

"Who says they're going to get married? I think you're jumping to conclusions."

And just as she said the words, Bob stepped into the center of the floor and grabbed a microphone. "Ladies and gentlemen, I have something I'd like to say."

A hush fell over the room. "Oh, God. I told you," Laura whispered. "Here it comes."

"I know this may not be the proper time or place," Bob continued, "but I have something I would like to ask Kim Montgomery, and if this doesn't go my way, I think I might need all you guys for emotional support."

Everyone chuckled. Laura went white and Becky grabbed her around the waist.

"Kim, if you're still out there, would you come up here please," Bob cooed into the microphone.

"Don't, Mom—please leave," Laura murmured.

But Kim walked right up to Bob, with Estelle close behind. Kim took Bob's hand, and he knelt down on one knee.

"Oh-God-oh-God-oh-God." Laura was almost frantic now. Becky had a tight grip on her, but she knew if Laura wanted to bolt, there was nothing she could do to stop her.

"Kim Montgomery," Bob began "I've loved you from the moment I first saw you. You were and are the most beautiful and loving woman I've ever known."

"Don't do it, Mom," Laura said over and over.

Bob kept going. "I would be the luckiest man on the planet if I was your husband." He pulled out a ring that Becky couldn't really see from her vantage point, but Kim seemed impressed. "Kim Montgomery, would you marry me?"

The room was silent. It was as if everyone had taken a collective breath and was waiting for Kim's answer before letting it out again.

Becky saw a flicker of confusion in Kim's eyes. It startled her for a moment, as if Kim wasn't exactly sure of what she should say.

Laura closed her eyes and kept mumbling for her mother to say no.

Kim turned slightly and glanced over at Estelle. In that instant Becky could tell who had the final say in this matter and it wasn't Kim.

"Yes," Kim said in barely a whisper. "Yes, I'll marry you."

The room exploded with whistles and applause. Laura broke away from Becky and headed straight toward her mother. Becky tried to catch her, but Laura was too quick. She followed after her, running to catch up.

"Mom, you can't do this," Laura said as discreetly as she could. Becky stood behind her, knowing this was not the time, but Laura was a strong-willed young woman who hadn't yet learned how to handle her emotions.

Kim tried to dismiss her. "Sweetie, we'll talk about this later," she said in a terse voice.

"How can you marry a man who doesn't like your own daughter?"

This information was new even to Becky.

"Don't be silly, pumpkin. Bobby loves you just like his own daughter." All the while Kim kept trying to shake hands with well-wishers.

"Excuse me, but I've been waiting all night to have a dance with the prettiest girl at this party. May I?" Dylan held out a hand to Laura.

And there he stood, right in front of Becky, as if he'd just dropped down from the sky to rescue Laura from her distress.

Becky took in a sharp breath—shocked and elated at the same time. In a navy blazer and white slacks, Dylan looked way too appealing, and Becky was glad he would be dancing with Laura, not her. She needed a little time to get used to the idea that what she'd wished for had come true. Somehow Dylan *had* been invited to Estelle's party. Probably at Laura's insistence.

Laura took a deep breath as she gazed into his eyes, then she looked back at her mom as Dylan patiently waited for her decision. In a heartbeat, it seemed as if all of Laura's anger subsided as she stepped toward Dylan, who took her in his arms and swung her out on the dance floor.

Laura looked like a princess, her satin dress catching the light as she swayed to "Just the Way You Look Tonight," an old Frank Sinatra ballad.

One of Becky's favorites.

Becky watched them for a few more minutes as they laughed and talked, Laura looking completely at ease while her mom and Bob played the happy, newly engaged couple. Then Laura and Dylan disappeared into the center of the dance floor.

"Champagne?" a woman carrying a tray filled with bubbling flutes asked.

"Absolutely," Becky said, taking a glass.

As she drank down the golden liquid, watching the other

dancers on the floor, she wondered how he did it. How Dylan could change Laura's disposition and defuse her anger in one perfect moment.

The man was magic, and she wouldn't mind falling under his spell.

"Can I have this dance, Ms. Montgomery?" She heard Dylan's voice behind her and turned. He smiled. "My partner abandoned me for a younger man," he teased, "and unless you want me to be scarred for life, you'll rescue me with a dance."

For a brief moment Becky thought of refusing, but the woman with the champagne tray walked by and Dylan slipped Becky's empty glass from her hand and gently placed it on the tray. Then he enfolded her in his arms, pulling her in close, and whisked her away to Neverland.

TRACY'S HEART RACED as Dylan placed the empty glass down on her tray, never giving her a second glance. It had almost been too easy. She had traded clothing with a disgruntled waitress who was eager to meet her new lover in the crew bar belowdecks, and within ten minutes of the clothes swap Tracy had scored big-time. She'd found Becky Montgomery and was staring at the coveted pendant. Because this was a private party, the wait staff had been pulled from other restaurants, so the managers didn't know all the faces, which played to Tracy's advantage.

To her complete amazement she had succeeded much sooner than expected. And not only that, she now had a face to go with the pendant, thanks to Dylan, whom she had seen in the crew bar many times before.

All she had to do was to find a way to steal the damn thing from Ms. Montgomery's cabin or just rip it off her pretty little neck some night when she was out on deck alone.

How hard could that be?

She'd do it no matter what…for her son.

CHAPTER SEVEN

By THE END of the evening, Becky's head was spinning. Not to mention the fact that she was falling for Dylan. She couldn't be sure if it was the magic of the pendant or his charm that had captivated her. Conversation had come easily as they'd danced. Even when they had sat and chatted about silly things, it was as if she'd known him for a long time and now all they were doing was catching up.

Of course, some of the ease of conversation may have been due to the champagne she'd consumed over the last three hours, but what did that matter?

She'd forgotten how fabulous it felt to be in a man's arms. How safe, how sexy it made her feel. But somewhere deep down inside, she still couldn't relax. Couldn't surrender to the moment and simply enjoy Dylan's company.

By the close of the evening, she and Dylan had moved off by themselves, dancing in a secluded corner of the room where moonlight illuminated the walls as they swayed to the music. Dylan pulled back to face her during a rather seductive rendition of Sting's, "When We Dance." He didn't say anything. He simply gazed into her eyes. When her knees buckled and she missed a step, he pulled her up. "Did I tell you how beautiful you look tonight?"

Becky could feel a blush come over her face. Feel the heat of it. She was acting like a schoolgirl, and if she wasn't careful, she'd be having "sex under the stars" before the night was over.

The way the heat was pooling between her thighs, her body was definitely rooting for the event.

"Come on. You can do better than that," she countered, trying to tease him, but then she regretted having said it at all.

He gave her a quizzical look. "Okay. You're delicious-looking and you stir emotions in me that I thought I could control, but when I'm around you they come pouring out and I'm willing to risk everything for just one kiss."

The look in his eyes convinced her he meant every word.

She was almost swooning now, and the heat between them was palpable, but they were in a public area onboard the ship. Her kids were here, Estelle was here, and his boss had probably already written up the warning slip for being overly friendly with a passenger.

Nothing could happen between them. No kisses. No caresses. Nothing but dancing, and even that might have already caused Estelle heart palpitations, especially now that they weren't really on the dance floor anymore.

Part of her didn't want to care about any of that, but Becky was the responsible type, and even in her light-headed state, she knew what she had to do to keep them both safe from unwanted attention. She had to try to cool this thing down before they both lost all sense of control and did what their bodies craved.

"Better, but I'd say that's still not your best line," she teased, hoping he would follow her lead and lighten things up a little. But for some reason his body stiffened against hers and he pulled back to look at her.

"I get it. You think I'm making this stuff up to get you into bed."

"I…no…I just—"

The music stopped and Dylan let go of her. Suddenly his expression changed and he fell back into the role of cruise ship staffer. "It's late and I have a long day tomorrow. Thanks for the great evening, Ms. Montgomery, but I'll have to call it a night."

Becky wanted to reach out and pull him back into her arms,

but he was gone before her brain could send the proper message. Probably a good thing or she'd make a fool of herself.

Without his strong arms around her, her head was spinning so fast that if she didn't sit soon, she'd fall right over in a heap.

Laura came to her rescue. "You don't look so good, Aunt Becky."

"That's funny. Two seconds ago I was beautiful."

"That hasn't changed. You just look a little pale. Here…" She rolled over a black arm chair. "Maybe you should sit down."

"A brilliant idea," Becky said as she fell into the chair. "Do you think you could round up Sarah and Connor and then roll me back to my cabin now? I've had enough fun for one day."

WHEN BECKY MONTGOMERY left the party, Tracy had tried to follow, but had been forced to stick around to the bitter end of the gala in her role as waitress. At first she resented it until she spotted Bob, the new fiancé, working on a double bourbon while he sat alone at the bar. There was something about the way he looked at her and some of the other girls who worked the party that made her wonder if perhaps Bob was someone she could tap for information.

Her heart hammered in her chest as she thought about her son and all that rode on her mission to get that necklace. She reined in her emotions. She needed to be calm. Smart. Everything depended on it.

Keeping an eye on Bob, she followed him up to the observation deck once the party was over and casually leaned on the same railing. If Vegas had taught her anything, it was how to spot a chippy, and this guy would sell his own mother for a chance at a hot woman. Tracy intended to be just that woman.

"Nice night," Bob said, right on cue.

She ignored him. Guys like him liked a challenge.

He turned and stared right at her. She didn't flinch. "It's a beautiful night, don't you agree?" he said.

She nodded his way, then turned back to look out at the ocean. In her peripheral vision she watched him stare at her for a moment, then look away. Tracy continued to gaze out at the black water caressed by moonlight, knowing she was right about this guy.

Suddenly he turned to leave, and just when she was about to question her instincts, he was right behind her. "Got a light?" he asked, standing a little too close.

Satisfaction washed over her. "Uh-huh," she said, retrieving a lighter out of her pocket.

She lit his cigarette, the flame illuminating the sharp angles of his face, giving him a harshness that sent a chill through her on this balmy night.

He offered her one of his cigarettes. She took it and let him light it for her. Then he handed her the lighter, and smiled.

She had him.

They chatted for a while about the night, the ship, her performance earlier, and the activities onboard, which gave Tracy the perfect lead-in. "I noticed one of the women at the party was wearing the pendant. She seems to be really into the game."

"Yeah, but she's like that. She'll do anything her kids want her to do. They've probably got her convinced to sleep with it for luck."

"Maybe that's a good idea. It could be worth a fortune."

He snickered as though he knew she was joking.

"That piece of junk? Anybody can see it's worthless."

"It probably is, but there's a possibility it could hold a valuable diamond."

They were standing right next to each other now, generating body heat.

He turned to look at her. "No way. My mother-in-law can smell diamonds. Believe me, if that thing held anything real she'd be all over it like a fly on crap."

Tracy took a long drag on her cigarette, thinking of what to say next, deciding exactly how much information she should leak. "That might be, but did you know there was a smuggling ring working from this ship while it cruised the Mediterranean?"

"I think I read something about it in the papers, but I didn't pay too much attention."

"Let me fill in the details," Tracy said, and for the next twenty minutes or so she brought Bob up to date. She told him how the ship's owner, Elias Stamos, was set up to look as if he'd stolen Greek and Roman antiquities. Then there was Mike O'Connor, who'd impersonated a priest named Father Pat and smuggled some of the blackmarket pieces onboard and mixed them in with the reproductions he used with his lecture series. He and first officer, Giorgio Tzekas had picked up a few hot items on the side to pad their own bank accounts throughout the Mediterranean voyage.

"The whole thing was resolved after the last cruise around the Greek Islands when Italian and Greek police, the FBI and Interpol boarded the ship and found the artifacts. They had enough evidence to pin it on the right people, so Stamos was cleared of any wrongdoing, but the fake priest and the first officer, along with Stamos's ex-lover, will probably be in prison for a very long time."

"So what does all of this have to do with the pendant?" Bob asked, stepping away to crush his cigarette in a nearby ashtray.

"The pendant was among the reproductions left behind after the police investigation. What if it's the real deal hidden under all that cheap silver? It could be worth a fortune."

She was playing on his greed factor. To a man like him, it didn't matter if he was about to marry some rich chick with deep pockets or not. He was the type who always wanted more.

His disposition changed. He was suddenly interested.

"So you think there might be a real diamond in there—just like that stupid legend? How much could it be worth?"

"Enough to make somebody rich enough to own this ship."

"That would have to be some kind of diamond."

Tracy had no idea what the diamond was worth, but she

needed to be able to play it up as some rare stone to make this guy bite. "It is. Ever hear of a red diamond?"

He shook his head.

Fortunately, Tracy had read something about red diamonds on the Web before she came on the cruise. "They're the rarest of them all, and they cost about two million per carat. The one I think's hidden inside the pendant is supposed to be at least five carats."

Bob didn't move. His face didn't register any emotion. For a moment, she thought either he didn't believe her or she'd lost his interest.

"Yeah, right." He chuckled then he turned to face her. "So why hasn't somebody turned the thing over to the authorities to check it out?"

"That's just it. Everybody onboard thinks it's just a cheap piece of costume jewelry. Even the police passed it over."

"But you don't believe that."

"Let's just say I have access to some privileged information."

"And you picked me to share in the privilege? What would keep me from going to the authorities or stealing it myself?"

"Nothing, other than a hunch I have that you're not really in love with Kim Montgomery."

"What makes you say that?"

"The fact that you're out here talking to me when you should be in bed with your new fiancée on the night of your engagement." She moved in closer. "And that I know you'd much rather take me to bed than her."

She was taking a big risk now, but she was desperate.

He gave her the once-over. "You like to move fast, don't you?"

"We don't have much time."

"How do you intend we find out if the diamond is in there?" Tracy had him. He had used the operative word, *we*. She felt a rush of hope; she'd see her son again no matter what it took.

"I have a contact in Saint Thomas," she lied. "He can take the pendant apart and tell us all we'll need to know about its worth. We stop there in three days, and if you could somehow get your hands on that pendant…well, we might have the beginnings of a beautiful relationship."

She was thinking she could just call Sal and have him or one of his thugs meet her on the island for the trade. It would work. It had to. All she needed to do was get Bob to steal the pendant for her.

Simple.

He took a step away from her. "You'll have to excuse me, but I have to get back to my fiancée. She's waiting up for me." A large grin spread across his face, and his hand slid up her back to her neck. His touch made her almost ill. "We'll talk again," he said. "Till then—"

She turned, moved in close to Bob and ran her finger down the side of his cheek. When he walked away, she felt confident that he would do everything in his power to get that pendant.

For her son's sake, she hoped to God she was right.

"BUT I DON'T CARE ABOUT swimming with dolphins," Connor protested as he stood next to Becky's bed, wearing his favorite navy blue cotton pajamas with the San Diego Chargers' lightning bolt logo emblazoned across his chest. Sarah had joined Becky in bed somewhere around dawn and was now sitting cross-legged next to Becky's head, listening. "It's stupid. I'd rather play golf with Grandpa."

Becky was in no mood for Connor's protest. She had woken up with a throbbing headache, a queasy stomach, and the rather unmotherly temptation of abandoning her kids to the first surly-looking person she met on deck.

"Golf is what's stupid, Connor," Sarah countered, apparently deciding to enter into the argument. "Who cares about hitting a little ball around all day? You're just doing this 'cause you like to be contrary. You're just like Nemo and look what happened to him."

Despite Becky's irritation over their argument, she was impressed with Sarah's use of the word "contrary." It amazed her whenever one of her kids used a complex word. A fresh little wave of guilt spread through her as she admitted they weren't getting this stuff from her since she'd been working so many hours at the dress shop.

"Nemo was a dumb clown fish. I'm not going off by myself, like Nemo did. I'll be with Grandpa. No one's going to kidnap me and bring me to Australia."

"How do you know?"

"Because I just know, that's why."

"See what I mean? You think you know everything, just like Nemo. Stubborn and contrary."

"I am not."

"You are, too."

"Am not."

The kids went back and forth with their argument until Becky wanted to scream, but knowing that would probably blow off the top of her head, she did the only rational thing she could think of.

She got up and took a hot shower.

As the water caressed her tired body, the events of the previous night began to come into focus and she was certain she had somehow managed to offend Dylan…but she didn't know exactly how she'd done it. All she remembered was being in his arms, and then she wasn't, and he was saying good-night. But that "good night" didn't have a kiss attached to it. Instead, it had a "Ms. Montgomery" stuck to it and that couldn't be good.

WHEN DYLAN'S CELL PHONE rang the next morning, he knew it could only be one person, his older brother, Bear.

Dylan sat up in bed. "Hey, man. What's up?"

"I've been tryin' to get you for two days." Bear's raspy voice echoed in Dylan's ear. Bear had never completely lost that mix of an Irish and English accent prevalent in their region of Newfoundland. An accent that Dylan had worked hard to shed. Just hearing Bear's voice reminded Dylan of their father. His accent was so thick that at times even Dylan couldn't understand him.

"Yeah, this phone only works when we're docked."

"You should be gettin' a more powerful phone."

"Then I'd have to talk to you more often."

Bear laughed. "You should be so lucky."

"Where are you?"

"I'm lookin' dead-straight at your ship."

Dylan's stomach tightened. He'd known he would have to see his brother at some point on this cruise, but he hadn't thought it would be so soon.

"I don't know if I can see you today. I've got a couple tours I've got to do." Dylan really only had one, but if he told Bear the truth he'd be stuck meeting him for sure.

"I'm only gonna be here for the day. Then I'm off to St. Lucia. You need to see *Good Hope*. She's better than she ever was, and it's all thanks to you, little brother."

Dylan knew he needed to get this over with, but the thought of boarding their dad's fishing boat again was almost too much for him. He knew Bear had restored it. Hell, Dylan had sent him the money to do it, but in truth he never wanted to see it again.

"I can't. Not today. Sorry. Maybe we can catch up on my next cruise."

"You're gonna have to see her sometime, little brother. Besides, I got a lot to tell you about startin' our own business back home. I think we can do it now. The O'Brien brothers are givin' up their whale watchin' tours, so we can step right in and take over next season."

Bear had been trying to get Dylan to partner up with him in a tour business back home ever since he began restoring the fishing boat, but Dylan wanted no part of it. That place held too many sad memories. He'd left ten years ago and he'd made the decision he would never return, but his brother couldn't seem to get that through his thick skull.

"You know I don't want anythin' to do with goin' home," Dylan said with more edge to his voice than he had intended, and with his own accent creeping in.

Bear sighed. "Don't be gettin' your drawers in a tangle. I get that you don't want to see this tub, but I got all day to wait around for you to change your mind. So if you do, just give me a holler. I ain't seen you in a long time, and I'm missin' you, Dylan. Dad wouldn't have wanted it to be this way. You know it for a fact just like you know you'll take another breath."

And he hung up.

"Damn him!" Dylan said out loud, and got out of bed.

Not only was his brother giving him a rash, but he'd awoke thinking about Becky and what she had said to him last night after he'd poured his guts out. He hadn't expected that reaction, not when they'd spent most of the night getting to know each other. Not after he'd risked his job to dance every dance with her while his boss was in the same room.

But, he told himself, the woman was probably right to react that way toward him. She couldn't know he was being honest. In the long run, she'd undoubtedly done him a favor. If he had danced with her any longer, Patti would have called him bright and early to give him an official warning.

Okay, so maybe he was a little bit grateful to Becky for thinking he was giving her a line. It just might have saved his job.

Now all he had to do was try to stay away from her for a few more days, and he could go back to his life.

But what the heck was he going to do about Bear?

AFTER DROPPING OFF Connor with Mark and giving her son a last-minute lecture on the virtues of cooperation, which he completely ignored, Becky met Laura in her cabin and they all headed for Coral Cove on Artemis deck. Becky wanted to apologize to Dylan before they had to board the tender.

It was an absolutely beautiful morning, not a cloud in the sky, and the sea looked as smooth as liquid glass. They were docked about half a mile off Tortola Island's Parquita Bay, which looked enchanting off in the distance. Mountains rose up against one of the bluest skies Becky had ever seen. She had to stop to take in the splendor of the moment.

A warm breeze caressed her as she leaned on the ship's railing to stare at the island, the sky and the textured colors of the sea. As she fingered the pendant hanging around her neck, a sense of well-being came over her making her realize she was indeed happy to be aboard the ship, surrounded by people who also seemed happy. It was the same feeling she used to get years ago whenever she went to the beach in La Jolla back home in San Diego—all those jovial people enjoying themselves in the sun.

"Come on, Mommy. We're going to miss the boat and we'll never get to see the dolphins," Sarah said, demanding Becky's attention.

"Yeah, we probably should get going," Laura agreed.

Becky wanted to linger a little while longer, but Sarah and Laura were right. Plus, she wanted to catch Dylan before she left for the day. When they arrived at the outdoor pool and she couldn't see him anywhere, Becky asked a member of the dive staff she recognized from her last visit to this pool if he was around.

"I'm sorry," the smiling water polo instructor said as she stood with a group of people getting ready to get into the pool. "But I think he had an excursion today and won't be back until late this evening."

"Thanks," Becky told her, disappointed. The smiling girl turned and dived into the pool along with about six people, causing one gigantic splash that almost engulfed Sarah. Laura snatched her out of the way in time.

"It wouldn't matter," Sarah teased. "I won't melt."

"Yeah," said Laura, "but then we'd have to take you back to the cabin to change and we might miss our boat."

"I wouldn't want to change. Red is a power color." Sarah

looked down at her red tee and matching shorts. Even her swimsuit was red. "Miss Carol told us red is a primary color and a power color and we should wear it when we want to be noticed. If I'm going to get in the water with really big dolphins, I want them to notice me a lot!"

Miss Carol was Sarah's second-grade teacher.

"Actually, Sarah, I read online that dolphins might not be able to see color at all," Laura said.

"Then I need to practice my dolphin calls," Sarah announced just before she started screeching in a high-pitched voice, sounding just like a screaming baby.

Becky watched as Laura grabbed Sarah's hand and ran toward the elevators, laughing all the way, while Sarah continued with her dolphin calls. They really needed to hurry and get down to sea level, where they would board the tender with everyone else going ashore for the day.

When Becky caught up with them, Sarah had thankfully stopped screeching.

"So, why are you suddenly looking for Dylan?" Laura asked as they approached the elevators. "I saw you two dancing last night. Is that pendant finally working its love magic?"

"Don't be ridiculous," Becky remarked a little too quickly. She knew Laura was a sharp kid, and hoped she hadn't picked up on any of the emotions that were stirring up inside Becky.

"Come on, Aunt Becky. I can tell when there's something going on with you."

Sarah pressed the down button.

"Okay, I might have said something…" Becky began. "I mean I might have acted a little…I need to talk to Dylan. That's all. Nothing more than a friendly conversation to straighten a few things out. He seems like a nice enough guy, but I'm—"

"Confused?"

Becky turned to face Laura to disagree with her, but the elevator doors opened and about a dozen people stared out at them, including Dylan.

JUST WHEN HE THOUGHT he was free to have a good day, Becky Montgomery squeezed in beside him on the crowded elevator. Seeing her again made him realize it was useless to try to stay away. One look and he was hooked all over again, and this time he knew he couldn't stop this thing. His attraction was too powerful.

"Mommy was looking all over for you, Dylan," Sarah told him. He could tell by the look on Becky's face that this information was not something she had wanted leaked. "Why weren't you at the pool like you always are?"

"I have an excursion today, Sarah." Dylan tried to ignore the fact that Becky's arm was touching his. "And it's a really exciting one."

"Are you going to play with the dolphins like we are?" Sarah asked, but Dylan was focused on Becky, who was staring straight at him.

As they dropped through space, she leaned in closer to him and whispered, "I can't remember exactly what I said last night to make you leave, but whatever it was, I didn't mean it."

That was all he wanted to hear. He was right. She did feel something for him.

"Then you didn't mean it when you said you love me?" He decided to have some fun with her; he liked teasing her and seeing her cheeks turn pink when she was a little embarrassed. And maybe she was blushing for other reasons. A man could certainly hope.

The woman standing right behind them, wearing a bright pink visor, a matching tee and huge pink sunglasses, peered right at Becky, waiting for her answer. He knew the elderly woman was probably making Becky nervous, but he didn't want to let Becky completely off the hook for last night...at least not yet.

"I, um, I said that?"

She swallowed, hard.

"How can you play with my heart like this, after all we've been through?" He was whispering just loud enough for the lady in pink to hear him, but not Laura and Sarah, who were standing in front of the doors chatting about dolphins.

Becky shifted her weight from one foot to the other. He could tell she was trying to remember the previous night.

"But what about the promises you made to me?" he asked.

"I made promises?"

She was starting to get it now, that he was teasing. Her face brightened.

"Yes, and unfortunately, those promises are dust in the wind, sand on the beach, shells in the ocean."

Becky smirked and one eyebrow went up. The cutest darn thing he'd ever seen.

"I'm sorry," she added, "but it simply wasn't meant to be."

The elevator stopped and a senior couple got on. He and Becky moved in even closer, her body tight up against his.

He could smell her subtle perfume now, and wondered if it was actual perfume or simply her natural fragrance. She smelled like a bouquet of mixed flowers, sweet, but not overpowering. More like a hint of fragrance. He had smelled it last night when they were dancing, but he somehow wasn't as conscious of it as he was now.

She was having more of an impact on him in this crowded elevator than she had last night while he'd held her in his arms.

"I don't know if I can go on," he said, trying to sound sad, but he was loving the fun of this.

"You must. The passengers need you."

"Yes, duty calls."

As three more people squeezed into the elevator, Becky was forced even tighter against Dylan, and he was loving it. Fortunately the kids were pushed farther away, and Dylan was conscious of Becky's breasts pressed up against his chest, her long legs resting against his. And she was making no moves to put any space between them. If the elevator doors didn't open soon he'd have a full erection going.

"This is cozy," she whispered, and he wanted to die right there. It was as if he was being tortured for any and all of his past sins.

He couldn't talk, so he smiled and nodded.

Finally, just when he thought he couldn't take it one more second, the doors opened at sea level and everyone gave a little cheer as they poured out of the elevator. Becky and the kids followed the rest of the passengers as they made their way through security to board the tender.

The lady in pink said, "I don't know what went on in that elevator, but I haven't had a hot flash like that in years. Take my advice, honey. Forget about your duty to the passengers. That woman's hot for you, no matter what she says, and you'd be a fool to let her go." And she walked away fanning herself with her pink visor.

CHAPTER EIGHT

ONCE THE TENDER arrived on shore and a few hundred passengers went off to their various adventures, Becky and the kids boarded a small green bus with about thirty other people. It was a relatively short journey to the private lagoon where the trained dolphins awaited their latest visitors.

On the way, Sarah mastered her new dolphin calls, and Laura made friends with a few teens. Becky had thought she might get to spend time with Dylan, but he was simply too popular with the passengers. A blond babe had lingered outside, stepping on the bus at the last minute so she could sit next to him, and four other model types occupied his every moment. Occasionally, Dylan would look over at Becky and smile, but he was playing the cordial escort, so his attention had to be focused on his group.

As she watched the attractive young women talking and laughing with Dylan, she wondered why, if he could have any one of them, he would bother to pursue her. Not that she was unattractive, or even matronly or close to it, but she simply wasn't a young hot babe.

She hadn't been positive Dylan was still interested until the incident in the elevator. Becky knew when a man was turned on, she knew the body language, the look, the talk, and she could actually feel the heat radiating from Dylan's body. Unlike the previous night, there was no champagne to make his temperature rise.

Becky had been a bit surprised at her own reaction to him

in the confined space. Up until that moment, she had worked hard to convince herself that her attraction to him was a simple crush on a cute guy, but being that close had made her realize this little crush might be something more.

But what?

It was an impossible situation. For one thing, if it was just the sex she wanted, she had her kids with her, and no matter what Lacey had said, she was not going to let it happen. It would be way too irresponsible on her part.

And if she was thinking of an actual relationship, she was kidding herself. The guy worked on a cruise ship that sailed the Caribbean and she lived in San Diego. What kind of relationship could there possibly be?

When Ryder died, she was certain she could never feel love for another man again…not that she was in love with Dylan. Heck, she hardly knew him, but there was just something about him, something in his eyes that fascinated her. And she didn't want to let that fascination go.

At least not yet.

THE LAGOON was beautiful. Lush mountains in the background and azure water welcomed them to this private section of the island. Sarah and Laura couldn't wait to get in the water, and for that matter, neither could Becky. The dolphins swam around in groups of three to five, bursting through the water's surface every now and then to chatter their welcome. Of course, Sarah answered right back, trying to mimic their sounds, which caused everyone around her to clap and chuckle at her abilities.

Becky caught it all on her camera.

Dylan and his two assistants, a woman who looked vaguely familiar, and a guy Becky hadn't seen before, went off with a small group for some other type of dolphin encounter.

Becky's group was seated on the sand on the small private beach for a brief history on the bottle-nosed dolphin, combined with instructions on how to handle the magnificent creatures. The instructor, Bonnie, an athletic woman in her late twenties, tanned with sunstreaked hair and delicate features, asked a few questions and got everyone laughing. She eventually informed the group about the pod of dolphins they were about to meet.

"Our dolphins love to play, especially with people," Bonnie said. "So don't be surprised when they give you an underwater body rub, or want to shake your hand. Most of their behaviors are up to them. We can coax them to do tricks, but some tricks are things that they decide to perform while we're all in the water together."

"How will we know if they don't like what we're doing?" Laura asked.

"They'll either swim away from you, or if they really don't like it they'll make a bubble cloud with their blowhole. If you see this, it's time to stop all activity, but if you're gentle they will be friendly and gentle right back. We have a one-year-old calf in the water with us today. Her name is Molly, and she's quite a character. She tends to stay with her mom, but every now and then when she's feeling comfortable, she'll come up for a kiss."

"I want to kiss her," Sarah yelled. "But does she bite?"

"Just keep your hands away from their mouths as a safety precaution. Dolphins don't typically bite, especially humans, though they sometimes scratch other dolphins by raking their teeth over their skin, so that's why you want to keep your hands away from their mouths. But don't be scared," Bonnie reassured her, "and just try to remember that you want to wait for the dolphin to come to you. And keep in mind these are still wild animals, even though they seem to love the attention from us humans."

While she told everyone about a dolphin's unique dorsal fin, that it was like a fingerprint, and that the creatures could swim at six to seven knots, dive more than one thousand feet, and live an average of twenty years, Becky watched Dylan several yards away as he instructed his own group. She noticed that he helped a woman slip on a mask and secure a snorkel on her head, taking the time to instruct her on every aspect of the procedure, making sure the equipment was securely fastened. Then he helped the next person and the next. When he was finished, he said something and they all laughed.

His kindness and his humor weren't the only things she noticed while he stood half-naked on the beach. He had a fabulous body, all muscle, with a flat stomach and legs meant for intertwining with a woman's. She wondered how that would feel. How his naked chest would feel against hers.

How his hands…

There was a tug on Becky's shirt. "Mom, are you listening to me?"

Becky came out of her daydream. "It's time to go in the water," Sarah demanded as she stood in front of Becky, clad in her red bathing suit and an orange safety vest, her curly hair drooping in her eyes.

"Hmm?" Becky murmured.

"I think that pendant is finally working," Laura teased.

"What?" Becky began her descent into reality. "Pendant? What are you talking…don't be silly."

"You've been staring at Dylan for the past five minutes," Laura said.

"Mom, it's time to go. You can stare at Dylan on the ship, right now I want to pet Molly."

Becky stood up. "I was not staring at Dylan. I was gazing at the beautiful lagoon. Isn't it magnificent?"

The girls looked at each other, then back at Becky. "Yeah, sure…beautiful," Laura said sarcastically.

Sarah giggled.

"You guys are jumping to conclusions," Becky declared, sliding the pendant back and forth along the chain. "This necklace isn't doing a thing."

"That reminds me. Bonnie said we have to remove all our

jewelry before we can go into the water with the dolphins," Laura instructed, nodding toward the pendant. Laura removed her watch and gold hoop earrings. "If we have anything valuable, they said they could lock it up for us inside the life-guard shack. But otherwise, our stuff is safe here on the beach."

Becky hadn't heard the instructor mention anything about jewelry, but it sounded reasonable to her, so she unclasped the pendant and slipped it into her large white canvas bag along with Laura's jewelry. She didn't have any zipped pockets inside her bag, so the pendant and jewelry sat at the bottom under a hat and a couple towels.

"You shouldn't take it off, Mommy," Sarah scolded. "It might be bad luck,".

"She has to," Laura countered. "Didn't you hear what Bonnie said?".

"Yeah, but I know she didn't mean the moon goddess's teardrop."

"I think I better put it away just in case one of those dolphins likes teardrops," Becky said. "Or do you think I should take the chance?" Whenever she could, Becky liked to allow Sarah to come to her own rational conclusions. This was one of those times.

"You're right, Mommy. They'd get really sick if they ate your pendant, wouldn't they?"

"Yep."

"Okay, but as soon as we're done, you have to put it on again or the moon goddess won't be able to work her magic."

Becky was curious what Sarah thought would happen. "What kind of magic are we hoping for again? I forget."

"Oh, Mommy, sometimes you're so silly."

Becky had a funny feeling she knew what was underneath all this.

"You miss your daddy, don't you?"

Sarah nodded.

"The moon goddess can't bring him back, sweetheart."

"I know, but maybe she can find someone that's kind of like him. Just for a while. I miss him, Mommy."

Becky hugged Sarah. "So do I, baby. So do I." Emotions swelled up in Becky, but she got herself under control. She'd cried for months over Ryder, and no amount of tears could bring him back. Plus, her daughter needed her to be strong.

"Come on, you guys," Laura said, running toward the rest of their group. "Those dolphins are waiting for us!"

She and Sarah pulled apart, and Becky was thankful for Laura's reminder, relieved that she'd gotten through the moment. She knew her kids really missed their dad, but in time they would come to terms with the hurt, just as she was beginning to do.

Sarah ran off with Laura, while Becky dropped her bag on the sand next to the rest of their things. Actually, she was thankful she could go without wearing the pendant for a while. The clasp wasn't very secure, and she felt as if she might lose it at any moment. If that happened, Sarah would be so disappointed. Becky would also have to tell cruise director Patti Kennedy, who seemed enchanted with the whole myth of the moon goddess and unrequited love.

Becky suddenly felt as if she wanted to lock her bag up inside the shack. Then she realized there were a lot of bags, shoes, hats and various articles of clothing strewn around the small private beach. Three lifeguards sat in front of the red shack right behind her, watching over both the belongings on the beach and the people going into the water, so she decided to just leave everything and ran up the beach to join Laura and Sarah. Grabbing Sarah's hand while Laura took the other, Becky and the girls ran down to the pier to meet a few friendly dolphins.

DYLAN COULDN'T KEEP his mind off of Becky no matter how hard he tried. And it didn't help any when he noticed she was staring at him while he tried to do his job. He knew he might end up fired, or really hurt, but he was like the proverbial moth to the flame, and this flame was red-hot.

As he gave his talk to his own small group about swimming with dolphins, his mind was on Becky.

He caught glimpses of her standing on the wooden pier gazing out at the dolphins while they danced backward half out of the water. Everyone was laughing at their antics.

His own group eagerly waited for him to take them out into the deeper water so they could begin their swim with the sea creatures. These dolphins didn't have to perform. It was their down time, and Dylan's group would be instructed on how to observe the dolphins and also swim alongside the agile creatures.

A thought suddenly flew into his head and he couldn't let it go. If he had to see Bear, why couldn't he bring Becky and the kids along? It might be against the ship's rules, but it would be his afternoon off. It seemed the perfect solution to his Bear dilemma, and besides, he was determined to find a way to get to know Becky Montgomery and her family.

He approached his two assistants. "Sorry, guys, but I think we have one more passenger to take with us. Apparently she went with the wrong group. Could you guys fill in for me? I'll only be a few minutes."

"Sure," his female assistant said with some reservation in her voice, but Dylan didn't have any time to question her response.

He left the group in the capable hands of Joe Bonner. Tracy Irvine, a dancer, was filling in for his other assistant who had come down with a nasty cold. Tracy didn't know the first thing about swimming with dolphins, but she took directions well and seemed eager to help, so he had agreed to bring her along. Having another warm body to keep an eye on the passengers had been the only real responsibility of the additional assistant anyway, and Tracy was doing just fine at that. He knew many of the staff looked for extra shifts during cruises, liking the overtime wages.

Dylan took off down the beach, and when he reached the pier, he walked toward Becky, Sarah and Laura. They were standing a few feet away in shallow water in the lagoon. "Ms. Montgomery," he called. "Can I talk to you for a minute?"

Becky turned and walked toward him wearing a black swimsuit that hugged her body in all the appropriate places and accentuated her full breasts. He told himself to concentrate on her face, but his reaction to her was instantaneous.

"Yes," she said, squinting into the sun as she pulled herself up on the pier to stand next to him.

"I know this is last-minute, and I understand if you refuse, but I really would like to get to know you and I can't do that while I'm working. Anyway, my brother is here and we'd love to take you and the girls out on our boat this afternoon. But I completely—"

Just then two male passengers walked up and stood behind Dylan.

Dylan wanted to give Becky all the details, but now it would be impossible. He wouldn't blame her if she told him to bug off, but he so wanted her to join him. He'd have to make something up for the benefit of the passengers behind him.

"I have room for three more on a trip out to the reef later this afternoon, and was wondering if you and the girls would like to join us." It was a believable scenario. There was a fantastic reef not too far out that he'd love to show her. "It's complimentary because of the pendant, of course."

"This afternoon?"

"Yes," he confirmed.

She smiled, looked down again as though she was considering his offer, and he knew instinctively she wanted to join him.

"Is this a snorkeling excursion?"

She sounded official.

"Yes," he said.

"But what about Sarah? She's too little to snorkel in the sea."

He had to think fast.

"There's lots of fun things she can do on the boat."

He stared at her lovely face. She seemed to grow more beautiful with each passing moment. In the bright sunshine, he noticed a light dusting of freckles across her nose and cheeks, just like Sarah's. It gave her a playful, mischievous look that made her even more endearing.

"Okay. What time?" she asked.

"About one," he said, thrilled that she had agreed.

"Sounds good," she answered.

"Perfect. I'll meet you back here in about three hours," he told her, then turned and ran up the beach toward his group, elated that she had said yes.

Now all he had to do was to contact Bear to tell him about the party he had planned with three passengers from *Alexandra's Dream*. He didn't care if Bear minded the added company—heck, if his brother wanted to see him badly enough, he wouldn't object.

TRACY WATCHED Dylan and Becky as they stood on the wooden pier, talking, but her real focus was on that white canvas bag. She'd seen Becky remove the pendant and slip it inside, giving her the perfect opportunity, but then Dylan had left her and Joe in charge of the group.

Part of her wanted to scream and tell him she had a purse to snitch and if she didn't get her hands on that damn pendant she may never see her little boy again! But she'd kept her cool and managed to act like a professional.

It was perhaps the perfect opportunity. The only clear opportunity she might get, but instead she was left with a group of anxious people asking her a million questions that she couldn't answer. That was Dylan's job anyway. He was the dolphin expert, not her. She was grateful that Joe was here to cover for him.

She glanced back at the white bag just sitting on the beach, leaning on another bag, a couple towels and God only knew what else. There was probably someone in that lifeguard shack watching all the stuff, just as there were a couple of lifeguards behind this group. She figured she would tell them that the passenger had asked her to retrieve the bag, or some such lame excuse. She just needed to get her hands on that damn pendant.

When there was a little lull in the chatter, Tracy said, "Perhaps you can tell everyone what else you know about dolphins, Mr. Hughes."

Mac Hughes, a high school teacher from Ohio, took it from there and entertained the group with his dolphin expertise.

In the meantime, her attention flew back down the beach to where Becky and Dylan were still talking. She wondered what, if anything, was going on between the two of them. Their body language didn't exactly give anything away, but she found it quite odd that he would suddenly hold up his entire group just to talk to her.

Then there was the party the night before. Dylan had danced with her almost the entire evening. She didn't quite know what the connection was between them, but she needed to try to stay as close to that pendant as possible, and for today, it looked like Dylan was her ticket.

Tracy had taken a chance that morning in volunteering for Dylan's excursion, hoping she could take advantage of whatever was going on between him and Becky to help her out. Bob was a good contact, and perhaps he would come through, but he had his own agenda that Tracy couldn't be sure of. So, for now, wherever Becky went, Tracy needed to figure out a way to follow.

But at the moment, Myra Wellington's goggles were slipping down the front of her tiny, crinkled face. Somebody had to help the sweet woman. She had come on this cruise all by herself, and today she wanted to celebrate turning ninety with the dolphins—a perfectly fine ambition. And if Dylan hadn't run off down the beach after Becky Montgomery, he could be helping Mrs. Wellington with her goggles and Tracy could be pinching Sal's diamond from that white beach bag.

BECKY AND THE KIDS had a wonderful time with the dolphins. She hadn't been all that enthusiastic about getting in the water with the huge mammals, but once she did and had gotten to know their personalities a little, she was completely blown away by their gentleness and intelligence.

"Look, Mommy," Sarah squealed. "Molly's giving me a kiss." Molly, the baby dolphin, who was much smaller than her mom, gave Sarah a kiss then chattered a little song to her. Sarah sang her own song and Becky caught it all on her video camera. The camera had been working overtime during most of the dolphin encounter—from handshakes with their fins and to dorsal rides for the braver passengers and Molly and her mom leaping over poles.

The lagoon was divided in two sections, a shallow end where everyone could stand and pet the dolphins as they swam by, and a deeper end where the dolphins did their tricks while people watched from the small wooden pier. Molly had come up to the pier, popping her head out of the water to kiss Sarah and a few other younger kids as they leaned over the pier, an instructor right at their sides.

"She feels like my rubber raincoat after a rainstorm," Sarah had said the first time she ran her hand over Molly's smooth body. "I love her, Mommy."

Becky only wished that Connor had changed his mind and joined them for the day. It saddened her to know that her son was missing out on such a special moment, and she promised herself that no matter how much he protested, she would do everything in her power to bring him on their next adventure.

When the time with the dolphins was over, Sarah didn't want to leave, but then she didn't like to leave any place she liked. She usually cried whenever they left an amusement park of any kind, and on her first day of preschool she cried all the way home and through dinner until Becky realized Sarah thought she was never going back.

The tears only flowed if Sarah thought she was never going to see or do something fun ever again.

"I'm sorry, sweetheart, but it's time for the next group to meet Molly and her friends," Becky told her as she escorted her out of the water.

Sarah's chin began to quiver. "But I don't want to go back to the ship yet."

Becky had an ace up her sleeve. "We're not, honey. We're going to do a little shopping and then Dylan has a special surprise for us."

Her face brightened.

"He does? What's the surprise, Mommy?"

"Yeah, Aunt Becky, what's the surprise?" Laura was curious, too.

"I don't really know. He wasn't too clear, but I think we're going out to a reef, and I think he has something special in mind for you, Sarah."

"I hope I get to play with more dolphins. They're silly, Mommy. And I love them."

"I do, too, baby. Just let me call your grandpa to tell him where we'll be, and to check on Connor. Then how about if we do a little shopping while we're waiting?"

"I spotted a great-looking gift shop on the way in," Laura said. "Let's go there."

"Can I get something special, Mommy?" Sarah asked.

Becky gave her daughter a hug. "As long as it will fit in our suitcases, you can get just about anything you want."

And off they went to find the gift shop.

CHAPTER NINE

"THIS IS LOVELY," Becky told Dylan once she and the girls had boarded the beautifully restored boat. It had to be at least forty feet long, with a huge wheelhouse and bench seating for more than twenty people up front. The deck was polished dark wood, as was the gunwale. The windows that encircled the wheelhouse had that rippled look, like fine old glass.

"Yeah. It's an old fishing boat. Been in my family for three generations. We had it dry-docked on Twillingate Island in Newfoundland."

Becky smiled. "That's where you're from, right? I noticed your name tag the first day of the cruise."

He nodded. "Born and raised."

"Too cold for me."

He chuckled. "A lot different from this part of the world, that's for sure. But when you grow up there, you come to like the cold and the change in seasons. You're more in touch with nature."

"Sounds like you miss it."

Dylan hesitated for a moment, then he said, "Sometimes I do."

"So, you said your brother brought this boat down?"

"Yeah, Bear's around here someplace."

He looked over at the wheelhouse. Becky couldn't see anyone inside. She was curious about this boat, and Bear, and how Dylan had ended up working on a cruise ship so far from his home and family.

"If you don't mind my asking, why aren't you or your brother fishermen, like the generations before you?"

He shook his head. "Can't make a living anymore. Not since the government put a moratorium on northern cod fishing in nineteen ninety-two. My grandfather and father caught a lot of cod off this boat, but now my brother has other plans for it."

Unhappiness flickered in Dylan's eyes.

"This is great!" Laura announced as she looked around.

"This is better than great," Sarah corrected, holding on to a stuffed dolphin that was almost as big as she was. Becky had tried to talk her out of it, but in the end, Sarah had won the argument. Now all Becky could hope for was that by the time they left for their flight home, she could figure out a way to stuff it in a suitcase.

A mountain of a man came out of the wheelhouse to greet them, blond tousled hair, a shaggy beard, Paul Newman eyes and a big warm smile. He loomed over Becky and had shoulders that she was sure could move boulders. He wore a battered straw hat, a bright yellow T-shirt, khaki shorts and deck shoes.

"I'm Bear, Dylan's big brother on some days and a thorn in his side on others." He slapped his arm around Dylan's shoulders with obvious affection. Dylan grinned, then laughed at some shared joke. "You must be Becky," he said with a Newfoundland accent.

They shook hands.

"You have a fabulous boat," Becky said. "Thank you for inviting us along." Bear's hand completely engulfed hers, from his handshake, she knew he was as gentle as a kitten.

He looked at Sarah and then leaned down almost to her level. "And who is this dazzlin' creature, and where did you get that dolphin? I need to get me one."

"I'm Sarah Montgomery, and my mommy bought it for me in the gift shop where Molly lives."

"Who's Molly?"

"She's a baby dolphin who likes to kiss people. She kissed me right here on my chin." She touched her chin.

"And what a pretty little chin it is," he said, and Sarah giggled.

Then Bear turned his attention on Laura. "And you must be Laura." He put out his hand and she took it.

Laura's smile couldn't get any wider. She was positively glowing, and Becky could see a hint of a blush creeping up her face. "Thanks. Yes. I mean, I'm Laura."

"Pleased to meet you, to meet all you gorgeous ladies. Dylan told me he was bringing some guests aboard, but I didn't know how pretty they'd all be."

He turned to Dylan. "Now," he said, smiling. "Let's go find us some wild dolphins and take a swim. They're gonna love you guys."

Dylan slipped a small life vest on Sarah, then Bear walked off to the wheelhouse with Sarah and Laura in tow. He entertained them with wild dolphin stories and what pod they were most likely to meet out over the white sand ridge that was a hot spot for dolphin encounters.

Soon the fishing boat roared to life and Bear maneuvered it away from the small dock in the lagoon and out into the open water.

Becky was now totally curious about Dylan, his brother, this boat and their life in Newfoundland. She had a million questions brewing, and now that they were alone, she couldn't wait to begin getting to know him better.

She and Dylan sat together on a bench seat close to the stern, water splashing up the sides of the boat as they glided forward. And just when she felt her most comfortable, ready to finally get to know this fascinating man, the woman Becky had seen on the beach with Dylan earlier that day walked up from belowdeck.

"I thought I heard voices." She approached Becky and Dylan. "Hi, I'm Tracy, and you must be Becky," she said with a sugary-sweet smile. But something in her eyes didn't quite match all that sugar. "I'm Dylan's assistant for this outing. If there's anything you need, don't hesitate to ask."

Then she plopped down right next to Becky, so close that she had to put Becky's bag on her lap.

"Oh," Becky said, somewhat confused. Dylan had told her this was a private outing. "Then this isn't…I mean, this isn't—"

Tracy stared at her.

"What I'm trying to say is…" She looked into Dylan's eyes, hoping there would be some sort of explanation. She had thought for sure when he'd asked her out on this adventure that it was personal. He had said he wanted to get to know her. How could she have been so wrong?

"So is this, um, because of the necklace?"

Still, Dylan gave no hint of a response.

Instead Tracy cleared things up. "It is! You found the lucky pendant and this is all part of your winnings. Isn't it wonderful!"

"Yep! Just fabulous," Becky lied, then she went to grab her bag from Tracy, but Tracy clung to it.

"Let me stow this somewhere where it's safe and out of the way," Tracy said as she stood, still holding Becky's bag.

"Thanks, but I might need something out of it," Becky countered, reaching for it. Tracy backed away, still gripping the bag.

"I'll just put it in the wheelhouse for safekeeping. That way you'll know exactly where it is." And she walked away.

Becky thought it odd that Tracy was being so helpful, or maybe she just wasn't used to this much attention.

Tracy returned in less time than Becky had to take a deep breath.

Dylan sat quietly next to Becky on her right, while Tracy sat close by on her left. Becky was beginning to feel penned in and couldn't wait to get into the water.

She stared out at the vast sea, thinking how long it had been since she'd mined the dating field. She guessed it would take her a little longer to figure out how guys worked these days.

As for Lacey and her "sex under the stars" suggestion, which popped into her head every time she sneaked a glance at Dylan,

Becky knew it was never going to happen on this vacation, at least not without a guidebook. She had been out of the game for so long, she could no longer recognize the signals.

THE ENTIRE DAY was turning into one great big bust for Dylan. Why he had thought he could somehow combine seeing his brother and getting Becky alone was beyond him. Not only had his brother pressured him about returning to Newfoundland with him, but Tracy Irvine had refused to leave his side. She had sneaked onto the boat, and Dylan hadn't the heart to create a scene.

Why had she wanted to come along anyway? This outing had nothing to do with the cruise ship.

And then there was Bear, who kept saying he had come all the way down to the Caribbean to personally convince Dylan to return with him to Newfoundland.

Okay, their dad's boat had turned out great. All the money he'd sent home to Bear had gone to good use, but that was the extent of his contribution—and any obligation—to Bear's dream of running whale-watching tours off the islands. There were enough companies to satisfy the tourists, even if one was folding.

Granted, Bear had some good ideas to make their tours different, but Dylan didn't want to participate. At least not now. It just wasn't the right time for him to go back, and Bear would understand…eventually. He'd just have to. It wasn't as if he was leaving his brother high and dry. Bear was perfectly capable of running the operation himself, or finding another partner if he wanted to. He didn't need Dylan. Not really. Bear merely liked the idea of both of them working on their dad's boat again, telling him over and over how Dad would have wanted it that way.

A pang of sadness washed over Dylan.

It was true. Their dad would have liked them to work together, and he would have wanted them to take care of their mom, which Dylan was doing, at least financially. But he hadn't seen her in so long her face was slipping from memory.

There was a grain of truth in Bear's arguments, he had to admit. Part of him wanted to help Bear with that whale-watching business more than anything, but the other part of him couldn't face the hardships they would encounter, at least in the beginning. Any new business took time to become solvent. Dylan had more than paid his dues in life, and he just did not want to ever be poor again.

Of course, the way he'd been acting around Becky could get him fired, and working with Bear might become a necessity. Not to mention this unauthorized expedition. If Tracy so much as hinted at it to Patti, he could be fired on the spot.

Acting on his emotions had taken him down a dangerous path.

"We should be out over the ridge in about fifteen minutes," Bear announced over a loudspeaker.

"Tracy, if you could help Laura get ready, that would be great," Dylan said. "We need to be back aboard *Alexandra's Dream* in about three hours, so that doesn't give us much time."

"Sure," Tracy agreed without hesitation in an overly cheerful voice. "And I'll stay aboard with Sarah when you guys go in. I'm not much for swimming in the sea."

"That's really kind of you, Tracy," Dylan said.

This was good news, he thought. The further away from Tracy Irvine he could get, the better. The woman was beginning to annoy him. He couldn't quite put his finger on why, but there was something about her that didn't quite add up. He was probably just imagining it. She seemed pleasant enough, but she was always underfoot.

"I think Sarah will be disappointed if she has to stay on the boat," Becky said.

"I can bring her to join you after I get you and Laura squared away. That's no problem."

Becky's face lit up and he had the strongest urge to kiss her, but of course, there was no way that would happen with Tracy looming over them.

The boat began to slow, and Dylan knew they were getting close to the ridge.

"We better get ready," he said, standing.

Laura and Sarah came toward them, excitement written on their faces. "Bear says we need to get ready, and you're going to give us some instructions," Laura told Dylan.

Sarah didn't seem very excited. Actually, she had a look of terror on her face. Dylan knew that look well. He used to feel it plenty of times when his dad took him out fishing as a kid. He used to think a giant cod was going to jump up out of the water and pull him under. It was a ridiculous fear, but when you were a kid with an active imagination, anything was possible. And from what he'd already seen, Sarah's imagination knew no bounds.

When he was a kid, his brother was the only person who could calm him during those moments. Now it was his turn to calm Sarah.

He knelt to her level. "So what do you think about the idea of swimming with wild dolphins, Sarah?"

She bit the nail on her index finger. "I liked Molly. She gave me a kiss."

"I bet she did. Tell you what. I need you to stay right here on deck with Tracy. She's kind of scared about going into the water and I think she needs a little company. Would you mind if you didn't get to swim with these dolphins?"

Sarah instantly removed her finger from her mouth. "Oh, no, and I'd be happy to stay with Tracy. I don't think anybody should be scared."

"Thank you, Sarah," Tracy told her.

"It's all right. I get scared of things all the time and my brother, Connor, always makes me feel better. Now I can 'pay it forward' just like Trevor did with Mr. Simonet. You'll be my first good deed."

Dylan didn't have the slightest idea what Sarah was talking about.

However, Tracy suddenly came to life. It was as if someone

had finally turned on a light and she could now see in the dark. "I loved that movie! I think Haley Joel Osment is the best little actor around. And Kevin Spacey, well, he's such a great actor. But how did you know it, Sarah?"

"My teacher, Miss Carol, explained it to us. If you do something nice for me, then I'll do something nice for somebody else, and then they do something nice for somebody else. I like that, don't you?"

Tracy led Sarah back to a bench as they chatted about the movie.

"Very much," Tracy agreed.

"I have Haley's poster up in my bedroom," Sarah told her. "Did you see him in—"

As their voices drifted off, Dylan said, "Okay, then. Now that Sarah's looked after, we have some dolphins to go find."

FIFTEEN MINUTES LATER, wearing snorkels, masks and fins, Becky, Laura and Dylan jumped into the clear water. Becky was in awe of the underwater beauty. She had seen various small reefs around the world on the Discovery Channel but this close, the myriad of colorful fish that inhabited the reef was truly breathtaking.

Dylan motioned for them to follow him. Laura and Becky did what they were told. Becky was astounded at the way the light reflected off the stunning colors of the reef. At times, there were so many schools of fish that she and Laura could barely see each other through the haze of bright blues, yellows and silvers dashing around them.

As if on cue, a pod of eight to ten bottle-nosed dolphins swam by, three babies straddling their moms. Becky skimmed the surface to let them pass, but Dylan motioned for her to begin swimming along with the pod. As soon as she did, it was as if the dolphins knew she had joined the group and began body rubbing her ever so gently. It was happening to Laura, as well, and to Dylan.

Becky swam effortlessly, breathing through her snorkel and arching her body to match the contours of these wonderful creatures. She could look them in the eye she was so close, and the way they looked back at her, it seemed they somehow understood her, understood the loneliness she kept hidden just beneath the surface.

The water was so crystal-clear Becky could see Laura right ahead of her, swimming with two smaller dolphins along the reef's edge. She watched her niece glide through the water, knowing she would never forget this moment.

Unexpectedly, two dolphins came up on either side of Becky, as if they were her escorts into their world. She followed their lead, not really thinking, just being in the moment. She felt the weightlessness of her body, heard the gentle rumble of a motor in the distance and delighted in the antics of these two gentle creatures as they led her right to Dylan and the rest of the pod. Dylan reached out and touched her hand, but a dolphin swam between them, breaking the connection, almost as if it wanted to play some kind of game. Then it twirled underwater and swam off.

The whole experience was almost surreal, and as Becky swam back and forth along the outer edges of the reef, she began to feel a sense of calm that she hadn't experienced since Ryder died.

Suddenly she wasn't quite so alone anymore. It was as though something had changed while she'd swum with the gentle creatures. As if something inside her had finally relaxed.

CHAPTER TEN

TRACY WAITED PATIENTLY for opportunity to come knocking once again.

It had been a miracle that she'd overheard Dylan talking to his brother on his cell about taking Becky and her family for this little excursion. With the good fortune of having the afternoon off herself, she had immediately decided to sneak onboard.

She had the distinct feeling that this whole thing was something Dylan had cooked up to be near Becky. She'd decided there really was something brewing between them, evident in the way they acted when they were around each other. But she was the last person to squeal on him. Everyone deserved a little happiness, in her book, and it wasn't their fault there were rules against staff/passenger romances. She was just glad he hadn't had a fit when she'd appeared on deck.

When Bear finally took over with Sarah, showing her all the dolphins swimming around the boat, Tracy had the perfect opportunity to check out Becky's bag more thoroughly. The first time she'd had it she'd did a quick search, but couldn't find the pendant. This time, she would go through everything. It had to be there. She'd seen her take it off and slip it inside before she'd gotten into the water.

All she had to do was grab the pendant, then call Sal when she got back on the ship and set up a trade to get Franco and her life back.

When Tracy stepped inside the wheelhouse, the white canvas

bag was nowhere to be found. Panic-stricken, she began searching under things and in overhead compartments, thinking Bear
might have moved it. Laura's things were there. Her straw bag
and a couple of plastic bags from shops on the island, but
Becky's bag was simply gone.

Now what?

She had to think fast. Dylan, Becky and Laura had been in
the water for at least a half hour and Tracy knew they would
be coming up soon.

Standing by the front window, she carefully scanned the
entire bow, and there, sitting on the port side of the deck was
Becky's bag. Who had taken it out from the wheelhouse and
why hadn't she noticed?

But she didn't have time to think about that now. She had
to concentrate on getting it.

She slipped off her flip-flops and walked back out on deck.
Bear was busy entertaining Sarah with fishing stories from
when he was a kid. Sarah seemed to enjoy Bear's company and
was completely captivated by his every word. Fortunately, both
Sarah and Bear had their backs toward Tracy and the coveted
bag.

Her heart raced. She wasn't cut out for this kind of thing,
but she thought of Franco and how scared she was for him. Sal
had totally fooled her in the beginning, but now she wouldn't
put it past him to hurt his own son when money was involved.
And there was no telling what his partner, Kirk Rimstead,
would do.

Tracy reached out and snatched up the bag, then swiftly
walked back to the wheelhouse. There was a small bathroom on
the starboard side where she could search for the pendant. She
slipped her flip-flops back on her feet, went in and locked the
door.

Standing in front of the mirror, she emptied the contents of
the bag onto the narrow counter. A tube of lipstick fell into the
sink, along with a white brush and two Hot Wheels cars. Tracy

stopped to pick up the cars, one blue and one red. Franco had the same ones. She remembered the afternoon they had spent at the store picking them out. Franco loved toy cars, and carried them around with him wherever he went. She wondered which ones he'd shoved into his pocket the morning Sal had taken him. The thought brought up a wave of emotion that she forced back.

She needed to concentrate on finding the pendant. It had to be somewhere among all the junk.

Tracy shuffled through damp towels and T-shirts, suntan lotion, hair clips, a digital camera, two sweaters—a tiny one that obviously belonged to Sarah—and a pair of pink flip-flops. She opened a stuffed makeup bag and dumped everything out, but no pendant. Just out of curiosity, she opened Becky's wallet to find the usual pictures of her kids and one of a guy sitting inside a car, smiling up at the camera with a silly grin on his face. Connor looked just like him and so did Sarah. Tracy slid her finger over the photo and wondered why he wasn't on the trip with his family. If she had a guy like that, she wouldn't leave him alone for a minute.

She snapped the wallet shut, put it down in the sink with everything else and felt inside the bag again.

Nothing.

"It has to be here," she said out loud. "I saw her put it in here."

She riffled through Becky's things once more, hoping she'd somehow missed it. That perhaps it was caught inside a T-shirt, but it simply wasn't there.

Tears began to slip down her cheeks as she hurriedly shoved everything back inside the bag. She had thought it would be so easy. That all she had to do was stick with Dylan and he would lead her to Becky and the pendant, but she'd been wrong.

The tears now streamed down her face and she could hardly control herself from sobbing. Her father was right about her. No matter how hard she tried, she couldn't seem to do the smart thing. When she had first started dating Sal, her father had warned her that he was trouble. Her mother had even tried to get her to stop seeing him, but Tracy had always been the rebellious type, especially when it came to her men. She married Sal, not because she especially loved him, but because she had wanted to show her parents they were wrong about him.

Well, she'd showed them, all right. And now she had to lie to them about this whole thing. Nobody could know what she was doing or she might never see her son again. For all her parents knew, she and Franco were on a long vacation.

There was a knock at the door and Tracy froze.

"Excuse me, I need to pee," Sarah moaned.

"Just a minute," Tracy yelled, wiping the tears from her face then blowing her nose.

"But I need to pee bad!" Sarah insisted.

"I'm coming, honey." She flushed the toilet, shoved everything back in the bag along with the lipstick, grabbed the cars and opened the door.

"It's all yours," Tracy told her. Sarah ran right past her, pulling down her swimsuit as she went.

Tracy closed the door behind her, hoping against hope that Sarah hadn't noticed Tracy was holding her mother's white bag.

IT HAD BEEN A LONG but thoroughly rewarding day for Becky and the girls. On the tender back to *Alexandra's Dream,* Laura was asleep on the bench seat across from her, while a sleeping Sarah was stretched out beside Becky, her head in her lap.

The only glitch in the day came right before they had boarded the tender, when Dylan and Bear had gotten into an argument. Becky had tried to catch some of it, but they were inside the wheelhouse with the door closed. When Dylan finally came out, she could see that he was distressed.

Now he sat next to Becky, staring out at the gray clouds gathering in a pale blue sky. It appeared as though it might rain soon. The water made the breeze extra-cool, so Becky had wrapped her sweater over her shoulders and covered Sarah with hers. She was glad she'd brought them.

Dylan didn't seem to mind the breeze. He sat straight, his gaze never faltering from the horizon. He hadn't said anything to her since they'd sat together. She was beginning to wonder if she should mention the argument. Perhaps she could help him get past it if he talked to her about it. That's what friends did, right?

"It was a fun day," she said.

He didn't say a word.

She tried again. "Thanks again for a wonderful afternoon, Dylan."

"Hmm?" he uttered.

"Thanks for the lovely experience. The girls and I loved it, and your brother seems like a great guy. Sarah really liked him."

He came out of his trance, taking in a deep breath then letting it out slowly. "Yeah, a great guy."

"Is there something you want to say…about Bear, I mean?"

He turned to look at her. "Suppose you tell me a little about yourself first. My life isn't very interesting."

She smiled, thinking she was going to get it out of him even if it took her the rest of the cruise. "Well, I like soft-serve ice-cream cones dipped in chocolate, See's candy and romantic comedies with Hugh Grant. I don't like gin, got sick on it once, butter flavoring on my popcorn and horror movies with Hugh Grant."

Dylan smiled and looked at her. "Was he ever in one?"

"I don't know, but if he was, I wouldn't like it."

That brought a chuckle out of Dylan. "I suppose it's my turn?"

Becky nodded.

"Okay. Let's see. I like Lucky Charms for breakfast, but only if there aren't any Cocoa Puffs—red wine, almost all types— and sprinkles on my ice cream. I don't like yellow cake, rough sheets and I especially don't like Hugh Grant horror movies."

They both laughed.

"We really had a great time today. Thank you for that."

"You're welcome. I had fun, too. Laura is quite the swimmer."

"Yeah, my husband, Ryder, taught her, along with Connor. The three of them could swim all day. I had to force them to come out long enough to eat. Now I can't get Connor to go in a pool, let alone the ocean. I thought this cruise would change all that, but so far, it's only gotten worse. He would have loved today."

"Laura told me about Ryder. I'm so sorry."

"Thanks. He was a great guy…most of the time, anyway." Becky's emotions were close to the surface, but she went on, feeling strangely comfortable talking with Dylan. "Except when he wouldn't let me have the remote, and he was a lousy poker player. He never showed me his cards when he won. Drove me crazy 'cause I never knew when he was bluffing. No little tells, or at least none that I could see. Of course Connor always knew. But they were close. It was almost as if they could read each other's minds, you know?"

"My dad and I were like that, too. I knew when he was tired, or angry, or when he needed to rest. And sometimes he'd say the very thing I was thinking. Checkers was our game. Of course, he'd always win, but every now and then I'd win and he never saw it coming. I would feel great for days, then we'd play another game and he'd win, and on and on we'd go. Drove my mother crazy."

"You sound as if you and your dad are very close."

"We were. He died in nineteen ninety-two, about six months after the Canadian government put that moratorium on cod fishing. My dad was an inland fisherman. That's all he knew. I was, too, and so was my brother. Actually we were the fifth generation of cod fishermen. That moratorium killed my dad as sure as somebody put a bullet in his head."

She could see the anger in his face, and the hurt in his eyes. The same look that Connor had whenever he talked about Ryder.

"I'm so sorry. Do you want to talk about it? I remember hearing something about that moratorium, but I never really understood it."

"According to my dad, it was because of the deep-sea draggers out on the Grand Banks. When a fishing company uses those things it's like underwater strip-mining. They vacuum up every last fish around. The inland fishermen warned the government for years that they were going to strip those waters clean, but they would never listen. The money was too good, and they thought the supply of wild cod was endless. As if any living thing could sustain that kind of slaughter. Then when the government put the ban on inland fishing, it was like something broke inside him.

"At first he would go to meetings with government officials and argue his case, especially when the compensation was two hundred and fifty dollars a week. As if anybody could live on that. Then when they banned cod fishing entirely, so that he and the other fishermen couldn't even catch a fish for their dinner table, I think it tore out his heart. Mine, too."

Dylan's eyes welled up with tears and he cleared his throat.

"It must have been a difficult time for your family."

"It was crushing. There were many nights when we'd go to bed hungry. My mom kept losing weight because what little we did have she'd give us kids. We never knew what she was doing. Finally, she took a job in the village working in a market. Bear got a job in St. John's and sent money home. We had food on the table again, but my dad just couldn't deal with it. Couldn't deal with the fact that his whole way of life was simply gone and he couldn't provide for his family. One morning he got up, showered and shaved and went out on his boat as he had countless times before, but this time he didn't return. My mother was frantic and sent Bear and me, plus a few of his friends, out to find him. It took two days, but we finally found the boat adrift. Apparently he'd had a stroke and died almost instantly. But I knew what really killed my father. The stroke was just a side effect."

"Is everything all right between you and Bear? I couldn't help but notice the two of you arguing earlier."

Dylan sighed. "Oh, that. Yeah, we're all right. It's just that Bear can't seem to get it through his thick head that I don't want to go back to that place. I left when I turned twenty and haven't been back since. It's too damn depressing."

"What about your mom? Have you left her, too?"

Dylan turned and looked at her. Anger flared in his eyes but faded as quickly. "I love my mom and I've been sending money home every month. But she and Bear think I belong there, running tours on my father's boat. They don't get that there's a whole world out here I want to see."

"Sounds as if you're running away from something you haven't resolved."

He slid back on the bench seat, stretched out his legs and chuckled. "Am I that obvious? Bear said the same thing."

Becky smiled and nodded.

"Maybe there is, but what about you?" he asked.

"I keep thinking I don't need to resolve anything, but who knows. Maybe I do. I work a lot, and sometimes my kids suffer for it because I'm not around as much. I own a dress shop, which keeps me busy. I run it and do most of the buying. That's one of the reasons I finally agreed to take this vacation during the biggest retail season of the year. I've heard there are some great dressmakers and designers on Saint Thomas Island. I'd like to check them out. It takes time and effort to keep a business going. I have to stay on top of it or we could fail and then what? What would I do then? I mean, I couldn't stand not to have something to do with my time."

And there it was. The very thing she had hated about Ryder's last few years, the thing that had eventually killed him. He'd been working way too many hours…and now she was guilty of the same thing herself. Why hadn't she seen it? Awareness washed over her. Why had it taken this man, this conversation, to make her see so clearly what she'd been doing?

Dylan took her hand in his as they both gazed out at the horizon, and this time there was nothing to come between them, nothing to break them apart. A comforting warmth swept through her as they sat together, holding hands, watching the water begin to embrace the ever-darkening sky.

They were the last people to leave the boat. Even Laura had gone aboard and was waiting for them on the other side of the gangway. Becky wanted to hold Dylan in her arms, but she knew she couldn't.

Not here.

Not now.

"I've never talked about any of that before—not even with Bear," Dylan said.

"Thank you." The words didn't seem like they were enough. "It means a lot that you chose me to share your feelings."

Dylan gently picked up Sarah from Becky's lap and rested her head on his shoulder. She squirmed for a bit, briefly opened her eyes, smiled, then fell back to sleep. "I'll take her," he said, and waited for Becky to slide out of her seat.

Once they were through security and aboard the ship, Laura went off to her cabin while Becky, Dylan and Sarah made their way to Becky's cabin.

"I've got the day off when we dock in Saint Thomas. I've been on that island many times before and know all the best shops. I'd love to be your guide for the day, Becky."

"I'm sorry," she explained, "but I can't leave my kids for a whole day without their mother. One-on-one with a grand-parent is fine, but not both. Besides, I just don't think it would be the right thing for us to do. The truth is, once the cruise if over, I'm going back home and you're staying on the ship. Nothing can come of this but a broken heart, and I've had enough sorrow for one lifetime." The words spilled out of her before she could censor them.

"It's just shopping with a friend, Becky. I'm not asking for anything else. You can bring the kids. It'll be fun."

Had she been reading more into Dylan's attention than she should have? She felt a little foolish. "Can I think about it?" she asked, buying some time so she could sort out her own feelings.

"Sure," he said, with an easy grin, but Becky could tell he was disappointed.

No one spoke after that. When they got to her door, she opened it and escorted Dylan into her bedroom. Sarah would sleep on her bed for the time being so she wouldn't be disturbed. That way Becky could close the door and she and Connor wouldn't wake her.

Becky pulled back the covers and Dylan eased Sarah onto the bed, then he slipped off her shoes and covered her with the blankets, lingering for just a moment to watch her sleep.

"I always thought I'd have kids of my own by now," he said. "I'd be fishing during the day, and tucking my brood into bed at night, just like my father, his father and his father before him." He turned to Becky, who stood so close that he brushed her body when he stood.

Sarah turned on her side, snuggled into the pillow and let out a contented sigh.

Dylan took Becky's hand in his and led her out into the other room. A fire ran through her body with his touch. She almost couldn't walk, but she did, and when she closed the bedroom door and turned to face him, she realized how much she wanted him. The emotions that ran through her were overpowering.

Without any further hesitation, he took her in his arms and kissed her. His tongue touching hers sent ripples of heat through her body. His lips were gentle yet hungry for the taste of her. His hand slid down to her breast, caressing it, causing her to let out a soft moan. She wanted him more than she could have imagined, but now was not the time nor the place. Sarah could wake at any moment.

She gently moved away from him.

"I can't—not here," she softly whispered.

"I know," he said, breathless. The cabin door clicked and she could hear Connor's laughter just on the other side.

"Damn!" Becky stepped away from Dylan.

"No kidding," Dylan agreed, and walked toward the door. But for some reason the door didn't open.

"Mom," Connor yelled. "Let me in! My card doesn't work."

"There is a God!" Becky murmured as she straightened her shirt and Dylan took a few deep breaths. "Coming," Becky yelled, grabbing the door handle and pulling it open.

Connor burst in with Mark by his side, along with a woman who was most definitely not Estelle.

CHAPTER ELEVEN

"THIS IS JAN MILTON," Mark said without missing a beat. "I think you two met at Estelle's Christmas party."

"Nice to see you again," Becky said, then she turned to Dylan. "This is Dylan Langstaff. Sarah fell asleep on the tender and Dylan offered to carry her back aboard."

Mark grinned, and Becky could sense he knew there was something brewing. She wanted to die right there…but before she did, she needed to know what was going on with Mark and Jan.

And did Estelle know?

That would be interesting to watch.

Jan, who had to be in her late forties or early fifties was dressed in a tight-fitting creamy yellow tee, white capris and sandals. Her dark blond-streaked hair was windblown and sexy, pulled back with a black hair band. She was attractive and had a warm smile. Becky was delighted to see her with Mark.

It was an awkward moment for Becky, but Dylan seemed to be able to handle just about anything. "I believe we met at the Montgomery party." He shook hands with Mark and Jan. "Nice to see you again."

Then he turned to Becky. "I better get going. I've got to check up on a few things for tomorrow's regatta."

He looked over at Connor, who had already made himself comfortable on the sofa in front of the new Apple laptop that Estelle had given him at the Christmas party. Both her kids got one, along with iPods that had tiny screens to watch TV shows, plus gift certificates for various stores. The digital camera she had given Connor was fit for a professional photographer, but at least Sarah's was a little more down to earth for a child. And as if that wasn't enough, they'd received the latest cell phones, one pink and one black, with a paid contract, of course.

Becky was still deciding if she was going to let them keep the cell phones. There was something not right about little kids and personal phones that could let them get through to the countryside in China if they wanted to, so for now, she had the phones in her suitcase.

"Hey, Connor," Dylan said. "I hope you and your mom signed up for the regatta off the coast of St. Maarten tomorrow. It's going to be great!"

Connor looked up, seemingly unimpressed. "What's a regatta?"

"It's a sailboat race. Like the America's Cup, only this one is a shortened version. I'm escorting a small group, and I think you and your mom would enjoy it."

"I don't know how to sail," Connor mumbled, showing no interest. Becky didn't think it was a good idea to put Connor on a boat with other people. Suppose he wanted to get off, or he got scared? They'd be trapped.

"There'll be special instructors aboard, and I'll be there to help teach you. Sailing is great fun. I have a feeling you'll like it."

"I don't know." Connor stared at the screen on his laptop, as if he were busy at work and didn't have time for play. At that moment, he looked a lot like his father.

Becky was just about to step in and put the skids on this whole conversation when Mark said, "I'll come with you, Connor. Your dad and I used to sail all the time when he was your age."

Connor looked up at his grandfather.

"Sailing is a fabulous experience, Connor," Jan interjected. "I don't think you'd want to miss it,".

Suddenly, Becky's mamma-bear claws came out. Why

was everyone making demands on her child? Becky knew what was best for Connor, and if he didn't want to go, then he shouldn't be pushed into it.

"You don't have to go if you don't want to, Connor," Becky said, and immediately knew it had been exactly the wrong thing to say.

She realized she needed to stop protecting him, but maybe not in this particular situation. Connor wasn't interested and she wanted to be his advocate when everyone else was ganging up on him. She knew her son better than anyone, and knew when he really didn't want to do something.

"I—" she began.

But Connor cut her off. "Did my dad really like to sail?" He directed his question to Mark.

"Very much so. We had a house in Sausalito then, and he couldn't wait for summer so we could go sailing almost every day."

Becky didn't remember Ryder ever telling her that he knew how to sail. This was as much of a surprise to her as it was to Connor.

"Okay, I'll go," he said mildly, looking back down at his screen.

"Great," Dylan said. "Then I'll see you guys first thing in the morning."

"I don't know," Becky said. "I'd have to find a babysitter for Sarah, and she may not like that."

Becky couldn't believe that Connor truly wanted to go. She was giving him a built-in excuse if he wanted to change his mind.

"But I want to go, Mom," Connor insisted. "You really don't have to come along. Grandpa will be there."

There was no way on this earth that Becky would send Connor off on any kind of water-related excursion without her. And, besides that, it wouldn't be fair to ask Mark to handle one of Connor's little fits if he changed his mind while they were out at sea.

"Estelle said something about taking Sarah and Laura out to the island for the day, Becky," Mark told her. "I think she has something planned for them."

Becky remembered the conversation she'd had with Estelle at the Christmas party. She'd have to check to see what that was, exactly.

"That's right, but I still don't think—"

Dylan interrupted her. "Then everything's set. See you guys in the morning. Have a good night."

He glanced back at Becky for a moment, smiled and let himself out.

Soon afterward Mark and Jan left.

Becky was in awe of what had just transpired. She had agreed to something that was sure to turn out to be the biggest fiasco of the trip. Connor could start crying as soon as they were ten feet from the shore, and then what?

She sat next to her son on the sofa, sneaking a peek at his screen. He was playing a NASCAR-type racing game. At least Estelle had had the common sense to load the laptop with something other than shooting games.

Her mind floated on the day's events as she watched Connor race his orange car around the track, bumping everyone out of the way as he went. She thought about Dylan and his kiss, and how he had pressured Connor to agree to this regatta tomorrow, even though he had to know how much she didn't want her son to go.

They had so much to talk about, but she knew there was no way that would happen inside her stateroom, or on a sailboat. She simply had to wait for the right moment, and waiting to see Dylan again, alone, was one of the hardest things she'd had to do in a long time.

She instantly scolded herself for thinking like a lovesick schoolgirl.

So he knew how to kiss, and his touch was like liquid heat, and she could still feel his hands on her body and…

"Mommy, I'm hungry." Sarah interrupted her thoughts as she opened the bedroom door. "Oh, and here's the moon goddess pendant. I kept it safe so you wouldn't lose it." She pulled the necklace from the pocket of her shorts, and walked to Becky, handing it over. Then she rubbed her eyes. "I need a huge chocolate gelato with lots of sprinkles or I won't be able to sleep ever again."

Becky chuckled.

So much for liquid heat.

TRACY USED A TISSUE to carefully dab at the beads of sweat that covered her forehead and nose while Bob pretended to want her autograph and she pretended to care. He had insisted on meeting her backstage between numbers during her show. Normally, it wouldn't be allowed, but Bob had come up with some lame rationale about making an impression on his future stepdaughter who supposedly wanted an autograph and a stagehand had let him in.

Now they were standing backstage, alone, next to some black curtains and a few folding chairs.

She was dressed in her Vegas-type showgirl costume, with a huge feather-and-spangles headpiece, matching red-sequined bikini top and a tight-fitting sequined skirt slit up to her waist. Bob was dressed in casual tan drab, the kind of man Tracy wouldn't even notice, but here she was shamelessly flirting to save her son. Plan A hadn't worked, and this guy was her Plan B.

"You look incredibly handsome tonight, Bob. Wish I wasn't dancing or we'd find a little hideaway and have some fun," Tracy teased while she scribbled her name on a show bill.

"Let's save that for the island. I figured out how to get away from the family for the day so I rented us a room."

Tracy's stomach turned at the thought. "A room? Aren't you moving a little fast?"

"It's my style."

"This is a business deal. I never said—"

"Get off it. If you want me to get that pendant, I need a little bonus to keep me interested."

"You've got the diamond to keep you interested."

"You're not even sure it's in there. Could be nothing's inside that thing. I don't risk my future for nothing. Either you give out, or find yourself another potential sucker."

She pasted a smile on her face and handed him the booklet. "We have to get that pendant before we dock," Tracy whispered. "Do you think you'll be able to do it?" She still couldn't figure out what had happened on the boat, and why she couldn't find the necklace in Becky's canvas bag. It looked as though she might have to depend on Bob after all.

"No problem. Everything's under control. You can count on me, baby." Bob's smarmy voice sent cold shivers up Tracy's back.

She wondered how a classy woman like Kim Montgomery could be in love with such a man. He was a two-timing gamer down to his rotting core, and if Tracy could see it, why couldn't Kim?

But she couldn't condemn Kim too much. After all, Tracy had fallen for Salvatore Morena, a man who was not only a thief, but who could use his own son as bait to get what he wanted.

"Okay, then. Just make sure you have the pendant when we go ashore at Saint Thomas. I have it all set up. My contact will tell us if that stone is in there and what it's worth. If it's the kind of diamond I think it is, we'll be set up for life…baby." And she said it with such conviction that Bob took a step forward as if he was going to kiss her right there.

She put her hand out, touching his chest to stop him. "Not here." She nodded toward the group of dancers waiting to go onstage. She was one of them. "Too many eyes. You'll get me fired, Bobby." She eased away from him. "We can do anything we want on the island," she cooed.

A female stage hand called out a two-minute warning.

"I've got to go," she said, and walked off to join the other dancers, hoping Bob would just vanish into the night.

Tracy hadn't wanted to depend on Bob, and the fact that he was her only recourse frightened her more than she wanted to admit.

"A friend of yours?" Tracy's cabin mate, Erica, asked while she gave Bob the once-over. Erica hailed from New York City, had danced off-Broadway a few times, but couldn't seem to land a big enough show to pay her rent. She looked a little like Britney Spears, only taller and with a much deeper voice.

"He's engaged," Tracy said.

"He doesn't act engaged. He's still watching you."

Tracy turned briefly to check, and sure enough, Bob was standing right where she'd left him. She nodded, smiled and spun back around, hoping again he would just disappear.

"Is he leaving now?" Tracy asked her friend.

"Yeah, but not before he gave you the once-over, a slow once-over that had a lot of nasty thoughts behind it. He's got it bad, girl."

Tracy was happy she had the creep on the hook, but felt sick to her stomach imagining his thoughts. "You know we can't have affairs with passengers, but besides that, I'm talking *recently* engaged. Like just the other night on this ship. He's traveling with his fiancée."

"It don't seem to make no difference with that guy."

"Believe me, there's nothing going on between us. He simply wanted my autograph for his future stepdaughter."

Tracy tugged at her headdress to make sure it was on tight, and checked her costume for potential malfunctions. She'd been at this dancing game long enough to know she didn't want any mishaps once she was onstage. She'd danced with a girl who'd lost her shoe during a number and it had thrown the entire company off. Of course, she'd immediately been replaced, and from that moment on Tracy always checked and rechecked her wardrobe.

"I saw the way you were looking at him—you want him, girl," Erica whispered, adjusting her top.

Tracy decided it might work in her favor to go along with whatever Erica said. "Was I that obvious?"

"Like birds have wings."

The lights dimmed and they walked onstage and got into position.

Tracy put on a big smile, not only for the full house in front of her, but because she had managed to fool her friend with this charade she was now living.

AS IT TURNED OUT, Estelle had planned a day at the St. Maarten Day Spa for the girls, and Sarah was all for it. She loved to get her nails polished and her hair curled, and to soak in a warm fragrant tub of swirling water. Laura offered to take care of Sarah, so Becky had happily sent her daughter off with her grandmother that morning.

But now Becky's focus was on a gorgeous man standing in front of her.

There was something incredibly sexy about a man at the bow of a sailboat, Becky thought as she watched Dylan and the rest of the male crew prepare to leave the dock in St. Maarten.

Connor and Mark were busy tying knots while she and Jan listened to a male instructor give them a crash course in sailing.

Becky wasn't really paying much attention. Besides the occasional glance at Dylan, she was watching her son and his grandfather. If this trip had done anything, it had brought the two of them closer, and for that, Becky would be forever grateful to Estelle.

"Let's see if I can remember this," Mark said as he sat next to Connor aboard the *Stars and Stripes*.

Connor studied his grandfather's hands as he demonstrated how to tie a bowline knot.

"The rabbit pops out of the hole, jumps over the log, runs behind the tree and jumps back down the hole. There." Mark proudly displayed the knot he'd just created. Connor took it from him, turning it over several times, as if he were making mental notes. It was uncanny how easily Connor learned something new once he decided to concentrate.

"Can I try it?" Connor asked, taking the bit of rope from Mark.

Mark gave it to him, but first pulled the knot apart. Connor's little hands began the process. "The rabbit pops out of the hole," Connor said, eyes intent on the rope. "Then he jumps over the log and runs behind the tree."

Mark gently guided Connor's fingers.

"And jumps back into the hole, just like that," Connor announced, and held up his perfect bowline knot.

"You're a natural," Mark said, giving Connor a hug.

Connor took a picture of his bowline knot, then one of Mark and one of Becky. He seemed to really be into his camera, and again Becky had to be grateful to Estelle.

Becky couldn't be happier as she sat on the starboard side of the boat. There were about fifteen people aboard with a crew of five, Dylan being one of them. Everyone was going to help sail this thing, eventually, but for now the four boys, all about Connor's age, and the one teenage girl, were getting a lesson in tying knots.

The first hour the kids had learned a few things about sailing, and about the sails themselves. They were taught how to move back and forth on the boat, or how to hike out, then were assigned specific places to sit on the rail to keep the boat from capsizing while they raced. And one or two of the braver kids were shown how to release the jib when the main sail started to luff.

Connor wasn't one of them, but Becky was holding out hope that by the end of the race, he might be.

Now the adults were being schooled in "coming about" and "jibing."

Apparently "jibing" could be dangerous, and when somebody yelled "duck," they were serious. A person could be knocked overboard by the boom coming across the middle of the boat, or be seriously injured.

After that little reassuring lecture, Becky decided to pay real close attention to her instructors from now on.

"Look, Mom, I did it," Connor yelled, holding up his second successful knot.

"That's wonderful," Becky called back, delighted that he seemed to be having a good time.

"Ready about!" a crew member yelled.

"Ready," Dylan yelled.

Suddenly the *Stars and Stripes* began to move away from the dock and as everyone raced from starboard to port the boom swept across the boat and the main sheet began luffing, and took on that beautiful billowy curve.

"Coming about!" another crew member yelled, and a wonderful thing happened.

The sailboat abruptly came to life and made its way out of the harbor with a steady whoosh. Becky became emotional at the sight of Connor sitting alongside Mark, watching as the sail captured the wind and took them out to sea.

It was as if he had found his true self, and as he sat on the rail, his orange life vest covering most of his upper body, he looked completely relaxed and happy.

Just a boy and his grandpa, enjoying the moment.

Dylan must have noticed Connor, as well, because when she glanced over at him, he nodded toward Connor and a wide grin warmed his face.

Becky took in a deep breath and began to relax, but as soon as she did the boat started to tilt upwards, the boom began another sweep and everyone moved to the opposite side.

So much for relaxing moments.

CHAPTER TWELVE

"I WANT TO SAIL AGAIN, Mom," Connor said as he took his seat at the round family table in the Empire Room on Athena deck. The Empire Room was the main dining room on *Alexandra's Dream*, and the most elegant. Everything seemed to sparkle with opulence from the fine china to the crystal wineglasses.

Estelle was in her element, dressed in a couture black gown, ruby earrings and matching necklace. Becky had chosen something a little less formal, a simple deep purple strapless gown, silver earrings, and of course, the pendant. Kim wore a gold-lace number that could only be Armani, diamond earrings that swept her shoulders with every turn, and a crystal-studded evening bag that screamed Judith Leiber. There was more money in accessories and gowns at their table than some small countries could generate in a year.

Becky slipped off her shoes under the table. She was exhausted. Who knew sailing could be so much work? What with all that jibing and tilling and pulling on lines and moving from rail to rail, she was worn out.

But not Connor. He had wanted to do the race again with the second group. Becky had actually considered it for a moment, but soon came to her senses when she realized she could hardly get through the first race, let alone a second.

"Do you think when we get home I can take lessons?" Connor asked from across the table. He sat between Mark and Sarah, while Becky sat between Laura and Bob. Not exactly an ideal seating arrangement for Becky, but one that Laura could live with.

Becky was just about to say yes to Connor's question when Estelle jumped in on the conversation. "Lessons in what, sweetheart?"

Up until that moment Estelle had been flirting with the captain as he passed by the table.

Mark was busy ordering his second Scotch. Bob and Kim were giggling while Laura entertained Sarah who had insisted on wearing her black boots with her red party dress because tonight she was Violet the Elastigirl from *The Incredibles*.

"Sailing, Grandma. I want to learn how to sail." Connor spoke with determination, and warmed Becky's heart to hear him talk about something with such excitement. "It was *so* much fun. Grandpa taught me how to make all the knots and how to use my weight so the boat doesn't capsize, and a lot of other things. But the best part was winning. We won the race by about ten feet. We were way out ahead of those other sorry sailboats. I was even at the helm for a little while. Have you ever been sailing, Grandma? It's awesome."

Connor's whole body vibrated with excitement. Becky hadn't seen her son this passionate about something since before Ryder died. She couldn't wait to get him into lessons. Like Mark said, he was a natural.

Estelle shook her head. "It's too dangerous, dear. Pick something else. Your father nearly died when—"

"Estelle!" Mark cut her off.

"Well, it's true. I warned you about this. You should never have taken him out there, Ryder *or* Connor."

"My dad nearly died? Sailing?" Connor turned to his grandfather. "But I thought you said the two of you went out every summer?"

"We did," Mark began, but Estelle cut him off again.

"Yes, dear, they did until Ryder hit his head on something and fell off the boat. Your grandfather nearly drowned rescuing your father, and if it wasn't for me calling the Coast Guard, who just happened to be in the area, I would have lost them both."

She pressed a hand to her heart.

"That's not exactly how it happened, Connor," Mark said. "Your dad—"

"Yes it is. That's precisely what happened. And your father instantly recognized the dangers of sailing. So he promised me that he'd never sail again."

"And he never did," Mark said, dejection evident in his voice.

Becky now realized why Ryder had never spoken about it. The Estelle scars ran too deep.

Connor's whole demeanor changed. Becky wanted to whisk him away from the table, away from Estelle's poison, but she knew it was too late. Connor had once again withdrawn into himself.

Sarah made two little fists. "I'll save you, Connor! Elasti-girl can jump deep in the water while my feet are still aboard the boat. I can stretch really far. You won't drown as long as I'm around." She stretched out her arms over her head as far as they could go, then punched the air.

"No," Estelle insisted. "I won't hear of it. There'll be no more talk of sailing in this family. Had I known that's what you were doing today, Mark, I would have put a stop to it. Now, let's have a pleasant evening, shall we?" She pasted on one of her fake smiles and settled in her chair.

Mark took a long swig of his Scotch, while Becky had to literally gnaw on her cheek to keep herself from lashing out at the woman.

Total silence fell over the group for a moment, until Bob suddenly stood and pulled a small digital camera out of the inside pocket of his suit coat. "You know, I don't think I have one good picture of my soon-to-be family. How about if we all squeeze in tight for a group photo?"

"That's a lovely idea," Estelle encouraged. "See how you

are? You're always thinking of ways to bring us together. You're such a dear, Bob."

"Yes, isn't he a love?" Kim added.

"A real treat," Laura mumbled.

Laura, Becky and Kim stood behind Estelle, Mark, Sarah and Connor for the shot, but just as everyone was about to go back to their seats, Bob insisted on a couple more pictures.

"I want a real close-up of this beautiful family," he said, and proceeded to click off three more shots, zooming in tighter with each one.

Becky wondered how everyone could possibly fit in the picture And from the angle of the camera and the way Bob gazed into the view finder, then up at Becky, she had the weird feeling that he was focusing in on only her.

But why was would he do that?

When Bob finally finished, everyone went back to their seats. The wait staff began serving a marvelous salad of pears, candied walnuts and baby spinach that Estelle had preordered, something she insisted on doing whenever her family dined out together.

Apparently dinner on a cruise ship was no exception.

"I've been thinking," Bob said, breaking the silence.

"Now there's a scary thought," Laura mumbled into her napkin. Becky turned and shot Laura a "not now" look to get her to stop the sarcasm before it ignited another family argument. Laura smiled and Becky knew she wasn't about to quit.

"I'd like to take the kids on the island tomorrow, and show them around," Bob said, surprising Becky. He hadn't shown much interest in Sarah or Connor—or Laura—so far. "I think there's even a sandcastle contest on one of the beaches. I'm an expert at sandcastles."

"That sounds like a wonderful idea, Bob." Estelle beamed over at her future son-in-law as if he were the reincarnation of Apollo. "I have an appointment to look at some emeralds in a little jewelry shop on the other side of the island, and I've asked Mark to join me. He's so smart when it comes to gemstones."

Mark didn't comment. He sipped his Scotch and gazed around the room as if looking for something or somebody. Becky thought it might be Jan.

"Bob, you never told me you've been on the island before," Kim said, holding a glass of French Pinot Noir.

"I haven't, actually, but I thought I'd give the mothers a rest tomorrow and step up to the babysitting plate."

"I don't need a babysitter," Laura hissed.

"Of course you don't, but I thought you'd want to come along so we can get to know each other a little better. I mean, I am going to be your dad."

"You might be a lot of things, *Bob*, but 'my dad' will never be one of them," Laura shot back.

"I will not allow you to speak to Bob like that, young lady," Kim said in a firm voice. "You will show him some respect and apologize."

It was as if the entire room suddenly fell silent and all eyes were on Laura. Becky hoped she would just apologize and let it go, but Laura was not one to back down easily.

"You can make me apologize because I'm still living under your roof, but you will never make me think of Bob as my father. My father lives in Arizona, and just because I don't see him very much, he's still my father, and no matter how many Bobs you might marry, I will still only call one man Dad." She turned to Bob. "I'm sorry, Bob, and I would love to go to Saint Thomas with you and Connor and Sarah, so you can show us around an island you know absolutely nothing about." She turned back to her mother. "There. It's done. Satisfied?"

Becky could tell that Kim wanted to leap across the table and wring Laura's pretty little neck. It was time for Becky to step into the quagmire with her own set of complications.

"I don't know, Bob, my kids can be quite a handful. It's a nice gesture, but I'm not sure—"

"I just thought, you three ladies work so hard and deserve a little time to yourselves. I really was just trying to be helpful, but if you have other plans, well, maybe some other time." Bob looked sad in an exaggerated way.

The difficult part in all of this was that Becky really did want to spend the day with Dylan, alone, but leaving Sarah and Connor with Bob somehow didn't strike her as a good thing to do. The offer seemed completely out of character.

Then Kim added her two cents. "I was hoping to stay aboard tomorrow and go back to the spa. Everyone will be on the island and I'll get all the attention. This is marvelous. Thank you, Bobby. You're such a generous man." She leaned toward Bob for an air kiss.

Mark sat forward. "So, Bob, why the sudden fascination with the kids? Somehow I got the impression you weren't interested in anyone but my daughter."

Bob put his fork down, wiped his mouth on his white napkin, took a big gulp of wine and said, "You're right, Mark. I've been blinded by my love for your daughter, and could think of nothing else. But then tonight while I was taking the pictures, it suddenly dawned on me that I want to get to know my future family, and what better way than to start with these great kids."

"This conversation is plain silly," Estelle said. "It's not as if he's asking to take the kids on a safari in Africa. They're simply going to Saint Thomas for a few hours. I think you're all making far too much of this." She looked at Connor. "I know you'll be a good boy and listen to your uncle Bob, now won't you, sweet pea?"

Connor gave a little nod.

She turned to Sarah. "And you, my little valentine—promise your grandma that you'll be your usual delightful self."

"I promise," Sarah said, chomping on a pear from her salad. Her hair was extra curly from her day at the spa, and her fingernails were painted a bright red. She looked so cute, Becky could eat her up.

"There, you see? Now, I don't want to hear another word. From anyone." Estelle gazed directly at Laura.

"Not a word, Grandma," Laura confirmed.

Then, as the soup course was being served and everyone slipped into separate conversations, Laura leaned over and whispered, "I'll take care of them, Aunt Becky. You don't have to worry."

"I know you will, thanks," Becky told her, feeling more comfortable with the idea.

And that's when she decided Estelle was right. She was making far too much out of the whole thing. Bob was going to be part of the family whether she and Laura liked it or not, and it was about time they both started trusting him…at least a little.

"IT'S ALL SET," Bob told Tracy as they stood in the shadows just outside the crew's lounge. He'd gone looking for her right after her last show, and Erica had not only told him where to find Tracy, but escorted him right to her. "I'll be waiting in the lobby at the Royal Garden hotel around eleven."

Tracy had removed her costume right after the show, and now wore stretch white jeans and a black tee. Her face, however, was still covered in heavy stage makeup.

"Did you get the pendant?"

"Right here in my pocket." He tapped at the bulge under his jacket, just beneath his heart. It could just as easily have been a couple of keys or some change.

"Why don't you give it to me for safe-keeping?" she suggested, holding out her hand, hoping that he would simply pass it to her so this nightmare could end right now.

He tilted his head, winked and grinned. "But, baby, it's my lucky charm."

He leaned in closer and pulled her into him, planting a wet kiss on her lips and then pushing his tongue into her mouth. Tracy had no choice but to go with the moment. She gave it everything she had, pressing her full body up against his, caressing the back of his neck, letting him cup her breast in his hand. When his hand started to slip lower, and dropped between her legs, it took every ounce of strength she had not to stop him, but she knew her son's very life might depend on her willpower.

When she thought he'd had enough, she pulled away, breathless from the strain. She could only hope he'd think the exact opposite.

She felt dirty, as if she'd just been raped, but she continued to play the sex kitten, her hand reaching for his suit coat pocket. If she could only grab the necklace while he was still recovering from their kiss, she….

He stopped her just as she was about to reach inside his jacket and pull the damn thing out. She wanted that pendant more than she wanted her next breath.

He grabbed her wrist and held it tight, almost too tight. Tracy filled her lungs with air, held it for a moment, then let it out, trying to remain calm. Trying to control the pain.

"Not so fast, baby. This necklace is my ticket to get your sweet little ass in my bed. Without it, I'm afraid you might not show up tomorrow, and I'd be very unhappy if that happened."

He brought her arm down and let go. She moved in even closer and, standing inches away from him, she reached down to his crotch and cupped his package. He winced and jerked back a little, but she held on tight.

"Believe me," she muttered in a sultry voice, even lower than the deep bass that was coming from the open door. "There's nothing in this entire world that could keep me away from you."

Then she abruptly let go, turned and casually walked back inside the crowded lounge.

The music surged through her like a million needles, causing her to become almost dizzy. She wished she could call her mom and ask her what to do next, or talk to her father about her fears, but they'd both probably tell her to call the cops and let them handle it, which was exactly the wrong thing to do when you were dealing with Sal.

Cops made him crazy. Made him want to go into hiding, or

worse yet, disappear. And when Sal wanted to disappear, no one could find him, ever. That was just another of Tracy's long list of fears. If she didn't return the diamond, Sal could take their son back to Italy and she'd never see him again.

Her stomach began to pitch.

Instead of returning to her bar stool and the vodka martini she'd been nursing, she headed straight to the ladies' room and vomited.

DYLAN'S CABIN PHONE RANG several times before he could actually focus enough to realize he should answer it. He was hoping his cabin mate would pick up and he could be spared the sleep interruption, but obviously the guy was still out partying.

"Hello?" Dylan rumbled into the phone. Whoever was calling him at one in the morning should be shot.

"Dylan?" an unfamiliar female voice whispered into the phone. He really didn't want to be bothered right now, no matter what chick was on the other end of the line.

"No. Dylan died when the phone rang and this is his ghost speaking. Call him back in the morning, and I might consider reviving him." He was dog-tired from sailing, and he really didn't need this right now.

"I'm sorry. For some reason I didn't think you'd be sleeping."

Dylan at once recognized the voice.

"Becky?"

"Yes. I'm so sorry, I—"

Dylan sat up to clear his head. He didn't want to scare her off since she'd taken the time to actually call him.

"No. Don't apologize. Is everything all right?"

"Yes, everything is fine."

"Good," he said in a more pleasant voice. His head was beginning to clear and his disposition was beginning to improve the more he thought about the woman on the other end of the line. Problem was, he didn't quite know what to say next. "Becky, are you still there?"

"Yes. Absolutely. I'm here."

"Good. That's good 'cause I thought you hung up."

"No. Not yet."

Silence.

Then, "I—" They both started at the same time.

Again, that awkward silence.

Finally, Dylan couldn't take it. "Did you want—"

"Yes. I'd like to take you up on your generous offer to take me shopping. I mean, how many straight guys would actually offer a girl a day of shopping? I'd be crazy to pass up the opportunity. My future brother-in-law is taking the kids tomorrow, so I thought maybe we—"

But Dylan was too excited to wait for her to finish. He couldn't take the chance that she would somehow change her mind. "I'll meet you on the dock at nine."

"Can we make it ten? That might be a little early for Bob."

"Sure, anything you want."

He thought that might have sounded a little desperate.

"Anything?" she teased.

"At this point? Yes, anything," he teased back, and she laughed. Her laughter felt like the sun coming out on a rainy day.

He got out of bed and began pacing, running his hand through his hair and over his stubbly chin.

The woman didn't know her own power.

"Do I need to bring anything other than some cash and a charge card?" she asked.

"Yes. You'll need some good walking shoes. Saint Thomas is a big island with a mess of shops, and a few of the good ones are uphill."

"Then I'll see you tomorrow," she said, exhilaration filling her voice.

"Yeah, tomorrow."

He hung up and slid back down into his bed, knowing full well that if he wasn't careful, this woman could change his entire life.

CHAPTER THIRTEEN

"HOLD STILL," Becky told Laura as she tried to fasten the moon goddess' tear drop pendant around Laura's neck. They stood in front of the mirror in Becky's bedroom getting ready for their day on Saint Thomas Island.

Connor and Sarah were watching *The Escape Clause* in the other room. Their laughter echoed through the doorway every now and then, reminding Becky of how much she had missed hearing that in the last couple of years.

"Are you sure you want me to wear this today, Aunt Becky?" Laura asked. "I mean, your luck might change if you're not wearing it."

"You're going to spend the entire day with Bob," Becky said as she fiddled with the clasp. "You'll need all the luck you can get, kiddo."

The clasp had always been a little loose, but for some reason, it seemed as if it was actually broken.

Finally, Becky got the delicate mechanism to close, and Laura turned to look in the mirror to check it out, but as she did, the pendant fell to the floor.

"I'm just not meant to wear it," Laura said, picking it up to hand it back to Becky.

"Then you'll just have to stick it in your pocket or bag and take it with you."

Laura stood holding it in her two hands as if it was something precious and she was afraid of breaking it.

"Are you sure?" she asked, obviously wanting Becky to re-think this risky enterprise.

"Yes, I'm sure," Becky said, closing Laura's fingers around the necklace. "The moon goddess would want you to have it today. Who knows, maybe you'll change your whole attitude toward Bob, and decide to embrace him as your new stepdad."

Laura got that look on her face as if Becky had just gone off the deep end. "You can't be serious."

"Okay, maybe there won't be any embracing going on, but tolerance always works."

"Out of all the potential stepdads I've had, this guy is wacked."

"Wacked?"

"Really bad."

"He's not your stepdad yet. There's still hope."

"Haven't you seen the way my mom looks at him? I've seen this before. I know that look. She's going to marry him and there's nothing I can do about it."

"If that's the case, then hold on to the pendant and repeat after me."

Laura did as she was told.

"Hear me, oh, kind and generous moon goddess," Becky said, and Laura repeated. "Allow me to accept the stuff I can't change, the nerve to change the stuff I can, and the smarts to know the difference."

Laura smiled. "That sounds like the serenity prayer for Alcoholic Anonymous."

"Kind of, but I modified it a little. But how do you know that prayer?"

"Potential stepdad number one."

"Oh, yeah, that Ron guy. He didn't last very long."

"Six months. As soon as he made Mom go to one of his AA meetings at our church and Grandma heard about it, that was the beginning of the end."

"He really wasn't a bad guy, aside from his drinking."

"Not if you don't count the fact that he would go on week-long benders and run around the house wearing Mom's underwear. No. He wasn't a bad guy."

"Okay, so your mom has a problem with the men she picks."

"Duh!"

"Maybe Bob is different."

"Yeah, and maybe pigs can fly."

Becky sat down hard on the bed. Laura was right. Bob was just another wrong guy in a long line of wrong guys.

"Okay. You've convinced me. I'm not sending my kids off with Bob today. I'll just have to call Dyl—"

Becky stopped talking and lay back on the bed. She so did not want anyone to know about her date with Dylan and now everyone in her family would find out.

She let out a heartfelt sigh.

"You're spending the day with Dylan?" Laura sounded incredulous. "Why didn't you tell me? Bob is great. Bob is good. He's the absolute best stepdad a girl could want. Don't listen to me, Aunt Becky. I'm just a tormented teenager who doesn't know crap."

"Don't swear," Becky said, raising her head to look at Laura.

Laura climbed on the bed and sat next to Becky.

"Crap is hardly a swearword."

"In some circles—"

"Aunt Becky! Don't change the subject. You've got to go out with him or the goddess is going to start crying again, and you know how bad that can be. I mean, come on, we're already floating on water."

"You'll never let them out of your sight for a minute and you promise not to tell anyone about Dylan and me."

"I promise. And besides, Bob can't be all that bad. This is the first guy that Grandma actually talks to."

"All right, but promise me you'll take your cell phone and if the good times start deteriorating, you'll call. I'll come find you and we'll spend the rest of the day together. And come back early. No later than four. No. Make that three. I'll feel better if we're all back here around three."

Becky sat up and pulled her legs in tight.

"I promise. And don't worry. I'll take good care of the kids."

This meant a lot to Laura on another level. She needed a self-confidence boost. She needed Becky to believe in her.

"I know you will, honey."

"But what about the pendant? Shouldn't you be wearing it?"

"Actually, I know this is silly, but I really do think it's good luck, and I'd feel better if you took it."

Laura slipped it into the pocket of her shorts and did up the button to make sure it was safe. "Then everything is right with the stars and moon. I'm going to make friends with stepdad-to-be and you and Dylan are going to…what are you going to do?"

Becky's mind raced back to that kiss the other night.

"Shop. We're going to do a lot of shopping."

Just then Connor and Sarah appeared and jumped on the bed. Laura grabbed Connor and tickled him while Becky grabbed Sarah and did the same.

Soon the small bedroom was filled with screams of laughter and Becky was sure the moon goddess was smiling down on her happy family.

The tickling and laughter continued until Becky caught a peek at the clock sitting next to her bed. If they didn't leave soon, she'd be late and Dylan would think she'd blown him off.

She slid off the bed. "Okay, you guys," Becky yelled over their giggles. "We've got to go. Bob is waiting."

"Bob's waiting," Laura echoed halfheartedly.

Nothing changed.

Becky really didn't want to stop the fun, but she knew if she didn't, Dylan would think she wasn't coming. She grabbed Sarah and pulled her off Laura, then she grabbed Connor, but he was relentless.

So instead she went in the other room and called Bob to come down to her cabin to get the kids.

Fifteen minutes later, he showed up at the door, and by then the kids were quietly sitting in a row on the sofa, waiting.

Laura had slicked down Connor's hair with a side part, pulled Sarah's hair back in little curly pigtails, and had purposely scrubbed her own face clean of makeup and put her hair in a sleek ponytail. She insisted they stop horsing around so Bob wouldn't be frightened away by their silly behavior.

"Well, look at this," Bob said as he walked into the stateroom. "They look like little angels." He turned to Becky. "Don't you worry about a thing. I'll take good care of your darlings."

Becky thought he sounded condescending, but he looked sincere. Besides, she had complete trust in Laura.

Laura and the kids sat with their hands folded in their laps, their shoulders back, chins forward, smiling up at Bob as if he was their superhero. Becky could see right through their little game. Those smiles were about as genuine as Estelle's compliments.

"I've got to get going," Becky said as she grabbed her white bag.

"We do, too," Bob said. "I'm taking the kids for breakfast first, then we'll go ashore after their tummies are nice and full. I believe a child needs a balanced breakfast every morning. It's what fuels them for their busy days."

What a crock, Becky thought, then felt a twinge of guilt. Perhaps he did think about such things. "You're so right, Bob."

She was going to be positive about him, at least for today.

Becky kissed and hugged the kids, told them once again to listen to Laura and Bob, then she left.

As soon as she walked out into the corridor, she heard the familiar chime of a pending announcement, and a pleasant voice came on to tell everyone that various island Calypso bands would be playing on the dock today.

Ryder had loved Calypso music.

What the hell was she doing going to meet another man?

She pressed the button for the elevator, and when it arrived she stepped inside. All the joy of the day had vanished, replaced by guilt.

When it came time for her to exit the elevator, and the doors opened, she simply couldn't step out, not while she carried Ryder's picture in her bag. It wouldn't be right.

She had to get rid of it. Had to take it back to her stateroom and lock it in her suitcase, at least for today.

Back at her cabin, Becky slid the card into the metal box on her door, the tiny green light flashed and she grabbed the handle and swung open the door. To her complete amazement, there was Bob standing over the dresser in her bedroom, rummaging through her things. Apparently he hadn't heard her come in.

"What's going on, Bob?" she asked as she walked toward him. Connor was in the room with him, on the floor in front of her closet.

Bob immediately stopped what he was doing.

"I want to bring my Hot Wheels with me and I can't find my blue car," Connor explained. "Bob was helping me look for it."

Becky noticed that the top drawer was open and a pink T-shirt was pulled out.

"I don't think you'll find his car in my dresser, Bob," Becky said, and closed the drawer. She looked right into his eyes. "You want to tell me what this is really all about?"

Bob smiled. "I was helping him look for his cars, wasn't I, Connor?"

"Yeah, Mom, but we can't find them anywhere."

Becky glanced at her son as he searched her closet floor.

"And what makes you think your cars would be in my closet?"

"Oh, I wasn't looking for the cars in your closet. Uncle Bob asked me to find the pendant."

She turned back to Bob. "You have my son snooping through

my things looking for my pendant? What the heck is going on, Bob?" She folded her arms across her chest.

"Look, it was innocent enough. I noticed that you weren't wearing your pendant today, so I thought it might be fun for Sarah to wear it. I sent Laura and Sarah to save us a seat in the dining room while we looked. I figured it must be on your dresser, or maybe you dropped it on the floor in your closet, that's all. It's really not a big deal."

"Yes, it is a big deal. My kids know better than to go through my things, and here you are not only prowling through my dresser, but encouraging my son to do something he knows he shouldn't."

"Don't have a stroke, Becky. Just give me the pendant and we'll get out of your hair."

Becky couldn't believe this guy. He had some kind of nerve.

"You must be joking. What kind of lesson would I be teaching my son if I rewarded him for doing something wrong?"

"It has nothing to do with that. It's just about letting your kids have some fun. You're hoarding all the fun by keeping that pendant to yourself. Think about the extra perks the kids could get by wearing it. You're not being very generous, Becky."

She wanted to slap that grin right off his face.

"Are you telling me how to treat my own kids, 'cause if you are, you're so out of line that I can't even begin to tell you what I think in front of my son."

Becky tried to hold back her anger because of Connor.

"Mom, I found a different Hot Wheels. We can go now. Sarah doesn't need the pendant. It's too big for her anyway." He turned to Bob, and took his hand. "Let's go, Uncle Bob. I'm hungry."

Bob didn't move. He just stared at Becky.

There was no way she was going to let Bob take the kids anywhere. "I don't—" Becky began, but Connor interrupted her.

"Uncle Bob, we need to go now," he said, pulling on Bob's hand.

"Sure, let's go," Bob said before Becky could respond, and headed for the door.

She wanted to stop them, but Connor seemed enthused about spending the day with Bob. Still, could she actually let her child go with this guy?

Bob turned to her. "Sorry if I caused you any grief, Becky. I was only trying to make it more fun for the kids. If you don't want me to take them on the island today, I won't. I can get Sarah and Laura right now and call the entire thing off."

Connor adjusted his hand in Bob's. "No, Mom, please. Uncle Bob promised that he could help us win the sandcastle contest. He knows how to make one that's three feet high, just like Dad could. Remember?"

Of course she remembered, but Bob was a poor replacement for Ryder.

Becky glanced down at her watch. She had exactly ten minutes to meet Dylan. She had to decide now.

Bob waited for her answer.

Connor waited for her answer, just as she was sure Dylan was waiting for her on the dock, maybe even wondering where she was.

She caved, reminding herself her kids were really in Laura's very capable hands. Laura would keep them safe. And Connor seemed set on winning the contest. "Go on and have a good time."

"We'll be back early," Bob said as they walked out of the cabin and the door slammed shut behind them.

Becky took a deep breath, searched for her wallet in her purse and opened it to remove the photo. But then she immediately closed it again, leaving the photo right where it was.

"No matter what happens today, I need you with me," she said out loud, and walked out of the room.

THERE WERE THREE large cruise ships docked in a row at Charlotte Amalia's waterfront on Saint Thomas Island. Each ship

probably carried several thousand passengers who now mean-
dered around the shops or the colorful vendor tents. Calypso
music danced through the breeze and the steep slope of the lush
mountainside rose like a backdrop. Everyone seemed relaxed
and having fun.

Except for Dylan, who paced back and forth along the dock.
He had already stored a picnic lunch in the back seat of the Jeep
that he'd rented earlier that morning, and now it was just a
waiting game.

He was beginning to have some doubts whether Becky
would show.

A woman like her didn't take affairs lightly, if this thing they
were about to embark on could be called an affair. No. It was
simply two people going shopping, and perhaps a picnic on a
quiet beach. That's all it was.

Maybe.

After all, he lived on a cruise ship and she lived in San
Diego. Nothing could come of this. And even if he decided to
work with his brother back home, Becky could never live in
Newfoundland. She owned her own shop, and besides, the
winters were too cold for her.

He stopped pacing and sat on a bench, realizing he'd just
considered going into business with his brother. The thought
was overpowering. After all this time, was he actually ready to
go home again?

"Hello," Becky said.

He looked up and at once his whole body reacted to the very
sight of her. They exchanged smiles, but he sensed the excitement wasn't mutual. Maybe his thoughts about affairs and romantic picnic lunches on a secluded beach were just pipe
dreams.

It didn't matter. She was here and he was determined to
make this a great day for her.

"Nice to see you again, Ms. Montgomery," he said in a formal voice for the benefit of other crew members who might be in earshot.

"You, too, Dylan," she said quietly.

At once he knew something was wrong and he wanted to find out what it was, but there was no way they could have any kind of private conversation this close to *Alexandra's Dream.*

He stood and she moved ahead of him. He watched as she casually chatted with the woman who walked up next to her.

Becky had the cutest way of tilting her head back slightly when she laughed, and wrinkling her nose. And he loved the way her chestnut hair caught the breeze and swirled around her face, but she didn't seem to notice.

Oh, yeah, he had it bad.

CHAPTER FOURTEEN

"THIS IS A GREAT SPOT," Bob said, stopping about fifteen feet from the water on the creamy-white sand. The beach was crowded with kids already in the process of building sandcastles. He dropped the blue canvas bag he'd been carrying and it landed in front of Laura with a thunk.

"There are shovels and molds, and all sorts of junk in this bag to make your castle. Have at it."

Connor looked up at him. "But aren't you going to help? We can't win without you."

"Your uncle Bob has something important to do. I should be back to help in a few hours, but if I'm not—"

"A few hours!" Laura interrupted, disgusted at the very thought that he was leaving them.

"Yeah, don't get excited. I'll be back, but just in case I'm not." He pulled out his wallet. "Here's a five spot to get you through."

"Five bucks," Laura protested. "You're leaving us with five dollars? That won't even buy one of us lunch."

"You all ate like pigs this morning. How much more food could you possibly need? You're kids. Pick up some candy bars and you'll be fine."

Laura knew she had been right about this guy all along. He was completely wacked.

"Listen, Bob. You can't just leave us here. Mom will throw a fit, and Aunt Becky will never forgive you." Laura tried to reason with him, but she knew it was going to be impossible. "And

Grandma, well, you really don't want our grandmother angry at you. It could get ugly…fast. Not to mention what Grandpa might do."

He nodded and tilted his head, motioning her to step away from Connor and Sarah. She followed him a short distance, her flip-flops picking up hot sand as she walked.

"How much will it take for you not to mention this to the family?"

She couldn't believe her future stepdad was actually bribing her.

"A lot. I'm part of the rich and famous."

He opened his wallet again. "How about a twenty?"

"You obviously don't want to marry my mother."

"Okay, okay. I get it."

He pulled out a hundred dollars.

"That's better, but the kids may need some new toys. They have expensive tastes."

"Look, I only have a couple hundred bucks. If I give you much more, I'll be out of cash."

"Ever hear of an ATM?"

She held out her hand and he gave her all the cash that was in his wallet. She folded it and stuck it in the same pocket with the pendant, making sure to fasten the button again.

"You drive a hard bargain, kid."

"I try to emulate whenever I can."

"Yeah, who'd you copy for this shakedown?"

"You," Laura said, and walked back to the kids, wondering what she was going to say to them.

Bob walked up the beach and out of sight.

"He's not coming back, is he?" Sarah said as Laura sat next to Connor.

"He might," Laura answered, trying not to let on that she was a little nervous about being completely on her own.

The sandcastle contest was being held on Megan's Bay Beach, which just happened to be on the other side of the island.

Not that Laura couldn't find her way back to the ship. All she had to do was jump on one of the open-air shuttles that came by periodically, so that didn't worry her a bit. But her real problem was telling Aunt Becky the truth. If she told her about Bob now, she knew her aunt well enough to know the date with Dylan would be over.

Laura really didn't want that to happen.

Besides, she was perfectly capable of taking charge, at least for a little while.

Connor sat back and crossed his arms over his chest, letting out a heavy sigh. "It's me, isn't it. He didn't want to spend the day with me."

Laura put her arm around Connor. "Don't ever think that Bob does anything because of any of us." Sarah crawled over to her and the three kids sat together in a huddle. "Bob has his own agenda today, and believe me, it has nothing to do with us."

"But he promised to help us win," Connor insisted.

"We don't need him, Connor," Sarah said. "If we all work together, we can do it by ourselves. We don't need an adult to help us."

"What movie is that lame idea from?" Connor asked.

"No movie. I just know it's true."

Connor kicked at the sand. "It's going to take a lot of work," he warned, but Laura could see the spark of determination in his eyes.

"That's okay," she said. "We can do it."

They had to be back on the ship by three, or was it four? She couldn't remember, but either way, they had a long enough time to win this contest.

"Let's get started," Laura encouraged.

"We only have a few hours, and we've already used up some of that time complaining," Connor warned, obviously won over by the idea of trying their best.

He reached for the blue bag, untied the string and poured

out the contents. At least Bob had been good enough to bring the equipment they needed; buckets, large plastic spoons and knives and ladles of all sizes, different-size round and square containers, tiny flags, shiny colored stones and a measuring cup or two. It looked as if he'd searched the ship for whatever he could find.

"Wow!" Sarah blurted. "We can make a castle that even Blackbeard would like. When we're all done with this, can we go and see where he used to live?"

"Who?"

"Blackbeard the pirate, silly. His castle is somewhere around here."

Laura whispered to Connor, "How does she know these things?"

"The Travel Channel."

"This kid really needs to get out more."

"Tell that to my mom."

"I will, as soon as we get back."

"THIS PLACE is unbelievable. Where do we begin?" Becky stepped inside the open red Jeep Wrangler. Dylan had parked it on a side street near the waterfront shops.

"Just lean back and enjoy. I'm taking you to the top of the mountain first. The view is amazing. You can see the surrounding islands and get a better sense of the history of this place. Did you know in the late sixteen hundreds the governor declared it a pirate refuge so the local merchants could sell and trade pirate booty?"

"Isn't this where Blackbeard built his castle?"

"So the legend goes. It's now part of a hotel. Don't know if Blackbeard had that in mind for his castle, but kids love it."

"I hope Bob takes my kids to see it. Sarah would be thrilled."

"What about Connor?"

"Not as much as Sarah. *Pirates of the Caribbean* is one of

her favorite movies, and every time we go to Disneyland she has to go on the ride at least three times. It gets a little old for Connor after about the second time."

"I've only been to Disneyland once, and that was last year. Living up in Newfoundland, I didn't get off the island much. I met Bear there—he'd never been, either. Had a great time. Have to admit, I went on Pirates at least twice. It was one of my favorite rides, that and Space Mountain."

"Me, too. I love Space Mountain," Becky said.

"Maybe we can go together sometime."

Becky wondered if that would ever happen, but she went along with the dream for the sake of the moment. "Anytime you're in San Diego, just call me and I'm there."

He tilted his head and smiled. "I'll be sure and do that."

Becky doubted it would happen. "Are there any shops at the top of the mountain?"

"Yes," he said after a moment, as if he were thinking of something else entirely. "There's a boutique I think you're going to like. I know the owner, Sonita. I made a call and she's waiting for us."

"Then let's go." Becky twisted her hair up into a clip. Excitement spun through her like cotton candy at a carnival and she couldn't help smiling. When she turned to Dylan, he leaned over and kissed her. His lips felt as soft as a whisper, and as sensual as if they'd just made love.

"I've been waiting to do that for days," he said in a low, sexy voice.

"Me, too," Becky whispered back while he ran his thumb over her lips and she gazed into his fabulous jade eyes.

The simple kiss had opened the floodgates. She wanted more and she wanted it now.

She leaned in and kissed him hard, moving her tongue to touch his, trying to tell him without words just how she felt, but she could sense his resistance. Feel him pull back.

"We better go," he finally said, moving behind the wheel then starting the engine.

"Yes, we should go." She felt a little embarrassed, as if she'd assumed something she shouldn't have. "I've got a lot of shopping to do."

Becky looked straight ahead at the young couple crossing the street, running in between the parked cars, carrying their bags of just-purchased booty. They looked happy and in love. When they got to the sidewalk, they kissed and she looked away.

He pulled out of the parking space into traffic and Becky got a taste of driving on the left side of the road. She'd never experienced it before, and at first it was a little unnerving.

They were soon buzzing up the winding roads of the mountainside, the drive was both exhilarating and…well, fun. Becky held on tight, knowing this could be the ride of her life.

"HE JUST WALKED INTO the lobby," Tracy told Sal on her cell phone. She stood at the far end of the massive lobby, behind a huge floral arrangement on a round table. She had the perfect view of Bob walking through the sliding front doors, but he couldn't see her.

"He better have my diamond," Sal growled.

"Don't worry. I told you he got it from her last night. Everything's cool. As soon as your guys get the diamond, I want my son on a plane headed back to Vegas."

"I'm on the way to the airport right now."

"Don't screw with me, Sal. I'm not the pushover I used to be. Put Franco on the phone so I know you're telling the truth." She didn't think he'd do it, but it was worth a try.

"Mommy? Mommy?"

Tracy's whole body went limp at the sound of his voice and her eyes instantly watered.

"Hi, baby. Are you all right?"

She had to sit, but Bob was heading right for her. She couldn't take the chance of him seeing her on the phone.

"I'm coming home today, Mommy. Are you going to pick me up at the airport?"

Tears streamed down Tracy's face. "No, baby. Grandma will pick you up. But I'll be there as soon as I can."

"I miss you, Mommy."

Bob had done a once-around in the lobby and was now standing about ten feet away from her.

"I miss you, too, baby. But we'll be together real soon, I promise."

"Okay."

Bob was looking in her direction. She ducked behind the large planter.

"I have to go, baby. I love you so much. We'll be back home soon. Okay?"

"Okay, Mommy. I love you. 'Bye, Mommy."

"'Bye, baby," Tracy said, but the phone had already gone dead. Sal had probably hung up on her.

Tracy snapped her phone shut, slipped it in her bag and wiped her tears away with her hands.

"You're late," Tracy said wearily when she casually walked up to Bob.

"I know. I couldn't get rid of those damn kids fast enough. First they had to eat, then I had to bring them all the way over to Megan's Bay for some kind of sandcastle contest and I—"

"What kids?"

He gave her a look as if she was treading on thin ice. "That's my concern."

"Where are they now?" Tracy suddenly thought of the little blond-haired girl and this guy. There was no telling where he'd left them. "Are you talking about Sarah and Connor?"

"How do you know their names?"

Her mind raced. "I met them out by the pool once."

He grabbed her arm and it felt as if he was going to pull

it out of its socket. "What's going on here? Are you being straight with me?"

She tried to stay cool, but the bellman must have caught the grimace on her face. He was staring right at them. "You better let go, or this place is going to come down on your frickin' head."

Bob looked around and caught the bellman's gaze. He laughed and let her go. "You better be straight with me."

Tracy rubbed her shoulder and regained her composure. "Have I lied to you about anything so far? I'm here, aren't I?"

"You bet your sweet ass you are. You want this diamond as much as I do."

"Probably more," she mumbled to herself. "Do you have it?"

"Why wouldn't I?"

"Because I'd like to see it."

"All in good time, baby. First things first." And he started walking toward the front desk.

"Later," she said. "There's a cab waiting for us outside and the meter's running. My contact can only see us before noon. We've got to go now."

Bob stared at her. She didn't know if he would buy it or not, but there was no way she was going up to any room with him. Not if she could help it, anyway.

He walked back to her, anger tormenting his face. "What kind of bull is that? Since when do diamond smugglers have hours?"

"I don't call the shots here, he does. If he says before noon, then that's what we have to deal with. As soon as we know if the stone is real, and how much it's worth, we'll come right back here."

She stepped in closer, put her arms around him and planted a kiss on his fleshy lips. "Don't you think I want you as much as you want me?" she purred.

"You bet I do, baby," he said, and they turned toward the door and walked out, holding hands.

"Have a nice day," the bellman said as they walked by, giving them a nod and a smile.

"I intend to," Bob answered with a suggestive lilt to his voice.

Tracy couldn't look at the guy or she'd start crying again. She could only keep up this tough-girl act for so long, and at the moment, it was wearing thin.

CHAPTER FIFTEEN

BECKY HAD BOUGHT up half of Sonita's shop. Silk-screened scarves, blouses and dresses, sweaters made of fine woven silks, floral skirts with hand-embroidery work the likes of which she'd never seen even on some designer garments, silver jewelry, and even a few hand-blown glass pieces featuring colorful local sea creatures that she planned on using to decorate her shop. She took down the names of the local artists who created all these wonderful things, and took Sonita's information, as well. Sonita herself was responsible for a purple, orange and blue silk-screened dress with an intricate detail that Becky would have thought impossible to create.

"My partner, Lacey, is going to love this one especially," Becky said, beaming. "Can you make more of these?"

"All that you want, *dawta*." Sonita's voice had that lovely island lilt to it, and Becky loved to listen to her speak.

The Jeep was loaded down with bags from Sonita's shop and a few others, as well. Becky had picked up some things for the kids, Lacey, the neighbors who were animal-sitting and a little something for herself—an actual bikini, something she hadn't worn in ages. Because of all the activity, she'd lost a few pounds. She planned to swap her one-piece for something a little more tropical for that picnic lunch on the beach that Dylan had promised.

"I'll be in touch," Becky told Sonita as they hugged each other goodbye.

"I'll be lookin' for dat e-mail," Sonita said, smiling. She was a beautiful woman in her early forties, with deep bronze skin and a face that lit up with delight whenever she spoke. She seemed to love people and fashion, the perfect combination as far as Becky was concerned. "Now you two go enjoy de island. She's got more to her than shoppin'."

"We will," Dylan said, and gave her a great big bear hug that Sonita seemed to love. "It was so good to see you again."

"You, too," she cooed. "You say hello to dat Bear for me."

"I will, but he'll probably be in to see you. He can never get enough of your shirts."

"He's a good one, dat Bear. Just like his brother." She turned to Becky. "Keep this one," she whispered, as Dylan walked out of the front door. "I know him. A good heart. He be magic."

It was the way she said it that caught Becky off guard. As if Sonita knew something about Dylan that Becky needed to know. She wanted to ask her why she thought he was magic, but Sonita's attention had turned to a woman wrapping one of her scarves around her neck and doing a bad job of it.

Becky walked out of the store and stepped into the Jeep. A moment later, they were headed down the other side of the mountain.

She couldn't get Sonita's words out of her head.

Was Dylan "magic"?

She would love to find out. Though he hadn't kissed her again, that comfortable feeling of being around him had returned. She was glad for that. Now she just needed to be patient and see where things led.

Twenty minutes later Dylan pulled onto a dirt road and Becky thought about calling Laura to check on the kids. As she took out her phone to make the call, she decided that would send Laura the wrong message. Laura would call her if something went wrong, and obviously nothing had. There were no missed calls and no messages.

Becky slipped her phone back into her bag and turned to Dylan.

"Where are we going now?" she asked, happy he was driving and she didn't have to decide where to go and what to do next. She had grown so accustomed to being in charge that she'd forgotten how lovely it was to simply let someone else make all the decisions.

It was a glorious feeling to be taken care of by someone she could trust, and at that precise moment, Becky trusted Dylan. And there was nowhere else on earth she'd rather be.

"One of the few waterfalls on the island. I thought we'd have a picnic there. I brought us a lunch from the ship. Sonita told me about the waterfall while you were trying on that bathing suit, and I thought it would be a perfect place for lunch."

He gave her a seductive little grin.

"Sounds good," she said, grinning right back at him. She was loving this game of cat and mouse, only she wasn't quite sure which one of them was playing which part.

She reached over and slowly ran her finger around his ear.

He drove the Jeep off the main road and down a dirt road until they came to a small clearing.

"If I have the directions right, the waterfall should be somewhere around here."

He parked and jumped out, walked around to her side and helped her out, then grabbed a basket and a blue blanket from the back. He threw the blanket over his shoulder and took her hand in his as he led her down a narrow path. When it opened up onto a sapphire-colored natural pool embraced by a spectacular waterfall, Becky sighed.

"This is so beautiful."

"Sonita's a good woman," he teased.

The pool was surrounded by lush grass and wildflowers.

"Magical. This place doesn't look real," Becky said over the sound of rushing water while she twirled slowly around. "I feel as if I'm in one of Sarah's movies. A Disney animation where everything sparkles and glows and birds sing recognizable songs."

But Dylan didn't seem to be listening. He was focused on setting out the blanket, the wineglasses, and opening a bottle of white wine. She watched him for a moment against the backdrop of the waterfall, studying the angles of his face, his fine nose, the arch of his eyebrows, the way his hair danced on his forehead in the gentle breeze.

Maybe he *was* magic. Once again, she felt bewitched. How could she be this attracted to him, this enchanted, just watching him spread a blanket?

It was more than that. They'd spent a perfect morning together. Though he hadn't kissed her, he'd put his arm around her waist while they'd walked from shop to shop, finding reasons to touch her or to take her hand to help her in and out of the Jeep.

This feeling inside her had been building all day. No. Since the moment she'd seen him that very first day…and every moment since.

Now the attraction had multiplied and was much more. Much, much more.

She watched as he poured wine into two glasses, stood and handed her one. They turned to face each other. He slid a lock of hair off her face and she let out a light sigh. It had been way too long since she felt such passion, such longing for a man's touch.

"Now, what were you saying about this place being magical?" he asked. The tune she was now humming in her head wasn't anything from a Disney animation, but "Let's Get It On" by Marvin Gaye.

Without allowing herself to think about it, Becky put the wineglass down and with trembling fingers slowly unbuttoned her blouse, untied her bikini top, slid them both off her shoulders and let them fall to the ground. He didn't have to say a word; everything she needed to know was right there in his eyes.

Without moving his gaze from hers, Dylan quickly shed his

own shirt so he could feel her skin next to his. He didn't want to wait another second to feel her breasts touch his chest, gently at first, and then he pulled her close, forgetting about any restraint he might have considered only moments before while pouring the wine. He kissed her neck then continued kissing down to her breasts, to experience the richness of her body.

"Hmm," he moaned. "You taste sweet."

She couldn't say anything in return. Instead she ran her fingers through his thick hair, and all the while the heat was spreading up her spine.

"Let me take off your shorts," he whispered, then he looked up at her, checking for her response, his lovely green eyes filled with longing.

She nodded, and he bent down on one knee. Slipping off her shorts and then tugging off her bikini bottoms, he nestled his fingers between her legs and pressed against her. A soft whimper escaped from somewhere deep inside her. He knew what she wanted. What she longed for.

She watched as he removed his own shorts and briefs, then she and Dylan lay down together on the soft blanket. And rather than worry even a moment about what her body looked like or the fact they were out in the open, about to make love, she felt perfectly comfortable as she spread her legs so he could take everything she had kept hidden for so long. She felt free with this man, free to let him pleasure her, knowing that her pleasure was his.

They shared a smoldering kiss, his tongue pressing against hers, making her heart pound against her breastbone. The heat taking over her body made her want him even more. Then, again, he kissed her neck, finding his way to her breasts, cupping them in his hands, slipping his tongue around each nipple before he continued downward. She shifted so he knelt between her legs, and when his tongue touched her, stroked her, it was too much pleasure to control and she felt the orgasm cascading through her body with complete abandon as she rode delicious wave after delicious wave. Soon she was gently tugging him upward, wanting more than anything to feel him inside her.

"Do you have a condom?" She sighed. Even though stopping at this point would almost kill her, her rational side won out.

"Yes," he mumbled as she watched him reach for his shorts, getting the condom and slipping it on. Then he turned to her and thrust himself into her body. The feelings were overpowering and she trembled as she came again, a deep moan escaping from the depths of her passion.

He kissed her and her scent mixed with his, sending soft waves tingling through her body as she felt his release.

Sonita was right. Dylan truly was magic.

They lay there for a few minutes, wrapped in a loose embrace, gazing up at the crisp blue sky, listening to the waterfall. Marvin Gaye's "Sexual Healing" popped into her head, and she simply couldn't hold back her laughter. The whole experience seemed surreal.

"I'm sorry," she said, "but it's been a long time, and I can't stop thinking of Marvin Gaye songs."

"Let's get it on, baby," Dylan said in a sultry voice, but with a little laugh. "You were humming it in my ear."

"Get out," she said, somewhat embarrassed.

He nodded, grinning. "It was very sexy," he said as he ran his finger around her mouth.

"Oh God, you must think I'm some kind of nut."

"No. Just that you like background music."

He stared at her for a moment, straight-faced, then they both started laughing, and Becky marveled at how completely relaxed she felt with this truly magical man.

"THIS IS A COMPLETE BUST," Bob said as the taxi came to a stop on the side of the road and smoke poured out from under the hood. "We've been driving around in circles looking for *your contact*, if there is such a person, for more than an hour, and now the car's wasted. Are you sure you know where you're going?"

The driver, a tall man with dark red hair and an American accent, got out of the car and lifted the hood.

"He's a busy man," Tracy argued.

"Yeah, right." Bob turned sideways. "Tell you what, I'll get out and take a look at this piece of shit and see if I can fix it. I used to work in a garage when I was younger. But once I get it going again, you have one more chance to find this guy, or we're going back to the hotel so I can get what I really came to this island for."

He grabbed her chin and kissed her while rubbing her left breast. She wanted to scream, but instead she took a deep breath. When he exited the car, she let it out, trying to relax with the exhale.

Sal had promised to send one of his thugs to get the pendant at their first stop, but when the guy didn't show, Tracy'd had no choice but to make something up. She was able to call Sal once, pretending she was talking to her contact, and he promised that his guy would meet her soon.

That was over thirty minutes ago, and so far no one had showed up at any of the places he'd told her to stop. Now the taxi had broken down. The chances of anyone finding them on this deserted road were nil.

She dialed Sal again, and just as she did a white car appeared and parked on the opposite side of the road. Two guys wearing island shirts, shorts and sandals got out. They looked as if they just stepped off a cruise ship and had been partying all night.

"What's up?" one of them yelled to Bob. The other guy slowed his gait, and that's when Tracy knew these weren't your typical tourists. They worked for Sal.

She hit the End Call button on her phone and shoved it in her bag.

Then she heard Bob explaining engine woes to the two guys as the driver got back into the car and tried to start the engine.

Nothing happened.

Completely dead.

Suddenly everything got quiet and she heard one of the guys ask Bob for the necklace.

Their voices escalated and the language got rough, but Bob refused to give up the pendant.

"Give it to them," Tracy yelled, getting out of the car.

Just as she went around to the front, Bob took a punch to the face and one to his gut. Blood squirted out of his nose, and he hunched over in pain.

"All we want is the necklace, and you and your woman can be on your way," the guy with the chiseled face said.

"Just give it to them, Bob," Tracy repeated, wanting to get this whole thing over with.

Another punch to the face. This time Bob's lip split open and more blood ran down his neck.

Tracy couldn't look. Even though she hated the guy, she didn't want to see him get beat up.

"I—I haven't got it," Bob mumbled.

"We know you do, Bobby. Now where'd you hide it?"

The guy doing all the punching grabbed Bob by the shirt collar and began going through his pants' pockets, but all he came up with was a small digital camera, a wallet and some change.

Tracy jumped back in the taxi to check if it had fallen out on the seat. "Where are you?" she said out loud as she shoved her hands in between the cushions. She pulled out change, dollar bills, a worthless ring, but no pendant.

The driver never moved or said a word. He had that look of icy fear. Tracy felt it, but her fear was for something other than her life. She was afraid Bob really didn't have the pendant, and because of him her son wouldn't be getting on a plane.

She slid out of the taxi and walked to the front, afraid of what she might see.

Bob lay facedown in a shallow ditch next to the road. She could tell he was breathing, but he wasn't moving. His shirt was torn and his pants were halfway down his legs. A trail of blood led from the car to the ditch.

Tracy froze.

"Your honey doesn't have the necklace," the man who'd beaten up Bob said, and he tossed her Bob's digital camera. "He only brought pictures of it on his camera."

Her whole body began to shake as the two men came toward her and pushed her to the side of the taxi, away from Bob. She hit her right hip on the door handle, but she refused to show them any pain.

"He told me he had it," she said, her bottom lip quivering.

"And you believed him? You're just as stupid as Sal said you were," the guy with the angular face said.

The two men looked like brothers; both had blond hair, ruddy skin and nasty dispositions.

The guy who liked to do the punching grabbed Tracy's hair and got right up in her face. She stared at him, expressionless. "If you ever want to see that kid of yours again, you better come up with that diamond, fast. Sal is not a patient man."

"I'm doing everything I can."

"Do more," he growled. His breath felt hot against her face and was tainted with the smell of stale beer.

He opened the back door, and pushed her inside.

"Get the hell out of here before somebody sees you," he told the driver, and threw him some cash. "Nice job."

The driver turned the key in the ignition and the taxi magically came to life. Apparently his car trouble had merely been a ploy.

"Wait," Tracy yelled as the man put the car in gear. "We can't just leave him here."

She pulled out her cell phone to call the local police.

"If you know what's good for you, lady, you'll forget about that guy in the ditch," the driver said as he sped away. "Or you'll be asking for trouble."

Gazing out the back window, she watched the brothers jump

into their small white car and pull out onto the road heading up the mountain. She thought about what the driver said. Thought about Sal and her son, and about Bob assaulting her the previous night.

Her hip was beginning to ache, and it was the first time she noticed that her lip was bleeding. She didn't even remember when that happened.

Tracy sat back for a moment, staring down at her open cell phone, as the driver sped back toward the little village of Charlotte Amalia and *Alexandra's Dream*, and as if she were suddenly in a hurry, Tracy snapped her phone shut and slipped it into her bag.

THE APPLAUSE AND WHISTLES rushed over Laura along with a burst of joy as Connor and Sarah held their silver trophy for second place in the sandcastle contest. She must have snapped two dozen pictures of the kids as they stood in front of their winning three-foot creation of sand and shells. Their castle was actually pretty astounding, complete with a drawbridge and gun towers, windows and courtyards, steps and an ornate wall around the entire creation.

Sarah had directed them, knowing exactly what she wanted, while Laura and Connor figured out how to fashion it from wet sand and shells. The castle was truly a team effort.

"I knew we could do it," Sarah said as the group of well-wishers now moved on to the third-place winners.

Laura hadn't seen Connor this happy since the cruise began.

"Wait till Mom sees this," he croaked, holding out the trophy, proud as a peacock showing off its feathers.

"And Grandma and Grandpa, and Auntie Kim, and everybody on the ship, and everybody back home and the whole world," Sarah spluttered, arms out, turning in a circle.

She stopped. "And Bob!" She began spinning again.

"Yeah, Bob," Laura said caustically.

"We didn't need him after all," Connor said.

"Nope," Laura confirmed. She remembered all the money he'd given her. "Hey, let's go celebrate. I've got a ton of money to buy anything we want."

"Can we buy some ice cream?" Connor asked. "And a pickle?"

"Absolutely," Laura answered as she began gathering up their things and throwing them in the blue bag.

Sarah stopped spinning. "Can we see Blackbeard's castle?"

"Anything you want. I've got plenty of cash. We can even buy some souvenirs to take home."

"Good. I want to buy Brad and Angelina a present," Sarah chimed in. "Something they can play with in their cage. They like to play and sing. Maybe a big shiny bell."

"And Lance Armstrong," Connor interjected. "He could use another toy to bat around. Maybe we can find a pet shop."

"And what about John Wayne?" Laura asked. "I bet he'd like a rubber bone or something."

"John Wayne doesn't do much," Connor said. "He's too fat. All he does is sit around all day on his raggedy old cushion and watch Lance Armstrong run around."

"We can buy him a new cushion," Sarah instructed. "A red one with gold tassels."

"All right, then. We're all set. We'll catch one of those big open shuttles, go to Blackbeard's castle, get some ice cream, pickles and go shopping. And we so deserve it," Laura reasoned. "But first we need to call your mom."

"Let me tell her about the trophy," Connor said.

"No, I want to tell her," Sarah protested.

"We can all talk to her." Laura scrolled through the numbers on the tiny screen and noticed that her battery symbol was bright red. She was always forgetting to charge her phone and her mom was always warning her about it, something that annoyed her. Laura tuned her out most times, but today, she so wished she had listened. "We have to talk fast, though."

She waited for Becky to answer. Instead her voice mail

clicked in. "Hi, Aunt Becky. Gotta talk fast. Battery's almost dead. Just wanted to tell you we came in second for the sand-castle contest! Yea! Took lots of pictures."

At the same time the kids yelled into the phone about winning the trophy. Excitement echoed in each word. Laura wished her aunt could see Connor's face. He was absolutely glowing.

When they quieted down a bit, Laura continued, "We're off to go shopping. Oh, and Bob—" Her phone went dead.

"Can we go now?" Sarah asked, dragging the blue bag that weighed more than she did.

"Absolutely."

Laura took the bag from Sarah and they walked off the beach, giggling with delight as they headed for an afternoon of adventure.

CHAPTER SIXTEEN

BECKY WAS TRYING to remain calm, but when she had returned to her stateroom and didn't find any evidence of the kids at three o'clock, she started calling Laura.

But Laura didn't answer so she left a dozen messages and even a text message.

No response.

A dozen times she listened to the cut-off message that Laura had left, and each time she heard it, her guilt for having left her phone in the Jeep grew tenfold. If she had only thought to bring it with her, she would know what Laura was trying to tell her about Bob.

By six she was frantic. With still no sign of the kids or Laura or Bob, Becky scribbled a note to leave in the cabin in case she missed them, and then went looking for Kim. She found her and Estelle covered in green seaweed masks, waiting to be detoxified with a Himalayan crystal salt bath at Jasmine Spa. The sight was almost comical, but Becky was in no mood for laughing.

"I'm sure they're having a great day with Bob, and they simply forgot about the time," Estelle said as she lay on a table with only a small towel draped across her hips.

"It's six o'clock. I told Laura to be back here by three, four at the latest. I'm worried sick that something happened. This ship leaves port in less than two hours. Did Bob at least call?"

Kim grimaced and removed the cucumber rounds covering her eyes. "No, actually, he didn't." She sat up and grabbed a towel off the table next to her. "One thing about Laura, she's always punctual."

"You girls are getting excited over nothing. They're probably bonding somewhere, and Laura lost all track of time." When Estelle spoke, nothing moved, not even her lips. It was as if she were a slab of green stone.

"Maybe we should go look for them," Kim said, getting up from the table. "Let me get dressed, and I'll meet you in your cabin in ten minutes."

On her way back to her stateroom, worry and guilt replaced the last traces of rapture Becky had felt over her day with Dylan. Up until the moment she had stepped into her empty cabin, she had thought it possible to once again let a man slip into her heart.

Dylan was that man.

But at what cost?

While she had been with him, she'd barely thought about her kids. She merely assumed they were fine, that Laura and Bob were taking care of them. But now she realized she had been deluding herself.

It had been so long since she'd shared a day with a man, made love with a man, felt his touch, his kiss, his affection that she'd lost all track of time and simply assumed her kids were fine.

How could she have been so neglectful?

Panic crept up her spine. Suppose something had happened to them? She would never be able to forgive herself.

She passed other families out on deck, laughing, teasing each other, enjoying themselves. A mother walked by with two small children, one on each side of her, holding hands, talking about their day on the island.

Precisely what Becky and her kids should have been doing at that moment, but instead, Sarah, Connor and Laura were missing. Perhaps it was time to call the island police. She reached for her phone, but then remembered she had left it in her cabin, in her bag...again.

What was wrong with her? This irresponsible behavior had to stop.

By the time Becky slid the key card into her cabin door, she had worked herself up into such a guilt-ridden, panicked state that she was next to tears. She'd made a thousand promises to any and all celestial beings, including the moon goddess and God himself, that if her kids were all right, she'd rethink this motherhood role and become more dedicated to their happiness. No more long hours, no more working seven days a week at the shop. She needed more balance in her life, more time with her family. Suddenly the cabin door swung open and Sarah's little face stared out at her. "Where were you, Mommy? We've been waiting forever for you to come home."

Becky swooped up her sweet little girl into her arms and tried to hold back the tears, but it was next to impossible.

Sarah pulled back to look at her. "Why are you crying, Mommy? Did you fall down, too?"

"No, honey. I'm fine." Becky brought herself back under control and stared at Sarah. "Did you fall? Are you okay?" She checked her daughter's little body for bruises or scrapes.

"I didn't fall, Mommy. It was Connor."

Adrenaline surged through Becky as she looked around the room for her little boy. When she noticed Laura sitting on the sofa, she said, "Do you have any idea how worried we were?"

"I know and I'm so sorry, Aunt Becky, but—"

"Where's Connor?"

"He's in the bathroom, but he's fine," Laura assured her.

"He had an accident," Sarah blurted.

Becky put Sarah down next to Laura on the sofa, but before she could take one step toward the bathroom, Connor walked out into the sitting room. "I'm okay, Mom. Really."

Becky went over and gave him a hug, stroking his tousled hair. He seemed all right, thank God.

"What happened, baby?"

Sarah and Laura walked up behind Becky.

"It was Blackbeard's ghost," Sarah began. "He tripped Connor on the stairs in his castle and Connor fell down."

Becky turned to Laura, anger taking hold of her. "What happened and why didn't you answer any of my messages? And why didn't you call me? And where the heck was Bob through all of this?"

"I'm so, so sorry, Aunt Becky—I called you once, but you didn't answer and then my phone went dead."

"Why didn't you find a public phone?"

"I wanted to but—"

"I didn't want her to call you, Mom." Connor said. "You'd get all worried and tell us to come back, and we were having so much fun. It's just a few scratches. I'm all right."

Becky leaned back to look at him. His forehead was scraped, his chin, both his knees and his left elbow. "I'm happy you were having a good time, but, Laura, you know you should have come right back to the ship. Why did you stay so late?"

"That was my fault, Aunt Becky. I got on the wrong taxi shuttle. It was some kind of tour, and by the time I realized what was going on, we were all the way at the far tip of the island. We got off, but the next shuttle back wasn't for another half hour, and that one was for another tour. By then, I really wanted to call, but we were stuck on the shuttle and I figured we'd be back soon anyway. None of this would have happened if I hadn't forgotten to charge my phone last night. I'm so sorry, Aunt Becky." Laura was visibly upset. "When Bob left us, I thought I could handle it, but my mom is right. I'm just hopeless. I can't do anything right."

Laura began crying, then Sarah rubbed her eyes and sobbed right along with her, and Connor wiped tears off his cheeks.

Becky felt as if someone had just ripped open her heart. "Guys, it's okay. I'm guilty, too. If I had kept my phone with me I wouldn't have missed your call, and all of this could have been avoided. You're all safe now. Laura kept you together and brought you back. I'm not mad. Honest. I'm happy you're here with me."

Laura and Sarah wrapped themselves around her and Connor. And then Becky also began to weep, out of relief and the joy of feeling her children's arms around her. But an angry thought shot through Becky.

"Wait a minute. Bob left you?"

"Yeah," Laura said, sitting on the floor. "Well, not officially. He said he was coming back, but he never did."

Sarah stopped crying and sat down on the floor next to Connor.

There was a knock on the door and Becky stood to answer it.

She was angry again, but not at herself.

"Maybe that's Bob," Connor said.

"It better not be 'cause he's a dead man," Becky seethed as she swung open the door.

It was Kim, dressed in jeans, a pink T-shirt, no makeup and her wet hair piled up in a clip. She looked almost human.

"I think we should call the island police," Kim said as she walked into the room. "I'm worried sick about the kids."

"Hi, Mom," Laura said.

Kim let out a heavy sigh. "Thank God." Her voice quivered and she walked straight to her daughter.

Laura and Kim hugged for a long time, then Kim hugged Sarah and Connor.

Becky stood at the door watching her uptight, critical sister-in-law display actual emotion toward her own daughter and her niece and nephew. Maybe under all that bravado was a loving woman screaming to get out.

"Yoo-hoo! Don't close that door yet." Estelle's voice echoed down the hallway. Could this be yet another loving woman screaming to get out?

As she passed Becky in the doorway, Estelle said, "You should put on some eye makeup, my dear. You don't want your children to know you've been crying. It scares them."

Perhaps the loving woman was buried a little too deep under

the straw hat she was wearing and the huge Dior sunglasses. Estelle had slipped on a yellow sundress and matching sandals for the occasion. Apparently, during a crisis of this magnitude, how one dressed was of the utmost importance.

"Bob left us on the beach," Laura said once everyone had gathered inside Becky's stateroom. "He told us he had somewhere else to go, gave me some money—that I had to blackmail out of him—and left. In all fairness, he did say he would be back, but he never showed."

"I can't believe he would do this," Estelle protested. "He was excited about spending the day with you and the kids. The darling man wanted to get to know you better, and Connor and little Sarah, of course."

Laura rolled her eyes.

"Well, Grandma, that didn't happen. He was only with us until we got to Megan's Bay, then he was out of there." She sat cross-legged on the floor.

"He didn't even stay for the contest?" Becky asked, knowing how much Connor had looked forward to it.

"No, but it was okay. We won a trophy, Mommy." Sarah was beaming. "Do you want to see it?"

"Yes, baby, but not right now. Mommy's too upset over Bob's behavior."

"Why didn't you call me?" Kim asked Laura.

"My phone was dead, and the kids—"

"There must have been a public phone you could've used, sweetheart." Estelle sighed. "But then, this is how your mother was at your age. No common sense."

Kim turned on Estelle, genuine anger on her face—an emotion Becky thought she would never see directed at Estelle by one of her kids. "Mother, now is not the time to find ways to berate me and my daughter. At least Laura managed to get everyone back here in one piece."

Estelle glanced over at Connor, who was getting out Spider-man bandages for his scrapes. "I wouldn't be so quick to give out any awards just yet. Did you get a good look at our poor little Connor?" She turned to her grandson. "What happened, darling?"

"He'll be fine," Becky grumbled.

"It wasn't Laura's fault, Grandma, it was mine and Blackbeard's," Sarah argued as she gently dabbed hydrogen peroxide on Connor's scrapes with cotton balls, and then helped him put the bandages on. Sarah was good with minor cuts and bruises. She liked to play super doctor and help with the healing.

"Now is no time for fantasies, sweetheart," her grandmother chided. "Blackbeard was a nasty old pirate and he's been dead for a long time. He couldn't possibly have anything to do with Connor's physical condition, which should be checked by the ship's doctor, by the way. Who knows if there are any internal injuries? If he were my son, he'd be in sick bay or whatever they call it on a ship."

Becky wanted Estelle to either leave or shut up. She was making the kids anxious. Just as Becky was formulating a way to tell her without offending her once more, Kim spoke up.

"Mom, don't you have somewhere else to be? There must be an appointment you're missing."

Estelle didn't budge. "Your father should be here. He'll know what to do." She pulled out her cell phone, pressed a number, then watched as the tiny screen searched for the connection.

"About what?" Kim asked.

"About finding Bob, of course."

"Bob's a grown man," Becky said. "I'm sure he can take care of himself." She hoped she never had to see him again. Maybe he'd found a better meal ticket, never to be heard from again.

Estelle held up her hand for silence as she put Mark on speaker. "Mark, darling. I'm here in Becky's cabin, and we have a situation. Would you please drop whatever it is you're doing and come on over?"

"I'm in the middle of something, Estelle," he said in a raspy voice.

"But you don't understand the importance of our concerns. Our dear Bob is missing."

Mark chuckled. "Don't worry. Guys like him don't drift very far from the money."

A woman's soft laughter echoed in the background.

Estelle disconnected the call. "Well, now we know how your father feels about all of this."

Her phone rang. She answered with a few uh-huhs. Then she disconnected again. "That was Mark. He says we should contact the ship's security, just in case Bob doesn't make it back in time and something nasty happened to him."

Becky had never seen Estelle look so glum. Her whole body seemed to cave in on itself as she sat on the chair next to the window.

"My dad's right," Kim said. "I'll call security."

Estelle turned to Kim. "Actually, he thinks it would be more effective if you, Laura and Becky go to the office in person and tell them everything you can about the day."

Becky sure didn't want to get into the details of her day, but if Bob was actually missing or hurt, which she doubted, she needed to be forthright about everything she knew.

"Will you stay with the kids?" Becky asked Estelle.

"Of course, but hurry and get back. I'm having dinner with Thanasi Kaldis, a sweet man and the hotel manager of this ship. I need at least a couple hours to get ready. Now run along and find our Bobby." She turned to Kim. "We don't want to lose him now. Heavens, I've already started the invitation list and I was planning on talking to Thanasi this evening about booking this marvelous ship for the event, although it may not be big enough. It can only accommodate a thousand passengers, but we'll deal with that later. Right now you need to find our Bob, and if your father wasn't busy with that Jan-woman, he'd be here with me right now, soothing my anxiety. This whole divorce thing is silly, anyway."

Kim stared at her mother. Becky could only imagine the

thoughts swirling around her mind. She didn't look any too happy with Estelle, but all she said was, "Relax, Mom. Put your feet up and order a cocktail."

Estelle sighed, moved over to the sofa and asked Sarah to bring her a book she could read to them. At least Estelle knew a little about how to be a good grandmother.

Kim motioned for Laura to come and join her. Becky gave another hug to her children, then three women walked out of the room, leaving Estelle to play grandmother, and no doubt dwell on "that Jan-woman."

CHAPTER SEVENTEEN

WHEN TRACY RETURNED to her cabin, Erica was asleep on the lower bunk. Meryl Streep's voice boomed from the small TV telling Ann Hathaway that she had no style or sense of fashion.

The Devil Wears Prada was Erica's favorite movie, and she watched it whenever she wanted to de-stress. Something that Tracy desperately needed to do herself.

She sat on the floor so she wouldn't wake her cabin-mate. She was still shaking from the events of the day and hoped the movie would work its magic for her, too.

Tracy had returned to the ship right after the incident with Bob, but had spent most of the remainder of the afternoon in the crew's lounge drinking martinis, hoping to relieve herself of guilt for having left Bob in the ditch, but so far they weren't working.

The whole thing was turning into some kind of endless nightmare. Once again she had been duped by a fast-talking guy into thinking he was the real deal. All that she'd gone through with Bob had proven to be just another ruse. She still couldn't believe he'd stepped on that island without the pendant. All he had really wanted was sex.

But she had been so sure it was the diamond he was after. It just went to show how naive she could be about men.

Bob deserved to be left in a frickin' ditch, but Tracy couldn't feel good about it. Perhaps it was her religious convictions or maybe simple human compassion had kicked in. Whatever the reason, she had called the island police as soon as she'd arrived back in town.

The cop on the phone had tried to get more information out of her besides the location, but Tracy knew better than to take that route. She could only hope that Bob was alive and back in the arms of his clueless fiancée.

"Is he still alive?" Erica mumbled, causing Tracy to jump at the sound of her voice.

"I, um, what?" The question startled her. Did Erica know about Bob? But how?

"Don't tell me you didn't meet that engaged guy on the island today. Why else did you go off by yourself? It certainly wasn't to shop. My bags are in the corner, but I don't see yours anywhere."

And sure enough, there were at least ten colorful paper bags stacked up in front of the closet.

Tracy couldn't admit she'd been with Bob. What if he was really hurt, or worse, dead? She had to come up with something plausible so Erica wouldn't get suspicious. She turned slightly to face Erica.

"I…spent the day on the beach," she began, and then she remembered what Bob had told her about Sarah and Connor. "I made a sandcastle for a contest. It was fun. You should've been there."

Erica didn't respond for a moment. Tracy hated lying, but she was getting good at it.

"Yeah, uh-huh, and you expect me to believe that?"

"Absolutely," Tracy said with conviction, turning back to the movie.

"Just tell me one thing."

"What's that?"

"Did you bite your lip, or did he? 'Cause either way, it must have been one hell of an afternoon."

Tracy sucked in her lips and felt the swollen cut. It had healed enough so that it didn't sting anymore and she'd forgotten about it.

She didn't quite know how to answer, so she decided to say nothing.

"Just what I thought," Erica said, then she made herself comfortable, punching her pillow and wrapping the wine-colored blanket around her shoulders.

After a while, Erica fell back to sleep, and Tracy noticed that the shaking had finally subsided. The more she watched Ann Hathaway struggle with the boss from hell, the more she began to appreciate the wonders of losing oneself in a good story.

It was much better than reality, especially her reality, which was fast approaching a long prison sentence.

"HOW LONG HAS IT BEEN since you've had contact with Mr. Ducain?" chief security officer Sean Brady asked Laura while they sat across from each other in a small office filled with sur-veillance monitors. There were two other security people in the room, a woman typing and a man was on the phone. Sean Brady entered everything Laura said into some sort of program on his computer. He had already taken down a description of Bob, and his vitals, and contacted the island police with the information.

His questions were now getting redundant.

"This morning on Megan's Bay Beach," Laura answered. "But I already told you that when we first came in here."

She was visibly shaken by all of this. Kim sat next to her and held her hand.

"Sorry, but I need to be sure you're telling me everything you know. Most of the time, in cases like this, the passenger loses track of time and we pick them up in the next port." He turned to Becky, who sat on a hard plastic chair behind Kim. Sean Brady was a big man, former military, Becky guessed, but he had kind eyes and a warm smile. He looked as if he really wanted to help. "And you say you were also on the island today, Mrs. Montgomery?"

Becky had already answered that question. "Yes, I did some shopping."

"It's a small island, but you say you never bumped into your children, or Mr. Ducain?"

Becky's stomach tightened. "No."

"It's a great place for shopping. It's duty-free. But Laura says she and your children were shopping, as well. Is there a reason why you didn't make plans to meet up with your niece and your children?"

"I don't see how this has any bearing on finding Bob."

He leaned forward, clasping his hands together on the desk, and smiled. "It might not, but you were on the island without your children, and Mr. Ducain was on the island without his fiancée and he suddenly leaves the children for 'something he had to do,' to quote Miss Montgomery. It makes one wonder…"

Becky finally got it, just as Kim spun around to face her.

"Y-you don't actually think—" Becky stammered.

"You're having an affair with my fiancé?" Kim protested.

"Mom, she's not having an affair with Bob."

"You always have to take her side, don't you?" Kim scolded.

Becky couldn't hold in the truth any longer, even if it did mean that Dylan might lose his job. Surely he'd understand. She simply couldn't allow Kim to think she was a cheat, and besides, Bob might really be in trouble somewhere. She had to tell everything.

"I was with Dylan today. Dylan Langstaff. He's in charge of the swim staff."

The man cracked a smile. "And was this personal, or were you part of a tour of some sort?"

Becky sighed. "It was personal."

Kim raised an eyebrow as she stared back at Becky. Her whole demeanor changed from anger to intense curiosity in a fraction of a second.

"Did Dylan happen to mention if he saw Mr. Duncan?"

Kim swung back around in her chair. "Look, Officer Brady, we're wasting valuable time here. Shouldn't somebody be out searching for my fiancé instead of grilling my sister-in-law?"

"We're doing everything we can right now."

"Well it obviously isn't enough, because you haven't found Bob."

"Actually, we have," an officer said from across the room.

He stood and walked closer, staring at a sheet of paper. "He's a little banged up, but the island police said as soon as the hospital releases him, they'll transport him back here."

"Hospital!" Kim shrieked. "Is he all right? What happened?" Laura put her arm around her mother.

The chief security officer skimmed the report. "Apparently he was mugged. The police got an anonymous tip, or your fiancé might still be out there. We'll do everything we can to hold the ship in dock until he returns. It should only be a short delay, if any. You can wait in your cabin and somebody will call you when he's brought aboard."

"Thank you," Kim said, and she stood to leave. "But could you please phone me in Becky's cabin. I'd like to be with my family right now."

Sean Brady nodded. "Will do."

Laura and Kim walked out together, followed by Becky, who wanted to crawl under a rock and stay there. She had essentially admitted to Kim that she and Dylan were together all day and now she would never hear the end of it.

By the time they returned to Becky's stateroom, the kids had eaten an entire cheese pizza and were both asleep in their beds. Estelle had already heard the news of Bob's imminent return.

"Those nasty people who mugged our poor Bobby should be shot," Estelle announced as she sipped on a Manhattan served in a martini glass.

Apparently a bartender had sent over two shakers filled with premixed Manhattans, courtesy of Thanasi Kaldis. Estelle was working on her second shaker.

It always helped to have connections.

"As soon as he gets here, I'm going to insist he go right to bed and rest," Kim said. "He must be awfully upset over the whole ordeal."

"That's a good idea," agreed Estelle, then she turned to Becky. "And what's this I hear about you and some male crew member spending the day together?"

"News travels fast," Becky mumbled to herself.

"It's a small world aboard ship. Everybody knows your business."

"I'll say," Laura agreed.

Estelle slapped her hand on the arm of the chair. "This is none of your concern, Laura."

Laura froze then slowly backed away. "I'm a little tired. Is it okay if I lie down on your bed, Aunt Becky?"

Becky nodded her approval, giving Laura a sympathetic smile before she turned and walked into the other room, shutting the door behind her.

"How could you even think about another man so soon after my son's death?" Estelle growled. Her whole body visibly shook with anger.

"My husband died more than two years ago," Becky shot back. "He'd want me to go on with my life."

"Right," Estelle said caustically.

Becky tried to remain calm as Estelle tore apart what little shred of happiness she had left. "I don't want to get into this with you, Estelle. You know how I felt about Ryder, but that part of my life is over."

"And what about my grandchildren? Is Ryder over for them, as well?"

"He was their dad. Nothing will ever change that."

"You seem to be giving it a good try. All they ever talk about is this Dylan character. They only talk about their father when I bring him up. It's not right. My son loved his kids and you should be preserving his memory."

Becky walked over and sat on the sofa, trying to keep her temper in check.

"For one thing, they happen to like Dylan, and for another, no one will ever take Ryder's place in their hearts. You above all people should know that."

"I only know what I see and I see a woman who has already forgotten about a man she supposedly loved."

Becky's anger grew tight in her chest. "I loved your son more than my next breath. If the choice had come for me to die or him, I would have gladly died so he could live. But it didn't happen that way. There was only a phone call in the middle of the night from Mark to tell me that his son, my husband, the father of my children had—how did he put it?—Ryder had slipped away from a massive coronary. I wanted to die right there, while I was on the phone listening to Mark sob. I wanted to fly away from that horrible moment and never think of it again, but I had two children to tell that their daddy had died. Can you even imagine what that might have been like?"

Estelle cleared her throat and tried mightily to hold back whatever emotion she was feeling, but Becky could see traces of empathy on her face. "I'm sure it was difficult, but that doesn't excuse your behavior right now."

The woman just couldn't give it up.

"Mother, stop it," Kim finally roared, tears trailing down her cheeks. Estelle stood and, ignoring what Kim had just said, walked over to Becky. "A man like that doesn't care about you. He just wants some temporary fun with a pretty passenger."

"I never thought it was anything else," Becky said, thinking that was exactly what her day at the waterfall had been—fun with a cute guy who made her feel like a woman again. It couldn't be anything more, no matter what she had felt. They came from two different worlds.

Estelle's eyes pooled with tears. "It's too soon, that's all. It's just too damn soon to think of you with another man."

Becky looked deep into Estelle's eyes and saw the pain, the intense emotion a mother must feel to lose a child. It had to be overwhelming. Becky had lost a husband, but Estelle had lost someone far greater. She had lost the baby she had felt kick at five months, who had the hiccups and kept her awake at eight months, who made her cry with happiness as soon as she held him in her arms. He was her child.

He was her Connor.

Becky's chest tightened. She couldn't breathe. The force was almost unbearable until Estelle, thankfully, turned away and walked toward the door.

Once she got there, she hesitated for a moment as if she wanted to say something else. But then she grabbed the doorknob, flung the door open, stood straight and walked out.

Becky watched as the door slowly closed behind her, and she knew deep down in her soul that she and Estelle had shared a moment that would forever change their relationship.

THE NEXT MORNING the Montgomery family met in Estelle's penthouse suite for breakfast. Estelle wanted the entire family to spend the majority of the day together. A healing time, as she had put it.

The large square table sparkled with the best china and flatware the ship had to offer. The room decorated in olive tones, with plush cream-colored carpeting, white drapes and light green accents was filled with the scent of freshly baked breads and sweet oatmeal cookies, Mark's favorite. A staff of two fluttered around the table keeping the Mimosa glasses filled with Dom Pérignon and freshly squeezed orange juice.

Everyone was there, even Bob, who had come aboard the previous night with the help of the local police. His normally ruddy complexion was dark with bruising, he had a swollen bottom lip and his right eye was surrounded with a deep purple and yellow combination. His left arm was in a sling, and he claimed to have three cracked ribs.

Despite all his injuries, he still had enough strength to keep everyone at the table entertained, especially Kim, who seemed to hang on his every word.

Becky wasn't buying most of it, but she was apparently in the minority. Even Laura was mesmerized by Bob's harrowing tale. "I had only intended to leave the kids for a little while, an hour at the most, but when I walked out of the jewelry store, these two guys came out of nowhere. The one bigger guy, who must have weighed two hundred pounds, pulled a gun on me. So what was I supposed to do? I had to go with them."

Kim ran her hand up and down his back. Affection oozed from every pore of her being as she stared at his battered face. "It must have been just awful for you," she soothed.

He slanted his gaze her way for a moment. "I have to admit, I didn't think I would ever see your pretty face again."

Estelle sighed.

Mark groaned, then covered it up with a cough.

"What happened then?" Connor asked, totally intent on getting all the facts.

"Then he punched those bad guys right in the stomach," Sarah explained, giving little air punches with her fists.

"Well, that's not exactly how it happened, but your uncle Bob sure gave those bad guys a run for their money," Bob said.

Becky wondered exactly when he had become "Uncle Bob."

"I don't know if I should go into all the gory details during breakfast," he said.

"That's a good idea, Bob," Mark confirmed. "Maybe you can wait until after we've digested our food."

"I don't care about digestion," Connor protested. "I want to hear how you got away."

"Well," Bob began. "After they drove me to some remote road on the island, and stole the diamond bracelets I'd bought for Laura and my Kimmy, and stole my wallet, they made me get out of the car with them. That's when I went into high gear and punched the big guy right in the nose and blood—"

"Please don't go into this kind of detail in front of my kids," Becky urged.

"I have to agree with Becky," Mark cautioned.

"You're right. I'm sorry. I don't want any of you upset. I'm just so happy to be back that I guess I get a little carried away. It's all too fresh."

"You should have been carrying this," Laura said as she held up the pendant. "It might have kept you safe."

Bob choked on the Mimosa he was drinking. Kim patted his back and held up an arm as if he was a child. Finally he got it under control. "You have the pendant?"

"Yeah, Aunt Becky gave it to me for good luck before we left for the island." As Laura dangled it above her plate, Becky noticed a strange look on Bob's face.

He started to reach across the table for it, but Estelle held up her Mimosa glass and Laura shoved the pendant back into her pocket.

"To Bob," Estelle began. "Who went through a terrible ordeal, but has safely returned to us."

Becky reluctantly held up her glass. Something was not right about his story, despite his broken ribs and black eye. It didn't match Laura's description of his leaving the kids on the beach.

She wondered if she would ever really know the truth. "To Bob," she chimed in, clinking her glass with Kim's, but Kim had a concerned look on her face as if perhaps she wasn't buying any of this, either.

CHAPTER EIGHTEEN

"HE STILL HAS his wallet," Kim told Becky as they sat out on one of the two teak verandas of Estelle's penthouse. The sky was a silky blue, but the ocean seemed angry. In the distance, rain plummeted from the clouds in a dark patch on the horizon. There was a slight chill in the air, but Kim had wanted to talk somewhere private, and the veranda off the master bedroom was the only place.

"That doesn't mean anything," Becky said. "They only wanted the bracelets."

"No, you're not getting it. He told us they stole his wallet. He told Security they stole his wallet, but I found it this morning in the inside pocket of his trousers. He has these special travel clothes. There's a hidden inside pocket for passports and such. His wallet was in there, along with five hundred dollars in cash and two ATM receipts. Why do you think he's lying about his wallet? I mean, he was obviously mugged."

Kim was visibly upset over her discoveries, but Becky didn't have the answer. "I don't know. Did the police track down which jewelry store he bought the bracelets from?"

"Well, that's just it. He says he can't remember which store, they all look alike, with similar names. The island police are still waiting for that information so they can question the shopkeeper."

Looking into Kim's eyes, Becky realized the woman really didn't want to hear the truth about Bob, at least not yet. She was in love with the man, and didn't want to believe he could be lying to her. "He was pretty beat up. I can understand if he can't remember the details. I've heard you can sometimes get a form of amnesia when you experience a trauma like Bob has suffered."

Kim brightened. "Maybe that's it. Maybe he can't remember his wallet *wasn't* stolen. It could be he's confused about the whole incident."

Becky didn't think that was the case, but for the moment, she was going with it. "Exactly. Give it a few days. He'll probably remember everything once you get him back home in his own environment."

"You're right. Thank you," she said.

"No problem."

Becky stood and turned to walk back inside, but Kim stopped her. "You know, I've been fairly harsh on you ever since you married into this family. I just want to say I'm sorry, and thank you for listening to me. It helped just to talk about it."

"You're welcome," Becky said.

The two women hugged. It was the first time Becky had ever felt genuine emotion for Kim. Perhaps they had finally come to terms with each other and could slowly begin an honest friendship.

PATTI KENNEDY had delivered the news to Dylan in a matter-of-fact tone, without the slightest trace of empathy. She told him about the mugging of Bob Ducain, and about Becky admitting to spending the day with Dylan.

"You know we have a strict policy against crew mixing with passengers. Therefore, in light of some rather disturbing information we've received, as of this moment, you are suspended from all your duties. We will review your case and inform you of our decision upon arrival back in Miami Beach. And one more thing, if there's even so much as a negative whisper about your behavior, you will be instantly dismissed."

She hadn't given Dylan the opportunity to challenge his suspension or to question what the "disturbing information" could be. She merely gave him the news and left his quarters. It was as if they had never become friends. As if she'd never confided in him about her mad crush on Thanasi or shared all the personal things they'd talked about.

But the potential of losing his job didn't seem to matter that much anymore. He had met a woman he would risk almost anything to be with, and getting suspended because of Becky only heightened his determination to somehow make this budding romance work out.

Dylan watched the rain fall outside his window. It cascaded into the ocean like a stream of sadness. He had to talk to Becky, but talking to her now would get him fired.

Unfortunately, he didn't have a choice in the matter. He had to know if she shared his feelings.

He called her cabin, but there was no answer, and just when he was about to go on deck to look for her, his phone rang.

It was Becky. "I need to talk to you," she said, but there was an urgency in her voice that threw him.

"Sure. Can we meet in your cabin?"

"Isn't that risky for you?"

"It doesn't matter."

"Ten minutes?"

"Sure," he said, and hung up.

WHEN HE ARRIVED at Becky's cabin door, the steward who was just finishing up her suite gave Dylan a nasty look. The news would probably get back to Patti before Dylan left the room.

"Come on in," Becky said when she saw him standing outside her door.

He wanted to take her in his arms. He'd missed her terribly, her fragrance, her touch, the silkiness of her skin. They hadn't seen each other or spoken since yesterday when he'd dropped her off at her cabin to meet up with her kids. But now he was getting a weird vibe from her, so he simply walked into the room and stood next to the door.

Becky headed for the far end of the room and crossed her arms across her chest, a body signal that told him to back off.

"What's going on?" she asked. "I thought you couldn't be seen with me while we were aboard this ship."

"I don't care about that anymore. Not after yesterday. I just want to be with you."

He took a step toward her. He couldn't stand being in the same room with her and not having her in his arms.

"That's what I want to talk to you about."

He didn't like the look on her face. Much too serious. He took another step forward. If he could just kiss her, he knew everything would be all right.

"Please don't come any closer. What I have to say is difficult enough."

Panic filled him. "We can make this work, I know we can."

Lightning ripped across the sky and thunder roared through the cabin. She shook her head. "It's just too complicated. This could never work."

"Yes it can. We can figure it out together."

She shook her head and rubbed her arms.

"Please, Becky, don't do this. We have something special. Let's not throw it away."

"It's not fair to Ryder's family. To Estelle. I'm breaking her heart. Ryder would never forgive me for that."

"Ryder's gone. It's time his family realized that. But you're alive and you deserve another chance at love. Let me be that chance, Becky. Don't turn me away."

Her face was wet with tears. It killed him to see her like this. He wanted her to laugh again, tease him again, love him again.

"I think you should go. My kids will be here soon, and I don't want them to see us together."

He stared at her for a little longer, hoping she would change her mind and tell him to stay so they talk this out.

But she didn't.

Dylan walked away from her, the rain causing the sea to play with the ship's stability like a rubber duck in a child's bathtub.

For the first time since he'd been working cruise ships, the motion made his stomach queasy and his head spin.

BOB HAD LEFT A MESSAGE for Tracy to meet him at the Espresso Bar on Bacchus deck. She thought it was rather bold of him, but at this point, she didn't care. It was his hide, not hers that was on the line.

The ship rocked back and forth, making it difficult for Tracy to keep her balance as she walked, but she liked the rain. Liked the smell of it, especially now when she was feeling a little sick from the rough seas.

On her way to the Espresso Bar, she passed the Chocolate café and was tempted to go in and buy half a chocolate cake and just pig out, but it wouldn't be any fun without Franco.

God, how she missed her little boy.

She had tried to get through to Sal last night about a hundred times, but he never answered his phone, and his voice-mail box was full. She was sure he'd done that on purpose, and it killed her. All she could think of was Franco at the airport, excited about going home, and then not getting on that plane for whatever sadistic reason Sal could come up with.

It broke her heart.

She ordered a hot chocolate, and when it arrived she sat at a small table next to a window so she could watch the rain hit the water, hoping the visual would calm her queasy stomach and somehow ease the pain in her lower back. She remembered how the streets in Vegas used to flood whenever it would rain too hard, and one time her father's car floated two blocks from home while she and her dad were still in it. He'd told her not to worry as they'd climbed out on the roof when the water got too high. He would save her.

And he did. They stayed right there on that roof, huddled together until the rain stopped and the water receded. Then they walked home and drank huge mugs of hot chocolate. She had never been so scared in all her life.

Until now.

"You enjoying your coffee?" Bob's voice made her jump. She hadn't seen him walk up to the table.

"It's cocoa, but yes, I am." She looked up at his swollen face, a reminder of Sal's power.

He sat across from her. "Who were those guys yesterday?"

"I don't know," she said. "They came out of nowhere."

"Don't give me that. I've got you all figured out, baby."

She took a sip of her cocoa, trying to regain her composure. The hot drink was sweet and went down easily. "I don't think you do, Bob. I had no idea anything like that was going to happen."

He leaned across the table, grabbed her wrist and squeezed hard. "I met you in this public place because I don't trust myself. All I could think of while I lay in that ditch yesterday was how I was going to get my pound of flesh, but you're not worth the risk. I know who has that pendant, and I know how to get it. If it's worth anything, you'll never see it. You were playing me for a fool, but playing time is over."

"People are staring, Bob," she said. "You better let me go."

He released his grasp, and she pulled back her throbbing arm. Her hand felt numb and her wrist carried his imprint.

"You've got me all wrong," she protested, leaning forward, allowing him a good view of her breasts. She had purposely worn a low-cut blouse knowing he got off on seeing a little skin. "I can help you. We're in this together, remember?" She was desperate now. She couldn't allow him to leave without finding a way to convince him she had nothing to do with his beating, but she knew her prospects weren't looking good.

He stared at her breasts, then smirked up at her. "Put your phony charm away. From now on, I'm flying solo, and if I see you anywhere within ten feet of my family I'll have to reconsider that risk factor."

He stood and left, and as he walked away, Tracy swore she

saw Connor and Laura leave right behind him. She stood to make sure just as the ship lurched. A wave of nausea overtook her, and her right side ached. She must have really smacked herself on the taxi's door handle yesterday because it felt as if a knife was going through her lower back. She sat, slowly.

She couldn't be sure she'd actually seen them. At the moment, she couldn't focus on anything other than how miserable she felt.

As DYLAN WALKED down a promenade to the Espresso Bar he passed a few boutiques, the Rose Petal tearoom, Marco Polo restaurant, Everyday Golf, the movie theater and Temptations Chocolate café, always a hot spot for passengers with a sweet tooth. Today was no exception, especially with all the rain.

He was on his way to the Internet café to e-mail Bear for a little brotherly advice. His queasy stomach had subsided and now all he wanted was a strong cup of coffee.

When he looked up, he saw Connor and Laura walking toward him. They were immersed in their own conversation so they didn't notice him.

"Hey, guys," he called.

"Dylan!" Laura answered almost as if she'd been looking for him. They ran right to him, breathless.

"We just saw my mother's fiancé, Bob, with Tracy," Laura whispered.

"Yeah, and they were talking about Mom's pendant like it was something important," Connor chimed in. He was almost shaking, but Dylan didn't know if he was cold or scared.

"They must think those rumors are real," Dylan suggested.

"What rumors?" Laura asked.

"That there's a real diamond hidden inside that pendant."

Laura pulled the necklace out of her pocket and they studied it for a moment. She shook it out and turned the pendant over to reveal a bad soldering job. Dylan held it up to a light fixture thinking he might be able to see through the silver teardrop, but he couldn't. The piece looked like something you'd find at a discount store.

"Not!" he and Laura said in unison, then he handed it back to her.

"Bob was mean to Tracy," Connor told him. "We couldn't hear everything he was saying, but he was holding her arm really tight. And it looked like he was hurting her." Connor was visibly shaking.

"Let's get you warmed up, buddy," Dylan said.

He walked Connor and Laura inside the coffee shop, ordered three hot cocoas and paid for them with his key card. When they arrived he gave each kid a steaming mug, then found a small round table to continue the conversation.

"Okay, now let's go over this again," Dylan said once everyone was seated and had some of the hot liquid in their bellies. "And this time tell me the whole story from the beginning."

Laura and Connor told him everything they'd seen and heard. They also told him about Bob's mugging, and how Laura could tell her mom was a little skeptical about it, but wouldn't come out and say so. And how mean Bob had been at Megan's Bay Beach and that he couldn't wait to get rid of them fast enough.

When they finished talking, Dylan asked, "What do you guys want to do with this information?"

"I want to tell my mother, but she won't believe me. She's in love with Bob, and now they've decided to get married as soon as they get home. Grandma wanted to book this entire ship for the wedding, but I heard Bob tell my mom that he wanted to elope as soon as possible."

"Okay, so what we have to do is prove to your mom that Bob is not the man she thinks he is."

"Yeah, he's a sleazeball," Connor said.

"Good choice of words," Dylan agreed. "And she needs to learn this information on her own, with our help, of course."

Laura nodded. "Sounds perfect, but we have to convince our

gram, too. She really likes Bob, and she'll persuade my mom to marry him no matter what my mom says."

Dylan's mind raced with different scenarios. "What does your family have planned for tonight? Are they going to the dessert party at Mermaid Lagoon?"

Connor nodded enthusiastically. "Yes. I even uploaded some of my digital pictures of the excursions we went on for the show tonight. Laura helped me. Mom said it was okay. Some of them are really funny."

He giggled, and Dylan noticed how much he had changed from that uptight little boy he'd met on the first day.

"I can't wait to see them, Connor," Dylan said, smiling and sitting back in his wooden chair. "I'd forgotten all about the passenger digital slide show Patti is planning to run in the background tonight. It's a new thing. Something she's trying out to see if the passengers like it."

"We're all supposed to meet there because it's Grandpa's birthday tomorrow," Laura told him. "Grandma wanted everybody to ignore it, because he's spent most of this cruise with Jan Milton, but Aunt Becky wouldn't let her. Connor and I were looking for a gift for Grandpa when we spotted Bob, who was supposed to be so battered and bruised he could hardly move. He seemed to be moving just fine, so we followed him."

"And then he sat down with Tracy," Connor said. "We didn't think he'd ever met her before."

"That's when we knew something wasn't right. So we snuck around to the table next to them to see if we could hear what they were saying, but we only caught bits and pieces. The rain on the windows kind of drowned everything out."

Dylan had an idea of how this whole thing should come down. He had grown fond of Becky's family and would be happy to see Bob exposed for who he was. Dylan had never trusted the guy. He didn't know Tracy very well, but he sensed she was a good person who had probably got caught up in Bob's web. He didn't want to use her in some on-board scandal that would get her fired. He knew she had a kid to support, so he had to concentrate on using the worthless pendant as bait, and not Tracy.

"Does Bob know you have the pendant?" he asked Laura.

"Uh-huh. I showed it to him at breakfast."

"Why aren't you wearing it?"

"The clasp is broken. Aunt Becky has to give it back to Patti Kennedy tonight at the dessert party, so I thought I'd find somewhere to get it fixed, but so far there doesn't seem to be anybody who can do it."

"Perfect. The safest thing for you to do is to make sure you find a way to let Bob know you found someone to fix it. Heck, tell him you gave it to me. That way he won't mess with you today."

Laura handed him the necklace, and he studied the broken clasp. "It doesn't look too bad," he said. "The clasp just needs tightening. I can fix it."

"Now what?" Connor asked.

Dylan sat back in his chair and slipped the necklace into his pocket. "This is when it gets a little tricky. I have to figure out how to lure him into doing something that's bad, while he's thinking it's good, at least for him, then we show Laura's Mom and your grandmother what a *sleazeball* Bob really is."

He looked at Laura. "You need to get your mom to invite me to the dessert party tonight in Mermaid's Lagoon. And she has to have it okayed through the cruise ship director, Patti Kennedy. Do you think you can do that?"

"Grandma will have a stroke, but I think my mom will do it anyway. Sure. I'll figure it out."

"Okay then, let's come up with our game," Dylan said. "I think I have an idea, but we'll need you, Connor, to make it work."

Connor leaned forward. "Just tell me what I have to do."

CHAPTER NINETEEN

BECKY, CONNOR AND SARAH headed for Estelle's private table next to the indoor pool in the Mermaid Lagoon. Kim and Bob walked in front of them, with Laura and Estelle leading the way. Mark was running late, according to Estelle, and would meet them later.

The event was formal, so Connor wore a gray pinstriped suit, with his orange T-shirt sticking out above the collar of his white dress shirt, and Sarah had chosen her favorite red silk taffeta party dress. Becky wore her deep purple gown with one of Sonita's silk scarves.

A small orchestra featuring traditional string instruments plus a beautiful golden harp serenaded the guests from a wooden platform surrounded by elaborate flower arrangements. The azure pool reflected the soft lighting, and the light scent of sweet chocolate filled the air. Dessert tables set up along one side of the pool featured chocolate fountains, dark– and white-chocolate sculptures, and cakes tied up with chocolate bows. There was enough chocolate to make a chocoholic swoon.

More tables lined the far end of the pool and were stacked with aromatic herb breads, pungent cheese and intricate ice sculptures of sea creatures.

Two giant screens continuously flashed pictures and video snippets taken by cruise passengers of their shipboard vacation. Becky could only hope Connor's pictures were flattering to the family, and if they weren't, Laura would have had the sense to edit them out.

"Wow, Mommy, is this a party for the moon goddess?" Sarah asked as she looked up through the mostly glass ceiling.

Becky followed her daughter's gaze, and sure enough, the sky had cleared enough for the full moon to peek through gossamer clouds. It had stopped raining a couple hours ago, but wispy clouds still drifted in the sky.

It almost seemed as if the goddess was looking down on *Alexandra's Dream.*

The thought gave Becky a shiver, or maybe it was the whisper in her ear. "You look beautiful tonight."

His voice was deep and raspy, reminding her of their day on the island, of their lovemaking, of how much she longed for his touch.

But she couldn't think about that now. She'd made her decision and she was determined to stick with it.

"Dylan, what are you doing here?" she asked.

"Your sister-in-law Kim invited me. I'm her guest."

Becky couldn't believe Kim would actually defy her mother so blatantly and invite Dylan. It was somewhat of a tiny miracle.

Connor took his hand. "Will you sit next to me?"

Becky was working on a bad case of separation anxiety and she wanted it to continue. Sitting with Dylan all night would only make her reconsider her self-imposed angst. This was not good.

"I'd love to sit next to you, Connor. Thanks for asking." The two went off to find seats at the Montgomery table.

Estelle would never forgive Kim for this.

"Mommy, let's get our seats. I want to sit next to Dylan, too," Sarah insisted as she pulled Becky along behind Dylan and Connor. "He makes me laugh."

Once they were at the table Becky helped Sarah slide out the white wooden chair to sit. Estelle, who sat directly across from Dylan, was scowling. Becky knew she was in for a horrible evening.

She took a deep breath to prepare for the confrontation.

"My stars—he's with that Jan-woman again," Estelle grumbled, trying not to look conspicuous as she glared across the room.

Becky turned to see Mark walk in with the beautiful and stylish Jan Milton on his arm. Jan was a vision of perfection dressed in a white, gold-trimmed chiffon and satin gown.

Estelle was not impressed. "I'd like to rip that woman's head right off her scrawny body."

"Mother, you and Dad are divorced now," Kim cautioned Estelle. "He can date anyone he chooses."

"You're right, of course, but I'd hoped this cruise would bring us back together. Little did I know he would meet *her!*" Estelle was flat-out staring now. "Look at the way he's ogling. This could get serious." Estelle's expression changed. She pasted on a smile. "God, I can't believe he's bringing her over here."

Dylan and Bob stood as Mark and Jan walked up to the table.

Estelle calmly slipped one hand under her regal chin and rested her elbow on the table just as they approached. "Mark, my dear, I'm afraid we only have one more seat at our family table. Your friend will just have to move in on another family."

Mark softly chuckled. "I just stopped by to say hello to everyone. Jan and I are sitting with the captain this evening. Seems that he and Jan are old friends." Mark looked at the kids. "If any of you want to see the bridge tomorrow, just let me know. I have the inside track." He glanced at Jan.

All three kids expressed their desire to see the bridge.

"I'll get Nikolas to give us a private tour," Jan said enthusiastically. "You're all welcome to join us. You too, Estelle."

Becky could see the storm brewing on Estelle's face. "No thank you. If you've seen one bridge, you've seen them all."

"But, Grandpa, we have a surprise for you. You have to sit with us," Sarah pleaded. "Jan can take my chair and I'll share Connor's chair. You just have to sit with us, Grandpa."

Sarah had a knack for knowing exactly the right moment to speak up.

Estelle guzzled the glass of white wine that had been sitting in front of her.

Jan softly mumbled something to Mark, and he answered her in the same low tone. He turned back to the kids. "Tell you what, Sarah, for you, Grandpa will sit here. I just have to go and make my excuses to the captain."

"Thanks, Grandpa, 'cause I think Grandma really wants you at our table. She just doesn't want to tell you in front of Jan."

Estelle choked a little on her wine as Jan and Mark walked away.

"Well!" Estelle sighed.

"Seems like you should be wearing that lucky pendant tonight," Bob said to Estelle.

She glared at him. "Don't insult my integrity, Bob. That little game is fine for Becky and the kids, but I wouldn't be caught dead with something like that around my neck. I'm just thankful that Becky isn't wearing it tonight."

"And why aren't you?" Dylan asked playfully. He was so amazingly cute when he smiled.

"The clasp is broken," Becky said. "I really did want to wear it, considering I have to give it back to Patti Kennedy in a few hours." She turned to Laura. "I hope you brought it with you."

Laura didn't get a chance to answer before Connor said, "Mom, I'm hungry."

Dylan stood. "I am, too, buddy. I can help him, Becky. I've been through this party before and know all the good stuff. Let me bring over a few plates for everyone."

And before Becky could argue, they were gone.

Bob said, "Laura, your aunt asked you a question about the pendant. Did you bring it with you?"

Becky thought Bob's voice was a little too harsh.

"I wouldn't forget something as important as the pendant," Laura replied crisply. "Of course I have it. I was planning on returning it to Aunt Becky so I slipped it into my purse. Dylan delivered it to us this afternoon. He fixed the clasp. I'm sure I have it."

She fished through her beaded purse, and then when she couldn't find it, she emptied everything on the table.

No necklace.

She sighed and sat back, looking dejected. "I must have left it on my dresser, or it could be on my nightstand. I can't remember which. I'll just run back to the cabin and get it."

She started to get up, but Bob was on his feet before she could swing around in her chair. "I'll get it. I forgot my camera anyway and this gives me a good excuse to get them both. Besides, the doctor told me to do some walking today, and all I've been doing is sleeping or sitting."

"Only if you're sure you can make it, Bob," Kim said.

"I'm fine, Kimmy baby. Really."

"You should go with him, Kim," Estelle insisted.

"No," Bob said before Kim could even react. "I, um, I want to take a brisk walk on deck first. Clear the cobwebs out of my head from all this pain medication, and it might be a little too cold for you in that gown. But I'll need your key card to get into your room."

Kim fished it out of her purse and handed it to him.

Becky found all of this rather curious. Kim wore a soft blue backless gown, with a matching shawl draped over her chair. She was well prepared for a brisk walk, but for some reason, Bob insisted on going alone.

"We don't deserve you, Bob," Estelle said. "There you are, all bruised and battered, and you're putting this family first before your own pain." She turned to Kim as he hurried away from the table. "Do you realize just how lucky you are to have this man?"

There was a split second of hesitation before Kim spoke. "Yes, Mother, very lucky."

CONNOR AND DYLAN let themselves into Kim's stateroom with the key card that Laura had given them. They knew they didn't have much time, so they went right to work without saying a word.

Dylan took the pendant from his pants pocket and placed it inside a small red leather box filled with costume jewelry on the nightstand next to Kim's bed. It was at a perfect angle from the slightly open closet door where Connor set up his camera on a tripod Dylan had borrowed from his roommate earlier that day.

Now all Connor had to do was press the auto button before they left, and for fifteen minutes his camera would toggle between two minute intervals of video and digital stills. Dylan had discovered this advanced feature when he and Connor were trying to think up how to take the pictures from inside the closet without Bob finding them.

That was, of course, if Bob fell for the trap. That depended on Laura.

And right on cue, Dylan's cell phone vibrated in his shirt pocket. It was Laura giving them the signal that Bob was on his way.

"Hit the button, Connor, it's time to go," Dylan said.

Connor slipped into the closet. Dylan waited.

"Darn," Connor said.

"Darn's not a good word right now, buddy."

"I know, but I pressed the button and that little red light didn't come on."

Dylan walked into the closet to check it out. "Did you set it to automatic?"

"Yes," Connor said, visibly upset.

Dylan didn't want to add to his concerns. "Okay, let's take a moment to go over everything."

"We don't have a moment," Connor said. "I knew I couldn't do this. My dad was right. Without him I can't do anything."

"Now wait a minute, little man. I really doubt your dad said anything like that."

"Well, he did. The day he left for India and never came back."

"What did he say, exactly?"

"We were in the pool, and he was showing me how to rescue someone if they were drowning. I thought it was a stupid thing to learn because everybody in my family knew how to swim and they were the only people who ever went in our pool. But he said that someday I might be in an ocean or in somebody else's pool where everybody didn't know how to swim. But I still didn't want to learn it, especially from him. I was mad because he was going on another trip and wouldn't see me in my school Christmas play. That's when he said how a boy needs his father to show him how to do stuff, like all the things he learned from Grandpa. He said those were the things that were important. What he could teach me. But then he died before he could teach me everything, and now I'm going to grow up stupid, and my mom won't be able to depend on me and neither will Sarah, and I can forget about ever getting married or having my own kids or—"

"Whoa, you're not even in middle school yet. I remember when my dad died, I felt kind of the same thing. It's a fantastic world out there, and if we stop enjoying it and learning as we go, then our dads would be very sad. We need to keep enjoying it every day. That's what our dads would want us to do."

"Do you really think so?"

"I know so. I used to be just like you when my dad died, but my brother Bear taught me to cheer up. I bet Sarah wants you to cheer up, but you resist her."

Connor nodded.

"You're her big brother. She needs you to set the example. To show her that it's okay to miss your dad, but it's also okay to laugh and have fun again."

"Sarah always has fun."

"Maybe so, but she wants you to have fun, too. She loves you and looks up to you, just like I do with my big brother.

How would it be if Bear was grumpy all the time? How do you think I'd be?"

"Grumpy."

"I know you don't want Sarah to be grumpy."

"No way. She makes me laugh."

"Absolutely. Tell you what. Let's take a look at the camera and see—"

The lock in the door clicked.

IT WAS POSSIBLY THE LAST BIG PARTY on the cruise, the last chance Tracy had to get the pendant, and there she was in bed in the completely empty infirmary high on drugs, hardly able to keep her eyes open or focused, suffering from a moving kidney stone.

"But I've got to get to the dessert party," Tracy told Brenda, the nurse with the kind face and the sympathetic smile. "I've got this thing I have to get. You've got to let me go."

Nurse Brenda smiled and tucked the white sheets tightly around Tracy. "There, honey. The drugs will calm you down in a few minutes and you won't care about the party. Now you just get some rest and I'll check on you in a bit." And she walked out of the room.

"You don't understand," Tracy called after her. "He has my boy. I need to get my boy back."

But Brenda didn't respond.

Tracy tried to cry, but the tears wouldn't come. It was hard for her to focus and was getting more difficult with each passing moment. The drugs were doing their thing and she was feeling less and less anxious.

Matter of fact, she couldn't seem to remember what she was yelling about, but it had something to do with the two Hot Wheels cars sitting on the rollaway table next to her.

"Oh, that's right," she said out loud. "Franco needs to come home, but…hmm…why in the world does he need a necklace?"

Suddenly her left kidney stopped hurting and she felt a calm wash over her as she stared up at the TV to see Meryl Streep looking down at her, or was that Erica?

She really wasn't sure. Maybe if she closed her eyes for a moment the picture would clear up.

"THERE'S BOB NOW," Becky said to Patti Kennedy as they stood together next to a long table with a cascading chocolate fountain at the end that was taller than they were. Estelle's table was within striking distance from where they stood. "He should have the necklace."

"Great. I want to make a little announcement about it. I have a special gift for you in exchange for the pendant." Patti seemed excited about the whole affair.

Becky wasn't in the mood for any kind of recognition. So far the night wasn't going very well. Earlier, Mark had dropped a bombshell on Estelle: he was flying back to L.A. with Jan when the ship docked in Miami.

So much for his surprise birthday party; now he and Estelle were no longer even speaking to each other.

Dylan and Connor had disappeared into the crowd of people who were vying for desserts. Kim was busy on her third vanilla-flavored vodka Martini, while Sarah had become totally mesmerized by the slide and video show on the big screen.

Plus, seeing Dylan again had brought on a bout of gloominess that Becky was trying to shake. It just wasn't fair. But she'd learned that lesson a long time ago. Life really wasn't fair.

"I won't have to give a speech or anything, will I?" Becky asked.

"Not if you don't want to, but it's going to be fun. I promise." Patti waved to Bob, but he pretended not to see her and kept walking toward the Montgomery table.

"Bob," Becky yelled, waving.

Laura appeared and stood next to Patti. "I hope he found it."

"I do, too," Patti added, then she turned to Laura. "So, did you have a good time on the cruise?"

"The best," Laura answered, but Becky could tell all her focus was on Bob, who was fast approaching. He had a slight skip to his pace, and even though he wasn't smiling, he seemed to be one happy man for someone with his arm in a sling and three broken ribs.

When he finally got close enough he said, "Are you sure you left the necklace in the cabin?"

"Yes. Why?" Laura asked. "It was either on the dresser or on my nightstand, like I told you."

"Well, I couldn't find it anywhere," he said, shrugging his shoulders.

Just then Dylan and Connor showed up, each carrying two platters piled high with an assortment of treats.

Becky turned to them. "Where were you guys? I've been looking everywhere for you."

"Getting food. The lines were long." Connor held up the overflowing platters, then walked over to their table and placed them in the middle along with Dylan's.

"Wait a minute," Laura said to Bob. "You didn't find the pendant?"

Dylan and Connor returned. Dylan stood next to Patti, who gave him a woeful look, while Connor took Becky's hand.

"Nope. Sorry. Maybe it fell out of your purse on the way over." Bob glanced at their table. "Wow. That food looks great. I'm starved."

He turned to walk to the table, but stopped in his tracks when Sarah came running up to the group, all excited. "Look, Mommy, we're on TV." She pointed to the big screen, and sure enough, there was a huge picture of Sarah and Becky on the beach petting stingrays, then one of Mark on the sailboat making knots, a couple shots of the winning sandcastle, and a short video clip of Sarah dancing in circles around the castle, clinging to her award.

The room erupted in applause and laughter.

"Those are great shots, Connor," Becky said. "Your pictures are wonderful." Everyone was looking at the big screen now.

There were also photos of Estelle at her Christmas gala, shaking hands with Thanasi, and Patti and Jan Milton. Becky could only imagine what Estelle was feeling at the moment—intense self-loathing, no doubt, for having invited the woman to her party in the first place.

Then another picture came up. This one was of Bob and Kim eating gelatos. It made Becky laugh when she remembered how Kim had ridiculed her for indulging in such a treat.

"We look good," Bob told Kim, who had joined everyone. "But I don't remember you taking that picture, Connor."

"Pictures are better when they're not posed for," Connor said.

"Did you find the necklace?" Kim asked Bob.

"Nope. It's nowhere in that cabin. And believe me, I looked everywhere."

Then another video came up, only this one was of Bob inside a cabin.

"What the hell?" Bob said as he watched himself shuffle through papers, combs, brushes and perfume bottles on a dresser. "What *is* this?"

"It's you in Auntie Kim's cabin," Sarah announced. "But you don't look too happy."

"Who took this? What's going on here?" Bob sounded panicky.

"Wait," Dylan said. "It gets better."

Bob glared at Dylan.

Then big-screen Bob opened a red box on the nightstand and pulled out a piece of jewelry. Becky immediately recognized the pendant. She turned and realized most of the people in the room weren't even paying attention to the screen, or if they were, nothing seemed to register on their faces. The same was true for Patti Kennedy. She was busy chatting with a few passengers in front of the chocolate fountain.

But at the Montgomery table…

"You lied," Kim said.

"No. I—" real Bob said.

"Son of a—" big-screen Bob mumbled.

Sarah gasped. "You said a bad word, Uncle Bob."

"I don't understand," Kim implored, turning to Bob. "Why would you lie about the—"

But Bob was already high-tailing it out of there, when suddenly he tripped over Dylan's foot, who just happened to put it in his way.

Bob stumbled, but tried to catch himself on the corner of the table. He steadied himself for a moment, but then got tied up in his sling and the tablecloth. His feet went out from under him, he grabbed at the tablecloth and the entire display of cakes, pies, chocolate sculptures and one very large chocolate fountain went plunging right into the sparkling pool…along with Bob. Fortunately, the plug pulled out from the floor just before the fountain splashed into the water.

Without hesitation Connor removed his jacket, threw off his loafers and jumped in after him before Becky could stop him.

CHAPTER TWENTY

ABOUT TEN PEOPLE HAD JUMPED into the now murky pool to save the flailing Bob, but it was Connor who calmly towed Bob to the shallow end.

The passengers surrounded the pool and cheered for Connor when he brought Bob to safety. Dylan and two other men jumped in to help Bob out of the pool. When that was accomplished, Dylan turned to Connor, but Connor didn't want to get out. Instead he swam back to the spot where Bob had fallen in.

Kim met Bob as he was dragged out of the pool, said something to him then stormed out of the area, clutching on to Laura for support.

Estelle never moved from her table. She simply poured herself another glass of wine and nibbled on the food Connor and Dylan had brought over, as if nothing out of the ordinary was going on.

The orchestra kept on playing, but the big screen went black.

When Becky looked around for Mark, she found him with Jan, cheering Connor on at the far end of the pool.

Becky wanted to call to her son and tell him to come out of the water, but she didn't. Instead, she anxiously watched him dive down in the deep end of the pool, come up, and dive again as cake and muck swirled around him each time he surfaced for air.

Finally he surfaced holding the coveted necklace above his head, grinning and looking totally triumphant. Then he swam on his back in tight circles, picking up a large chocolate dolphin along the way and putting it on his belly. It was a funny vision, and it made Becky both laugh and cry at the same time.

"Don't cry, Mommy," Sarah said, slipping her hand into Becky's. "Connor won't drown. He knows how to swim. Daddy taught him. Remember?"

She giggled at her brother's antics in the chocolate pool.

"You bet he did, honey," Becky said, and gave Sarah a big hug, holding her close.

Dylan walked over, his hair flat against his head, his blue shirt stuck to his chest and his pants clinging to his legs. He looked positively miserable. Somebody threw him a towel and he wiped off his dripping face. Becky picked out a strawberry slice from his hair.

"I can't believe there was all this fuss over that silly pendant," Becky said. "Why on earth would Bob want it?"

"It's a long story, but let's just say he was probably misguided into thinking it was worth something."

"Is it?"

"Only if you believe in the legend, but other than that, it's just an inexpensive reproduction."

"Did you take that video?"

"No, Connor is the movie-maker."

"But how did Connor—"

"It's complicated," Dylan said, wiping his neck with the towel. "But I'll tell you this much, the whole scam got a little intense for a moment, but Connor managed to come up with the perfect hiding place for us on the veranda at the last minute. And he even figured out how to make his camera work within seconds of Bob walking in on us. Actually, the sting was all Connor and Laura's idea."

"Well, at least Kim now knows who she's dealing with. She didn't look too happy when she saw Bob slip that pendant into his pocket after he told us he couldn't find it."

"Yeah, and she told him so before she left with Laura."

"What did she say to him?"

Dylan nodded over at Sarah. "I don't think I can repeat it."

Becky smiled, knowing that Kim would never take the guy back now, no matter what Estelle said. And she was happy for Laura.

Dylan turned to watch Connor swim around the pool. "That's one brave little boy, Ms. Montgomery."

"I know," she said. "He just needed the right mentor to break him out of his shell." She took his hand in hers as they stood side by side. "Thanks for giving me my son back."

"Believe me, he did it all on his own."

Becky smiled up at Dylan, knowing full well that between him and Mark and even Sarah, Connor was returning to his old self.

She glanced down at Sarah, and could see she was getting sleepy. Becky sat on a chair next to an empty table. Sarah climbed up on her lap and rested her head on Becky's shoulder. Within moments Sarah fell asleep.

Connor was being coaxed out of the pool by various crew members, so he swam to the shallow end and walked up the steps to get out. Becky and Dylan went over to meet him.

"Mom! Did you see me, Mom? I saved Bob from drowning. Dad wasn't here to teach me, and I didn't think I could do it, but I did. Want to know how I did it?" Connor was talking so fast he was stumbling over his words.

"Of course I do, but slow down a little."

Connor took a seat across from her, hardly able to contain himself. He placed the necklace on the table.

"Now, tell me everything," Becky insisted.

"Yeah, buddy. I've got to hear this," Dylan said.

"Well, first I remembered what Dad showed me, then I remembered what the sailing instructor said when we were on the boat, and what Sarah said when Bob left us alone on the beach. I put it all together, and when I jumped into the pool, I knew how to save Bob."

People were leaving and a cleaning crew had moved in. Becky

could feel the energy drain from her body. The whole incident had made her tense, and it was only now that she was beginning to relax.

"I don't understand what you're saying," she said.

Connor grinned at Dylan. Dylan gave him a nod and a smile. "I can learn stuff from everybody," he said, raising his arms in the air. He was beaming with excitement at his discovery. A discovery that was pretty sophisticated coming from a ten-year-old. But then he was almost eleven, so perhaps that accounted for it. The silly thought made her smile widen. Her son was on his way to becoming just like his analytical, logical-thinking dad, and Becky couldn't be happier.

He was giggling with joy.

"Well, young man," Mark said as he walked up to them, Jan by his side. "You should be proud of yourself. Not only did you save a drowning man, but you helped your aunt Kim make a pretty important decision."

"I do what I can," Connor teased, shrugging.

Everyone laughed.

Mark kissed him on the top of his head and left with his arm around Jan.

Estelle walked out not two minutes later, purposely ignoring Becky and the kids. Fortunately, Connor wasn't paying attention or he would have been devastated at the snub from his grandmother.

Becky wasn't sure if Estelle was angry at Connor, Mark or her. It was probably a little of everything, but either way, she was disappointed in Estelle's bad behavior.

"Some people never change," Becky muttered.

"Excuse me?" Dylan said.

She shook her head. "It's a story that always seems to end the same sad way."

"That's only if it's a movie or a book, Mommy," Sarah said in between a couple yawns. "Miss Carol said we can't change those kinds of sad stories, but we change real life stuff all the time."

And just as Sarah spoke those words, a flash of sparkling blue light came off the pendant. It only lasted for an instant, but it was so brilliant it startled Becky. "Did you see that?"

"Yeah, what was it?" Dylan asked.

Connor nodded. "That was weird."

Sarah pulled back and looked up at her mom. "It was the moon goddess, Mommy. She's talking to us. She wants us to all be happy again." Sarah stroked Becky's cheeks.

"You think that's what she's really saying?" Becky asked.

Sarah nodded. "Of course, silly. The moon goddess cast a happy-lucky spell on the pendant, and you found it."

"You're absolutely right, sweetheart." Becky thought about Estelle and how she had snubbed Connor. She turned to Dylan. "Would you mind sitting with the kids for a minute? I have something I need to do."

Becky moved Sarah onto the empty chair next to her and ran after Estelle. She caught up to her just as Estelle was getting into the empty elevator.

"I no longer wish to speak to you," Estelle said from inside the elevator.

"That's perfect, but you will not ignore my children," Becky warned as she stepped in beside Estelle.

The doors closed.

"Sarah can come to visit me anytime, but you've poisoned Connor and I no longer wish to associate with him until he apologizes to Bob."

"After tonight, I doubt that Bob will be part of this family."

"That's not true. He and Kim simply had a misunderstanding and—"

"The man is a liar and a thief, and now your daughter knows it. If she takes him back because of you, she'll have nothing but misery in her life. Is that what you want for Kim?"

"Of course not, but—"

"Let it go, Estelle. Stop trying to control this family. I know you mean well, but you have to stop this or you're going to lose everyone you love. You've already lost a son and a husband. Do you really want to lose the rest of us?"

She turned to face Becky. "You will never be a part of this family. I tolerated you because of Ryder, but he's gone now, and in my mind, so are you, especially now that you've taken up with that water boy."

Becky stared at her. She wanted to lash out and tell Estelle exactly what she thought, but instead she simply pitied her. Sarah's teacher was wrong. There were some circumstances you couldn't change in real life, and Estelle's stubbornness might just be one of them.

"That's fine, Estelle." She pressed the button and the doors slid back open. The elevator had never moved. "But don't contact either one of my children until you can love them both equally, and enjoy them for being who they are."

She walked out, but turned back to say one more thing. "Thank you for the cruise, Estelle. It allowed me to meet a kind and generous man, and I have every intention of seeing him again, if he'll let me."

The doors closed, and Becky stood there for a moment.

"Did you mean that?" Dylan said behind her. Sarah leaned up against his right side and Connor held his left hand.

"You bet I did," she said, staring into his beautiful eyes.

"Then take this." He slid the silver ring off his pinky and handed it to Becky. "It was my dad's."

"No. I can't—" She tried to give it back to him, but he closed her fingers around it.

"I want you to. You can give it back to me when you and the kids come up to Newfoundland. It's time I went home. Will you come?"

Becky nodded and slid the ring on her index finger. It fit perfectly. She was thrilled to hear he was going home. "But will you come to San Diego sometime?"

"Absolutely. Those winters back 'ome can be a bit cold," he said, using his native accent.

Becky loved the way he sounded, sexy and cuddly at the same time.

"Then kiss him, Mommy," Sarah said. "The moon goddess is waiting for a happy ending."

"Can't disappoint the moon goddess," Dylan said as he took a step toward her, letting go of the kids.

He took Becky in his arms, bent her back for effect, and kissed her tenderly.

"'Since the invention of the kiss, there have been five kisses…this one leaves them all behind,'" Connor and Sarah said in between giggles.

Dylan swung Becky back to an upright position. "I know that line. It's from *The Princess Bride*."

"How do you know that?" Becky asked as she pushed the button for the elevator.

Dylan blushed. "I own the DVD."

"You own it?" Becky's eyes widened as the elevator chimed its arrival.

"It's my favorite movie."

The elevator door opened, but no one moved. The kids stared up at Becky. Becky stared down at the kids, and without hesitation, Becky took Dylan's right hand, Connor his left and Sarah twirled into the empty elevator.

"What?" Dylan asked, obviously confused by everyone's reaction. "What did I say?"

"Let me tell you a little story about this family and *The Princess Bride*," Becky said, as they all piled into the elevator, giggling.

TRACY WOKE UP with a start to hear Nurse Brenda scolding someone behind the curtain in the bed next to her. "If you relax I can give you this shot, and we can all get some rest. You're in a lot of pain right now, and this will help."

"But I told you, I don't want a shot. I hate needles." It was a male voice protesting. "I just want to get out of here."

Tracy was still a little dopy from her own painkiller, but she swore the voice sounded just like Bob's.

"It won't do you any good to fight me on this. Dr. Latsis ordered it and I never go against her orders," the nurse said.

"Give me a break. I outweigh you by about fifty pounds. If I want to get up and leave, I will."

Tracy chuckled, knowing that no one could get by Nurse Brenda.

Suddenly there was a lot of thumping, a few clanging noises. The curtain moved and then there came a heavy sigh.

Tracy reached over and pulled the curtain back to see Bob sprawled out on his stomach on the bed, wearing nothing but a medical gown.

Nurse Brenda stood over him and poked a very long syringe right into his left butt cheek.

Bob screamed out as if she was killing him, until he saw Tracy glaring at him from the next bed.

"Damn," he said.

"Watch your language, sir," Brenda said as she yanked the syringe out of his butt. He flinched and Tracy knew that had to hurt.

Nurse Brenda turned on her heels and walked out of the room as Bob tried to cover himself with the flimsy blanket. He looked positively miserable, and Tracy couldn't be happier.

"Hi, Bob," Tracy said. "Rough day?"

A DAY LATER, as the ship docked in Miami Beach, Becky ran around in circles trying to gather up all the miscellaneous junk that hadn't made it into their suitcases the night before for the massive luggage pickup.

Connor held up a jar filled with shells. "I don't have any more room in my backpack. Can you take this, Mom?"

"We live in San Diego. You can get all the shells you want." She was really feeling the stress of going home with so much more than they'd come with.

"But these are Saint Thomas shells. They're different," Sarah argued.

"You're right," Becky agreed, caving as usual to her daughter's logic. Part of her totally understood the need to bring home something tangible from the trip, and, yes, these shells were indeed different than those they collected at La Jolla Shores and the Coronado beaches they liked to explore. Luckily she had brought a collapsible second bag to fill with all the things she'd collected for her shop, so she stuffed the jar inside. It barely fit.

"But we can't leave this behind." Sarah was, holding on to her stuffed dolphin, which was almost as big as she was.

"Well, honey, you'll just have to carry it on the plane," Becky said, "and you can use it as a pillow, okay? Now, do we have everything?"

"I think so," Connor said, standing by the door wearing his bulging backpack.

Becky gave the cabin one last look, checking the bathroom, under tables, behind sofas and inside closets. When she opened the closet door in her bedroom and spotted the silk hanger tucked in the back, she remembered the pendant and her stomach tightened.

"Did either of you happen to remember to pick up the pendant the other night from the table?" She walked out into the main room.

The kids looked at each other and then at her.

"Uh-oh," they said in unison. She couldn't imagine why she hadn't done it herself or why Patti hadn't asked her about it before this. After all, they had spent the entire previous day lounging around the pool and had bumped into her at least twice. Dylan had quit his job and had spent most of the day with them, much to the chagrin of Patti Kennedy.

Becky sighed. This was not good. "Well, we'll just have to tell Patti we lost it and offer to buy another one."

"But that one was special, Mommy," Sarah said. "A new one won't have the same magic attached to it."

"Well, honey, there's nothing else I can do now."

Becky opened the door and the little family filed out of the cabin.

"Maybe someone found the pendant," Connor offered as they headed for the elevators.

"Yeah, and now they'll be lucky," Sarah said.

Becky didn't want her kids to worry. "I bet that's what happened. Somebody found it, and the moon goddess is already working her magic on them."

PATTI SOMETIMES LIKED to bid farewell to the passengers as they left the ship. She knew it was a little corny, but it was those added touches of courtesy that she believed had gotten her this job in the first place.

As she stood smiling and thanking everyone for cruising on *Alexandra's Dream*, Thanasi Kaldis walked up to her, grinning. It was unlike Thanasi to want to be anywhere near the rush of outgoing passengers, and he was usually busy with last-minute cabin problems that only he could resolve.

He was holding something in his hand, something that looked a lot like her pendant.

"Did you lose something?" he said as he approached her.

She reached out and grabbed it from him. "Where did you get this?"

"A member of the cleaning crew found it under a table at Mermaid Lagoon," he explained.

"And you're just returning it to me now? Ms. Montgomery refused to take her gifts, and couldn't apologize to me enough. Even her kids apologized."

"It sat in Lost and Found for an entire day. The only reason I even knew about it was because one of my staff mentioned it to me and I went to retrieve it."

She softened. "I'm sorry. Thanks for bringing it down to me."

Patti had a hard time believing that Thanasi would take the

time to personally return it after he'd made such a fuss about the idea in the first place.

Why would he do that?

"You're welcome," he said, giving her a warm smile.

Patti shoved the necklace into her jacket pocket and watched as Thanasi said goodbye to the passengers.

Then, just before he left, he turned and threw her a smile. She returned the friendly gesture as a rush of warmth swept over her, causing a blush on her cheeks.

Was it simply her wishful thinking, or was he actually flirting?

Either way, Patti couldn't be happier.

* * * * *

MEDITERRANEAN NIGHTS

*Join the glamorous world of cruising with the
guests and crew of* Alexandra's Dream.
The voyage continues with

Island Heat
by Sarah Mayberry.

*While attending the Culinary Institute of
America, Ben Cooper seduced Tory Sanderson
in order to win a bet with their classmates.
Tory got her revenge back then, but eight years
later as a guest lecturer on* Alexandra's Dream,
*she finds herself sharing a kitchen with Ben.
Even though they've both found their own
successes as chefs, the past is still very much
with them. Ben wants to get even with Tory,
and Tory refuses to back down. But the more
time they spend together, the more Ben begins
to wonder if what he really wants is Tory
in his life* and *in his kitchen!.*

Here's a preview!

Island Heat

by

Sarah Mayberry

AFTER DESSERT, coffee and liqueurs were served. The captain invited his guests to move away from the formality of the table and take advantage of the couches and occasional chairs nearby. Ben heaved a sigh of relief as he at last moved beyond the range of Tory's perfume.

He'd had worse dinners—but not many. The meal itself had been fine, but being trapped next to Tory for two hours had been a new and exquisite form of torture. Every time he'd let down his guard and let his gaze wander, he's found himself studying the swanlike line of her elegant neck, or the golden curls teasing her delicate ears. Several times during dinner he'd heard her low, melodious laugh as she talked with the woman on her right, and the hairs on his arm stood on end.

Then there was the little tit for tat they'd played. He was still trying to come to terms with the hurt he'd heard in her voice when she'd talked about their date. And that damned bet…

He'd never been the kind of person who dwelled in the past. Besides, she'd gotten her own back. More then gotten her own back, in his opinion.

Glancing up, he saw that Nikolas was crossing the room to join him.

"Captain," Ben said with a half-assed attempt at a salute.

"Maître d'. Sorry, no, it's something else, isn't it?" Nikolas pretended to be confused. "Chef de something or other?"

"Close, but no cigar," Ben said dryly.

Nikolas grinned, his teeth very white against his olive skin.

"How are you finding working with Ms. Fournier?"

"Tory is very good at what she does," Ben said easily.

"Helena swears by her cookbook, She's fallen in love with your spicy Caribbean food."

"If Helena is interested in trying real island food, I'll give her some local recipes to try," Ben said.

Ever astute, Nikolas picked up on the reserve in Ben's tone.

"You don't like Ms. Fournier's cookbook?" he asked with the quirk of a dark eyebrow.

"It's fine. It's just not authentic, that's all."

"What do you mean it's not authentic?" an all-too-familiar voice demanded.

Ben turned to see Tory standing behind him, Helena at her side.

"I was bringing Tory over to meet you," Helena said to her fiancée, obviously trying to smooth over the awkward moment.

But Tory wasn't about to let his comment go.

"Well? What's not authentic about my book?" she asked again.

Her cheeks had flushed a becoming pink, the color flattering against her creamy skin.

"For starters, have you ever visited half the places you've written about?" Ben asked.

"No. Have you ever visited France?" she countered.

"No."

"Yet I bet you dare to serve a bouillabaisse in your restaurant, right? And I bet there are a host of other recipes cherry-picked from half a dozen other countries around the world on your menu."

He nodded. "That's true."

"I researched my book meticulously and I worked with dozens of expat islanders in New York. I may not have the same beach view as you have from your restaurant, but I know what I'm talking about."

"If I'm willing to concede that my bouillabaisse might not hold its own against a local offering in Marseille, will you conclude that as a born-and-bred islander I might just have the edge on you?" Ben asked.

Her chin came up and her hand rested on her hip. Despite how annoying he found her, a part of him couldn't help admiring her chutzpah. Did this woman never admit defeat?

"Nope. I'd pit my jerk chicken against yours any day," she said proudly.

"Sounds like a challenge." Nickolas was clearly enjoying their sparring.

"Why not?" Tory said.

All eyes turned to Ben. He shrugged nonchalantly.

"It'll be like taking candy from a baby, but if that's what the lady wants…" he said provocatively.

Tory didn't rise to the bait. Instead, she smiled a secretive, confident smile.

"Done," she agreed. "My jerk chicken versus your jerk chicken. Time and place of your choosing. And when I win, I'll expect a quote for the review pages of my next cookbook."

That nearly made him choke. He'd rather eat her damned cookbook then endorse it. But she was hardly likely to beat him.

"Deal. And it I win…" He couldn't think of what to say, because the only idea that popped into his head was so inappropriate and never-going-to-happen that it made him want to shake his head to knock the thought loose from his mind. "If I win, you give me your father's famous secret recipe for port wine glaze," he finally said.

"Still haven't worked it out, Ben?" she asked mockingly. "It's very simple, really."

Very aware of Helena and Nikolas watching their interplay like spectators at a tennis match, Ben stuck out his hand.

"Are we agreed or not?"

Her hand was warm and firm as it slid into his.

"Agreed."

Helena cleared her throat. "Aren't you forgetting something?"

Ben stared at her blankly and was aware of Tory doing the same.

"Such as?" he asked.

"Who is going to decide the winner?" Nikolas asked.

"Oh," Tory said.

"Of course Nikolas and I might be available…" Helena hinted with a glint of mischief in her eyes.

"Perfect," Ben said. "You two are the judges, and your decision is final. We'll use the cuisine center as a base. How does two days' time sound, after we've departed Grenada?"

Tory lifted a shoulder in a careless shrug. "If you need a couple of days to get your act together, by all means," she drawled.

Ben looked down at her, at the flush in her cheeks and the challenge in her blue, blue eyes.

"It's a date," he said.

Romantic reads to
Need, Want

...International affairs, seduction and passion guaranteed
10 brand-new books available every month

Pure romance, pure emotion
6 brand-new books available every month

Pulse-raising romance – heart-racing medical drama
6 brand-new books available every month

From Regency England to Ancient Rome, rich, vivid and passionate romance...
6 brand-new books available every month

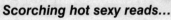

Scorching hot sexy reads...
4 brand-new books available every month

MILLS & BOON
Pure reading pleasure

M&B/GENERIC RS2 a

LOOK OUT...

...for this month's special product offer.
It can be found in the envelope containing
your invoice.

**Special offers are exclusively for
Reader Service™ members.**

You will benefit from:

- Free books & discounts
- Free gifts
- Free delivery to your door
- No purchase obligation – 14 day trial
- Free prize draws

THE LIST IS ENDLESS!!

*So what are you waiting for —
take a look* **NOW!**